YOU CAN RUN

L C GEORGE

INKUBATOR
BOOKS

Published by Inkubator Books
www.inkubatorbooks.com

Copyright © 2024 by L C George

L C George has asserted her right to be identified as the author of this work.

ISBN (eBook): 978-1-83756-320-3
ISBN (Paperback): 978-1-83756-321-0
ISBN (Hardback): 978-1-83756-322-7

YOU CAN RUN is a work of fiction. People, places, events, and situations are the product of the author's imagination. Any resemblance to actual persons, living or dead is entirely coincidental.

No part of this book may be reproduced, stored in any retrieval system, or transmitted by any means without the prior written permission of the publisher.

PROLOGUE
BEFORE

The experts will tell you there are warning signs, traits to watch out for in those who will grow to be labelled a psychopath. But those signs are only noticeable in those who aren't smart enough to keep them disguised.

People talk about spotting the warning signs right from childhood, and of course they are there, but a true expert won't diagnose psychopathic tendencies in a child. They placate themselves with notions of it being nothing more than a phase. It's those who continue the impulsive behaviour into adulthood that are a concern. Ironically, the ones who are to be feared the most are those of us who can expertly mirror and mask, blending in with those around us, fitting perfectly into society.

I believe more people have wondered how long it takes to extinguish a life than any of us would care to admit. How long you have to hold the pressure, exactly how much to apply as you witness the life-force drain from the body... the eyes to finally stop pleading. Just the same as the intrusive thoughts we have about hurling ourselves over the edge of that cliff we peer over.

For me it was never about death. There is so much more to life. It started with the neighbour's cat. Before the protests start, the creature lived to tell the tale. It wasn't even a particularly grizzly one. It fascinates me that people always seem so much more disturbed by the death of an animal than that of a fellow human. Doesn't that say something about the way we truly feel about one another? Anyway, I digress. I was only a child, around five years old, when they called to say it had gone missing. They were asking everyone on the street to look out for it as though it were something of value. I couldn't understand their distress. It was only a cat.

My parents told them we'd let them know if we found it. They checked our shed and anywhere it could have been hiding in our garden. I found the creature by chance. I could just make out the sound of it meowing through the fence and discovered it caught up behind the shed of the elderly lady next door.

When my mum was busy preparing our evening meal and my father was cleaning himself up from his job as a mechanic, I carried the cat around the side of the house. I had already prepared my story. If I was caught, I would claim I had just discovered it and was preparing to take it back to its owners. I slipped through our back gate and took it to our shed. It was such a trusting thing, purring at me quietly as I cradled it.

I locked it inside, sneaking back out numerous times over the following days to watch it as it slowly starved. Of course, my father discovered it before it reached the point of actual starvation. I have never felt emotions in the way others describe them, but I can still picture the look my father gave me as he carried that mangy cat past me through our house.

I didn't see anything wrong in what I had done, but it did pique my curiosity as to why my father seemed to avoid me after that, unable to meet my eye. It had fascinated me so much – watching that creature. I felt no empathy, only enthralment at witnessing it feeling all the things I never had. I was so desperate to hold that same kind of control again. But next time, it wouldn't be a cat that I'd experiment with.

1

I ran my fingers across the lettering engraved into the cold stone. A chill ran over me, causing my skin to break into goose bumps as the October breeze whipped itself around me. Placing the flat of my palm against the headstone, I closed my eyes for a few seconds, allowing the cold to seep in. It made me feel closer to them in a way I couldn't explain, like I didn't deserve to feel warmth while they lay in the cold, damp earth.

It had become habit to follow the gravel path round to the left, away from the small car park and deeper into the sea of headstones. I didn't need to search out her name anymore, finding myself arriving by her resting place on autopilot. The fresh carnations told me I wasn't her only visitor. Guilt gnawed at me. I knew I shouldn't be there; I couldn't imagine what her family would have to say if they found me hovering at her graveside and discovered who I was. Of course, my name had been changed, no photographs of me ever released, but I had seen enough pictures of my father to know there was more than a slight resemblance.

A gust of wind tossed my hair across my face, and I hunched my shoulders. The trees groaned, their branches bending as the storm gained momentum. It was time to leave.

It was ironic that I never uttered a word when I visited my mother and sister, always crouching in silence, hand on their stone as though it was connecting us. And yet without fail, as I left the final resting place of Naomi Wells, I felt compelled to whisper the same words time and time again.

"I'm so sorry."

Pushing myself up from my crouched position, I pulled my jacket tighter around me, allowing my eyes to linger on their names before turning and walking briskly across the graveyard. I'd never been one to talk to the dead, lacking the imagination to hold up a one-sided conversation, and I'd never been a believer in any sort of afterlife. My mother and sister were gone for good.

The thought of one-sided conversations left me batting away the images of my father's letters that fought to infiltrate my mind. It had been years since I had received one but I could still conjure up the pages without effort. The perfect block lettering, written so neatly across the stark white page, as if he'd painstakingly formed each individual letter with such care and attention. I supposed he had enough time on his hands. He had nothing better to do whilst he served his sentence.

They were nothing more to me than the words of a stranger. I couldn't remember a time in my life that my father had been present, and all he had left in his wake was a void where the memories of my mother and sister should have been.

I wished with all I had it was him laid in the dank earth instead of them.

I ARRIVED home just as it began to pour. Only a few steps away from the front door, and yet the relentless downpour had still managed to soak me through to my skin. Slamming the door closed behind me, I remained against it as though the storm may attempt to follow me inside, then blew out a breath, regretting my decision to linger in the cemetery as long as I had.

"Hey, Rach." My smile was genuine, my mood instantly lifting at the sight of my husband as he stepped into the hallway. Dan's hands were wrapped around his mug, clutching it close to his chest.

"Where've you been?"

My eyes dropped away from Dan's. "Just had some errands to run."

The heat rose to my face at the lack of shopping bags or anything else to prove the fictional errands, instantly wondering what more I would say if Dan pushed the matter. There was no real need to lie to my husband when it came to my visits to my family. It wasn't as though Dan would begrudge me the time spent with them, or wouldn't understand why I chose to go, but somehow, I felt guilty, dirty almost, for having been with them. Mentioning them would remind Dan of who I really was – a reminder we didn't need. Everything to do with my family felt sordid and I didn't want any part of the toxicity to poison what Dan and I had.

Thankfully Dan didn't press me, simply giving a small nod.

I regarded him, noticing the tightness to his eyes, the way his hands were clenching and unclenching around his mug, and his inability to keep his face still.

"Is… everything okay?" I titled my head, my white lie instantly forgotten as I tried to get him to meet my eye, the tightness that gripped my stomach telling me I already knew the answer.

"Erm…" Dan cleared his throat. "There's a letter for you." There was a pause as he fumbled over what he was trying to say. "It's from the prison."

My stomach went into freefall, and I felt as though all of the air had been forced from my body. I opened my mouth, a thousand questions in a rush to be answered. Nothing came out, so I snapped it shut, pressing my lips together and taking a second before I trusted myself to speak.

Swallowing hard, I fought back the nausea.

"Why would they write to me?" Obviously the simple answer was just to open the letter, but that would mean holding it in my hands, acknowledging it was real and facing whatever it contained.

Dan gave a small shrug. "I don't know. I don't work in that side of it, so I don't know much about it. It's probably best we just open it rather than speculate."

I nodded, pushing back a strand of wet hair from my face. He turned back towards the kitchen, and I followed him deeper into our home. The crisp, white envelope sat waiting on the kitchen table as I stepped into the room, the smell of coffee still lingering in the air as Dan drained the last of the contents from his mug and placed it by the sink. He winced and pulled a face the way he always did when he had left it too long and it had turned cold.

Pausing to draw in a deep breath, I plucked the letter from the table. There was little point in delaying the inevitable, and I needed to know why they would feel the need to contact me after so much time had passed. I silently reminded myself that whatever was inside the envelope couldn't hurt me. It was just words on a page.

Tearing it open, skim-reading, my hands trembled so hard I struggled to focus on the words. I stared at the page, watching the water droplets from my hair falling onto it, soaking into the paper and causing the ink to bleed.

"Well?" Dan's voice startled me from my transfixed state, and I blinked at him, unable to find the right words.

He took it from me as I held out the paper instead, observing him as his eyes darted across the page. His frown seemed to deepen, and his jaw tensed as he gripped the letter, finally looking up at me.

"He's getting out?" he hissed.

I nodded, biting hard on my lip.

"Seems that way." I shivered and sucked in a shuddering breath, no longer sure if it was from the cold or the shock.

Dan's nostrils flared and he shook his head. "How long has he served? Were you expecting it?"

"Twenty-seven years," I replied without hesitation. It had always been in the back of my mind that Dennis was likely to get out at some point. When you were serving a life sentence in the UK, that rarely meant you would actually die in prison. "I knew they planned to appeal but they've tried before and it's always been denied."

Dan nodded slowly, puffing out his cheeks and blowing out his breath. "He'll be on licence. Part of his parole agreement will be that he can't contact you."

I nodded, wishing that made me feel any better.

"Plus, he wouldn't know where to find you. You go by a different name now; you aren't in contact with anyone from... back then. Only the prison has your new identity, and there's no way they would allow him to get hold of that. This doesn't change anything, Rach. Not really." He stepped towards me, gripping the tops of my arms and looking into my face. I wondered whom he was trying hardest to convince.

After the incident, I had been placed with my maternal aunt who lived over a hundred miles away. As I'd gotten old enough to make my own decisions, I'd felt a strong pull to be back nearer my mother and sisters' resting places, to go back to my roots. Had that been a mistake? Made it easy for him?

"I can dig into it a bit, find out who his parole officer is. I'll contact them and..."

"No." I shook my head, Dan's hands rubbing the tops of my arms doing nothing to comfort me. "I don't want you dragging this into work with you. You said it yourself; it doesn't change anything. He doesn't know where I am, and if he tries to find me, they'll arrest him again, right?"

Dan swallowed hard, his features pinched. I didn't wait for his confirmation.

"I just want to forget all about it. Prisoners must be released all the time; this is no different. As far as I'm concerned, he's nothing to do with me and I want to keep it that way." I gave a firm nod, making it clear the conversation was over.

I turned away from my husband, unable to disguise the quiver of my lips.

It didn't matter how I tried to spin it, what anyone said; this *was* different, and I knew it.

The man who was due to be released from prison, who would soon be free to walk the same streets I did, was not just another prisoner. This man had murdered my mother. He had murdered my sister. His own wife and child. Dennis Raiker was a killer – and he was also my father.

2

THREE MONTHS LATER

Dropping down onto the sofa beside Dan, I lifted my feet and placed them into his lap. He jabbed the remote at the telly to start the film he had chosen for us to watch and subconsciously stroked my leg.

I took a minute to appreciate the moment. Dan often worked odd hours in his job as a detective inspector, meaning it wasn't unusual for me to spend evenings home alone. He loved his job and had been commended on his commitment to it on more than one occasion. It was hard to understand how he was able to disconnect from some of the horrific things he had to deal with, how he could come home and sleep, knowing what kind of monsters roamed while we believed we were safe in our beds.

The memory of the letter from the prison shoved its way to the surface of my mind, unwelcome in the serenity of the evening. It had been two months since Dennis had been released from prison, and although nothing had changed, everything felt different. I found myself checking and rechecking that I had locked the doors, anxious on the evenings that Dan left me home by myself. Checking over my shoulder to make sure the stranger behind me on the street was, in fact, nothing more than a stranger. Dennis hadn't even had to renter my life to have shaken it up.

"You okay?" Dan's voice startled me, and I wrapped my arms across my chest, feeling exposed somehow.

"Yeah, fine. Just tired."

He angled his body towards me, and I shifted under his gaze. At six foot two and with eyes that seemed to be able to bore into your soul, it was no surprise that Dan was so good at his job. There was no doubt Dan could have seemed intimidating, and although I knew that was the side that he presented at work, that wasn't who he was when it was just him and me. He rested his hands on my drawn-up knees.

"What is it?" He stroked my knee with his thumb.

"It's nothing." I shrugged, pressing my lips together and shaking my head. "Nothing's happened. I just have a lot on my mind." There was no way Dan wouldn't have noticed the changes in me since the release date, so there was no point in lying. "It's weird to know he's out there, free. After what he did. After all these years." Dan nodded, pulling me closer against his body and stroking my hair.

"I keep thinking I've seen him – in the supermarket or in the car next to me at the lights. He hasn't been near me, but he's everywhere, infiltrating everything. I forgot to do a referral for a patient at work. Things like that could have serious consequences. Why can't I pull myself together?" I dropped my head against his chest as he held me tighter.

"I just—" My words were silenced by the shrill sound of Dan's phone ringing. His body went rigid and I was propelled forwards as he lunged for his phone on our coffee table.

He cursed under his breath and threw me an apologetic glance, already pushing himself to his feet and accepting the call.

"DCI Thatcher." He was across the room before I had managed to sit myself upright, cold and abandoned with Dan's sudden desertion.

"When?" Dan's face had turned dark, his features pulled in tightly as he paced the room. Wrapping my arms across my chest, I made no attempt to disguise the fact that I was listening.

Dan pinched the bridge of his nose, screwing his eyes up as he listened.

"Okay. Yeah. Start processing the scene but don't move anything. I'll be there as soon as I can. Thanks, Clarky." He hung up and I stared at him expectantly.

He tapped the edge of his phone against the palm of his hand, seeming to weigh everything up, not meeting my stare.

My stomach knotted and I felt my heart rate increase watching him, aware from his hesitation that this was something big.

Dan and I had an unspoken agreement to share the burdens of our work with one another. We both worked in high-pressured and demanding roles where we were bound by confidentiality. We never gave names or details that were too specific, but we were one another's confidant, someone to open up to about anything and everything.

"What?" I pressed. "What's happened?" Part of me didn't want to hear the answer to my own question and I felt the urge to tell him to get going, that I didn't need him to tell me. But I did.

"There's been a body found. A woman. She was

murdered." My skin felt as though it had turned to fire, my blood to ice.

I knew there was more without Dan having to say so. It wasn't exactly a regular occurrence for him to be called out to a murder, but equally, it wasn't unheard of. I'd never seen him act this way.

"Right." It was the best I could manage.

"She was strangled." The words hung in the air as my mind fought to both process and reject this information. A few seconds passed before I felt able to speak again.

"Was it..." I cleared my throat, my words barely more than a squeak. "Was it him?"

Dan gave a small shrug. "We don't know yet. They're only just starting to process the scene. Obviously, his name's been mentioned, and they'll be bringing him in for questioning, checking if he has an alibi and all that."

"So, he's close enough? If you're being called out, it must be close to us. Does that mean he is too?" My voice was rising, my breath catching.

"I don't know, Rach." Dan didn't look at me.

I ricocheted between wanting to dissolve into helpless tears and the desire to lash out at something. I did neither, instead clenching my jaw, trying to think of something to say. I wanted to demand that he find out more, that it was cruel to leave me, terrified and alone, no longer able to convince myself that Dennis was probably the other side of the country.

But the shame of it stopped me. What kind of position was it going to leave him in as a high-ranking officer, having to instruct his team on interviewing his convicted father-in-law over a murder?

"I'm so sorry to have to do this to you, babe, but I have to go. Are you going to be alright? Do you want me to call one of the girls? See if they'll come over and sit with you or something?"

His suggestion caused the reality of the situation to crash down onto me with the same weight as though the walls of our home had just crumbled, imploding until they were almost suffocating me.

"No. No, God no. What would we even say?" I breathed, barely able to believe he had thought it a good idea.

"Yeah, no, course." He shook his head vigorously, dismissing it. "I was thinking we could just say you weren't feeling well or something... but..." He trailed off, both of us at a loss over how to deal with the storm we had just found ourselves thrust into the centre of.

"They'd know something was happening." I cupped my hands against my burning cheeks, part of me wishing Dan didn't have to leave, but also keen for him not to be present to witness me falling apart. "They can't find out, Dan. No one can. Promise me you won't tell anyone who I am, who Dennis is to me."

There was an edge of panic to my voice, and I fought to gain control of it.

"Of course I wouldn't." Dan closed the gap between us and had his arms wrapped around me in an instant. "I swear, I won't breathe a word to anyone that doesn't have to know. Everything's going to be fine, Rach."

I rested my head against Dan's chest, desperately trying to draw some comfort from his reassurances.

3

BEFORE

It didn't take me long to realise I just needed to mimic the others.

In the same way a child learns to speak, or to dress themselves, it was just a case of copying what I witnessed around me. I didn't understand why they saw my behaviour as such an issue. It felt bizarre to me that the other children didn't act the way that I did – or at the very least, strive to.

When the school scissors I'd hidden in my pocket didn't slice through Imogen Hill's hair in the way I imagined they would, I didn't let go, continuing to hack my way through her pony tail no matter how much she screamed or tried to yank her body away. Our classmates had watched on, but no one intervened. I had her hair so tightly wrapped around my fist it ripped from the roots when she fought against me.

The teacher had appeared in time to find me clutching the thick clump of hair, Imogen a pathetic, crumpled heap, sobbing on the floor of the playground, clutching her head. They'd asked why I did it, and I shrugged, telling her the truth – I wanted to see what happened. I was being honest;

that's what they had always told me to be. She had frowned at me and asked why I didn't stop when Imogen screamed and begged me to let go, and had gotten such a strange look on her face when I'd said it wouldn't have hurt if she had just stayed still. It seemed obvious that it really was her own fault.

My parents had come to collect me, and my father had given me the same look he had when he'd found that cat. I learned then that although I still got that sense of excitement when I inflicted the harm, it didn't come close to what I felt taking control of another, overpowering them and watching as they carried out my instructions. I also avoided the repercussions of the actions if I wasn't the one to get my hands dirty, as it were. It offered a buzz like nothing else – taking that control – leaving every nerve in my body tingling in a way that was indescribable to anyone that hasn't felt it themselves.

I overheard them talking, my father telling my mother that he didn't want me around my brother, that they weren't in a position to be able to 'deal with me'. I couldn't understand what he felt needed dealing with.

It didn't take more than a few tears to pacify my mother when she gently broached the subject with me. She and my father argued once again as she defended my 'behaviour' as childish antics, reminding my father of stories he had told her about things he and his brother had done to one another as kids.

As I got older, it intrigued me that the word psychopath was used as a negative term, discussed as though it was a characteristic you'd be cursed with. Of course, I had begun to recognise that I was different, but I had never been able to put my finger on what it was that made me so much better than my peers.

I can only assume it was similar to those who discover they are colourblind; they never knew there was more to see than what appeared for them. The others didn't know any different, didn't know what they were missing. They couldn't understand it was possible for another human to be immune to their sentimental crap, to possess so much freedom. I could do anything I wanted to.

4

It was the early hours of the morning by the time I heard Dan's key slide into the lock. I wasn't certain if I had slept at all. Every time I allowed my eyes to drift closed, images of my father's face had loomed behind them. Still only an infant myself, I had no memory of ever being in the same room as him, so the visions I saw consisted of the snippets of news footage and photos released by the press, merging with the earlier ones of him posing with us as a family man. My body recoiled at my own mind, my skin crawling.

It never failed to make my breath catch when I saw him in the news, unable to miss the striking resemblance I held to him. The constant fear that someone else might one day make that connection between us.

Dan trudged up the stairs. He seemed to believe he was quiet when he came home late, thinking he crept into our bedroom in near silence. The reality was, he always came in like a one-man band, keys rattling giving way to the big base drum that was our staircase, before he seemed to drop or knock over every item in our bathroom. It didn't irritate me, though. Instead, I found it a source of comfort to hear my husband's noisy routine.

He pushed open the door to our bedroom, using his phone screen to light his path, still managing to stumble and stub his toe on the edge of the wardrobe that had been there forever. Usually I'd have stifled a chuckle as he let out his string of expletives, but tonight was anything but usual.

It tends to be assumed that people with a history like mine would be afraid of the dark, that we would have to sleep with a light on, but that couldn't be further from the truth. I couldn't ever doze off if the room wasn't pitch black, so I had insisted on blackout blinds on all of the windows. I had never found the dark intimidating, actually preferring it to the artificial light that caused shadows and tricks of the mind, making you feel as though you were seeing things that weren't there.

Besides, my father had proved that awful things could happen to people at any time, regardless of the time of day or amount of light.

"Hey," I whispered.

"Oh, hi. You're still up?" Dan asked the obvious question, unable to believe he may have disturbed me.

"Yeah. Couldn't sleep."

"You okay?" The concern that laced his voice caused my heart to constrict, the conflict of needing him to tell me everything, to know exactly what was happening and if Dennis was involved, battling with the need to bury my head and just have him next to me in a moment of serenity. Not that anything had been serene since I'd received the letter from the prison.

The recurrent nightmares that had become so rare since

I'd shared my bed with Dan had started up again. They were never directly linked to my father or what he'd done, but I had no doubt about what was causing them.

"Yeah." We both knew it was a lie. "Was it him, Dan? Have they arrested him?"

Dan's belt buckle tinkled as he released it, slipping out of his trousers and letting them fall into a heap on the floor.

"It's too early to know for sure. I've still got officers working the scene but whoever this was, they knew what they were doing. We haven't found a single shred of evidence yet." Even without being able to see his face in the dark room, the edge to Dan's voice gave away his frustration.

The conflict of feelings that pounded me was staggering. The desperation I felt to hear that my father was back behind bars slammed up against the agony of having to hear that he had done it again. The man who had given me life, slowly snuffing others out for nothing more than his own sickening pleasure.

The mattress shifted as Dan lowered his weight onto our bed. The room lit up again briefly as he plugged his phone into the charger.

He slid his arm underneath my neck, and I shuffled over to him, curling into his cool body. I rested my cheek against his chest, the hairs on it tickling my nose.

"They've picked Dennis up, though. He's still tagged so can't be out past his curfew. We only have a rough time of death, but the murder happened during the daytime."

My body turned rigid, fear leaving me weak.

"So, it could have been him? He's here?"

"They're questioning him. That's all."

I sat up, staring at nothing but darkness. "Dan?"

"They haven't housed him close to us, Rach, but they do

think it is feasible for him to have travelled to the area of the murder. He isn't allowed to track you down, but equally, that means he doesn't know where you are. You have a different identity. He hasn't seen you since you were barely more than an infant. Even if it was him, it's just a shitty coincidence."

I was speechless, wondering if Dan – a man of evidence and science – actually believed anything he had just said to me.

We lay in silence, both at a loss for what to say.

It was only a matter of minutes before Dan's breathing seemed to deepen, not quite a snore but a low, even sound that left me in no doubt that he was already sleeping. I had always been envious of how easy my husband seemed to find it to switch off, even when working on the biggest of cases. His head would hit the pillow and out he'd go – but tonight, I was incredulous.

Could he really not see how significant this was?

I curled into a ball and squeezed my eyes closed, knowing sleep had evaded me completely now. I never slept well. My mind always seemed to use the time when I tried to switch off to replay the moments I most wanted to forget. I could never be sure if the memories I had of my family were based on my actual memories, or just what my mind had conjured up from everything I'd been told.

My mother hadn't been well before she died. That's the reason everyone believed my father had killed her. He'd cared for her for so long, until he couldn't take it anymore and finally snapped. No one could ever explain why he had also killed my sister, though, or why he had spared me.

Dennis had refused to speak after his arrest, and so we were never offered the comfort of answers.

I shuffled a bit closer to Dan, needing to feel the warmth

of his body. I hated the way Dennis was already coming between us, infiltrating our lives from different angles.

My father had been released from prison less than eight weeks ago, and once again, a woman had been murdered. Could that possibly be coincidence?

I hated myself for the selfish reassurances I tried to cling to. Dan was right – I was safe. One of the conditions of my father's release was that he couldn't look for me, or come anywhere near me or my home if he was to find out my new identity. He didn't even know where I lived or who I was anymore. There would be no reason for him to try to track me down. But how could I be okay with taking comfort from the idea of another being killed as long as he didn't come after me? Maybe I was like him in more ways than just our appearance.

But despite my attempt at self-assurance, I couldn't shake the cold fear that coiled itself around me. If it had been Dennis who had killed that woman, was it just because of some sort of addiction, an urge he felt to murder the innocent? Or was there more to it? Was this a sign, letting me know he was close, that he knew exactly where I was hiding? My instincts told me that tracking me down may well have been the only reason he had cared about getting out.

THE LIGHT from the hallway woke me as Dan pushed open the bedroom door, and I screwed my eyes up against its harshness.

It had taken me ages to finally drift into a fitful sleep, and last night's nightmares still lingered in my mind.

"Morning." Dan crossed the room, his towel wrapped

around his waist, his torso glistening with droplets, fresh from the shower, and his dark hair slicked back. "Sorry, I didn't mean to wake you. What time are you in today?"

I stifled a yawn with the back of my hand, the gritty feeling behind my eyelids making me desperate to close them again. I felt stale next to his freshly washed skin.

"Not until ten. I have the late shift."

The thought of working into the evening did nothing to lift my spirits. Although I enjoyed not having to be woken by my alarm, looking forward to a lazy start, I always found the later end to my day – watching everyone else leave – to be a drag.

I had taken the job share at our local surgery for the convenience of the location. They'd only had part-time hours on offer, a full-time job split between me and Janet, who had wanted to cut her hours and spend more time with her children.

Originally, I had only taken it as a stop gap, planning to search for a full-time post or increase my hours, but Dan and I had never struggled financially and I had to admit, I enjoyed the freedom of a shorter working week.

"In that case, you should try to get a little more rest." Dan made the couple of strides over to the bed and perched on the edge. "I know you haven't been sleeping and I can see how drained you are." His face was creased with concern, his smooth skin replaced with worry lines.

I sighed heavily, attempting a smile that I knew looked as forced as it was.

"I'm okay. Just... Stuff on my mind, you know. Work is busy and—"

"We both know this is nothing to do with work, Rach." Dan reached out and pushed my hair back from my eyes with his damp fingers. I avoided meeting his gaze. "I'm sorry I had to run out on you last night. I know this must be hard for you, and now with..." He trailed off, not wanting to voice the suspicions we all had. "There are conditions in place for his release. He *can't* contact you. If he even tries, we will throw away the key before he knows what's happening." Dan's hand moved to my cheek, gently turning my face, guiding me to look at him.

"I know." I nodded, wishing I could share his confidence.

"Let's go away, me and you. Once things have settled with this case. I wish I could take you now, take your mind off everything, but things at work are so crazy they really need us all on board right now."

"I know," I mumbled again.

"But when we catch this guy, as soon as we have him, let's book something, okay?" A look crossed his face as the same thought crossed both our minds.

As soon as we rearrest your father.

Forcing a smile again, I nodded. As lovely as a weekend away sounded, it felt wrong in the circumstances that I should be able to enjoy being away with my husband while everyone around us was still reeling – especially if it turned out to be from the actions of my flesh and blood.

5

"Mrs Richardson?" I offered her a bright smile as my regular patient looked up from her seated position, clearly in mid-flow, chatting to a young woman who had a red-faced toddler attached to her in a way that resembled a baby koala. The poor woman appeared frazzled enough by the whinging child without having to be humouring a lonely old lady. A look of relief passed over her face as the older woman gave a little wave in acknowledgement. Lorna Richardson placed a hand on the young mother's arm, giving it a light squeeze before rocking herself backwards and forwards, finally launching herself out of her seat.

"How are you, Lorna? How's that leg?" She'd had skin cancer and visited the surgery regularly. A nurse had requested I see her and review the wound after her last dressing.

"Oh, I'm fine, dear, just fine. A lot of fuss over nothing, this is." She gestured to her leg. "All of this terrible to-do with these poor young women – now that's something to worry about. It's almost enough to make you want to lock yourself away and not leave the house."

I froze, my breath catching, naively not having expected the murdered woman to be a point of conversation.

She didn't seem to notice, continuing on undeterred.

"Luckily for me, I'm old. Nothing like that would happen to me at my age, but it must be a terrible worry for you young ones."

She eyed me. I kept my full focus on her wound, refusing to meet her gaze.

"I do hope you are taking extra care. I was just telling that young girl in the waiting room, all of you young women, you must do whatever it takes to keep yourselves safe. I'm sure that husband of yours tells you the same thing. It must be reassuring to have a policeman around."

The thought of how often I was waking up alone sprang to mind, but I spared her the concern.

"I'm very lucky." I nodded.

"Still, it must be keeping him busy. That evil creature is moving quickly."

Pausing, I glanced up at her, catching the glint in her eye as she realised she'd snagged me.

"You have heard the news this afternoon?" She cocked her head, eyes searching my face. I stared at her blankly, the room feeling airless, while I waited for what she might be about to tell me.

"There was another death last night. Well, that's when the police found her anyway. Killed in the exact same way as the first, by the sounds of things. I think they wanted to keep it under wraps a bit longer, but the press got hold of it. A local girl – God rest her soul."

"But... it... it could be coincidence. They can't know the

deaths are connected this quickly, surely?" I breathed desperately.

She lifted one shoulder and pursed her lips. "It doesn't take a genius. And right when a murderer has just been released from prison too. Unbelievable, it is. I don't know why they call them life sentences when they barely get anything. He got away with all sorts last time, you know. I remember reading about it when it happened. He was sentenced for the murders of his wife and baby, but there were others too – a schoolteacher and a colleague of his. It was obvious to everyone he was responsible, but they just didn't have the technology to prove it back then."

I stared at her, aware my breathing had become too loud, unable to find an appropriate way to respond. I opened my mouth, closed it again, knowing I should say something.

"Are you okay, dear? You've gone awfully pale." She sat forward, her brow creased.

"Yes. Sorry. Yes, I'm fine." I pulled myself together although my voice was a pitch higher than it should have been. I took a deep breath, trying to focus back on the task in hand. "It's just awful. Not something I like to think about." I shook my head, not risking glancing in the direction of her face.

"Well, yes, of course. But you know, dear, it's important to know what's going on, and to keep yourself safe."

I ushered her from my room with a prescription for some antibiotics, needing a minute to gather myself. My bag was tucked under my desk, and I reached for it with trembling hands. As expected, there were multiple missed calls from Dan, plus messages requesting that I call him when I could. He would have wanted to spare me finding out like this. Unable to face hearing any more about it, I replaced my phone and dropped my bag back under my desk.

Sucking in air, I composed myself as best I could before making my way through to the admin office. The usually vibrant mood of the admin staff seemed tense and subdued, the room seeming uncharacteristically quiet.

"Afternoon, all." My greeting sounded too loud and I cringed at my false enthusiasm. A couple of faces glanced up, offering a small nod and forced smiles. I glanced around, feeling a sense of unease creeping over me, the same feeling you get when you've walked in on someone talking about you. I usually loved chatting with the admin gang, their warmth and openness always seeming to lift my mood. I understood why things would be sombre today, but it felt like more than that. Something was different, and I felt like an intruder.

I dropped my letters into the tray, ready for franking, and practically tiptoed over to Thomas, one of my favourite of the team.

"Hey, is everything okay with you guys? I know things are tough." I kept my voice low, barely above a whisper, as I leant in.

Thomas lifted his eyes to meet mine, something clouding his.

"We had a death called in by the hospital an hour or so ago."

I tilted my head, sympathetic but confused. Of course, it was always sad to receive notification of the death of a patient, but it wasn't unusual. It was part of the admin team's job to deal with the records of the deceased.

Thomas sucked in a breath, seeming to take a minute to

compose himself and his eyes stealing a fleeting glance at Millie as a prickling sensation crawled over my skin.

"It was..." He winced. "She was the latest victim of that evil bastard that's killing women." He scowled as though it left a bad taste even speaking of him. "And she was a friend of a couple of the girls here. They're obviously devastated. Plus, it's a shock for everyone, you know, being so close to home."

The room felt suddenly cold. I was unfortunate enough to know just how close to home it could get. Gripping the edge of the desk, I tried to force out visions of the faceless woman socialising with the girls I worked with before having her life cruelly snatched away from her, my father's face potentially the last she had seen. Millie could only be in her late twenties. I glanced over at her, noticing for the first time her red-rimmed, puffy eyes. She held her hand flat against her forehead, her elbow leaning on the desk for support, and stared, unseeing, at her computer screen.

Thomas jerked his head in her direction, keeping his voice low. "We've tried to tell her to go home, have some time, but she said she'd rather be here." He shrugged, sighing. "I don't think anyone feels safe being alone."

I nodded, unable to find anything useful to offer. Placing my hand on his shoulder, I gave it a squeeze. "Thanks, Thomas. You guys just take care of each other, okay?"

He nodded, looking up at me through watery eyes and perfect lashes.

Crossing the office in a few short strides, I reached Millie's desk. Lowering myself to crouch at her level, I placed my hands on her leg and moved myself into her line of sight as she looked around. She seemed startled, as though she had suddenly remembered where she was.

I had been the one that everyone avoided because they didn't know how to approach me, or what to say, even to a child. I wouldn't do that to Millie.

"Millie, I am so, so sorry to hear about your friend," I whispered to her, fighting to hold back my own emotions. I could feel the eyes of every person in the office resting on the back of my head. "Please know I am always here if there is anything I can do for you or if you'd like to talk about her."

Opening my arms, I held them awkwardly as Millie stared at me blankly for a few seconds. Before I knew what had happened, her full weight was pressed against me. She had crumpled into my arms and sobbed noisily.

I wondered how she would feel about me – if she would have still been so keen to accept my embrace – if she knew who I really was.

6

It was barely past eight in the evening, but I lay in the dim light of the bedroom, the TV on, sound barely up enough for me to hear. The weeks since my father's release had left me exhausted, feeling like both forever and no time at all had passed. It had become all I could think about. The continuous internal battle I faced was like carrying a weight. I ricocheted between desperation to hear of his arrest, to once again feel safe in my own surroundings, and silently praying, begging, pleading for some evidence to come to light to prove that he wasn't guilty.

If this was the work of my father, his kills were getting closer, homing in on my safe haven. Was he doing that on purpose? Some kind of game of cat and mouse? Had he requested to be located back in this area? That thought left me bitter. He had no right to be close to any of us.

It also left me feeling guilty by association. I barely knew anything about Dennis, so I could hardly try to predict his end game. Did he want to watch me die, be the one responsible as he squeezed the last breath from my body? Or was it bigger than that now? Had my survival as a child changed things, left him wanting to inflict more on me than just death? Did he know how afraid I was of the people around me connecting me to him? Was his plan to isolate me? Watch me lose everything, see my life implode around me before he ended it? My mind was in overdrive.

I saw his face everywhere, jumped at every sound and found myself double-checking every lock.

I was so desperate to tell Annie and Dalaja everything, unburden the ugly truth and find myself wrapped in the warmth of their support. They had been my best friends since college, the closest thing I now had to family. The moment had played out in my head countless times, picturing the looks of shock on their faces as I told them of my connection to the infamous serial killer they would have heard horror stories about when they were children. I imagined their acceptance, the reassurance that it didn't change anything. But reality crushed that idea each and every time I found myself basking in it, replacing it with images of my friends exchanging looks, avoiding meeting my pleading stare. In my mind, I watched them – supportive on the surface of it, but edging away from me, freezing me out. How could I blame them? Hadn't I been the one to hold back, to keep them at arm's length? Hadn't I always held myself on the outside, never trusting them enough to open myself up and allow them to make their own judgement on me and our friendship?

How could our relationship weather the lies I had allowed it to be built on? They would feel as though they had never really known me at all.

I was the daughter of a murderer. Of course they'd want to separate themselves from me. After all, it came back to that age-old question, nature or nurture – the abused who became the abuser, the child of the alcoholic who turned to the bottle. How could anyone be sure I wasn't just like him? A chip off the old block.

Thinking about him had left me spooked, with that same feeling you'd experience after you've watched a horror movie and find yourself afraid to turn out the lights or walk up the stairs. Although rationally you know watching a scary film isn't going to conjure up a monster, your head is still too absorbed by that feeling of it all being real to allow the fear to subside. I turned off the TV, aware what I needed most was sleep.

A pillar of light stretched out across the bedroom, casting its glow and making me aware of the gap in the curtains. I threw off the covers, springing from the warmth of the bed and dashing over to yank them closed. I paused, hovering at the window. Only seconds before I had felt horribly exposed, but the realisation dawned that, with my bedroom in darkness, no one would be able to see inside. That, plus of course the fact that I was on the second floor. I crossed my arms over my chest, attempting to retain some warmth, and rolled my eyes at my own paranoia.

I was allowing the fear I was working so hard to suppress to creep under my skin. My father was hardly going to be standing under the streetlight, waiting for me to look out of my window and spot him. I screwed up my eyes, shaking my head, and yanked the curtains together.

"You're being stupid," I scalded myself out loud, hoping the sound of my own voice in the quiet room would help me pull myself together. The near silence that followed only served to spook me further, reminding me that I was alone.

Shivering in the cool air of the bedroom, I scrambled

under the duvet and lay perfectly still, listening out for any sound, unable to switch off, wanting to hear Dan home, wondering if Dennis might be close by.

I must have drifted off, as a scraping sound broke through my dream, causing my heart to pound as I sat up with a whimper, straining to listen.

At the sound of the front door opening and being pushed closed again, I gripped the bedsheets, visions of Dennis creeping his way into my home filling my mind.

The thump of shoes being kicked off, hitting the wall, instantly diminished my fears. I highly doubted Dennis would have stopped to remove his shoes while breaking into my house. I drew in long breaths, willing my heart to return to a normal rhythm in the hope Dan wouldn't notice how jittery I was.

The room was filled with a glow as he switched on the landing light. Eventually, after his usual bathroom ritual, Dan appeared, a dark outline in the doorway to our bedroom.

"Hey," I called out, thankful I'd been able to hold the tremble from my voice.

"Oh, hey, babe. You're awake." He perched on the end of our bed, reaching out towards me. I pushed myself upright and linked my fingers through his.

"Yeah. Couldn't switch off. It's been a horrible day."

He turned to me, releasing a deep sigh, his features seeming to sag under the weight of it all.

"I tried to call. I wanted to be the one to tell you." He trailed off, seemingly lost for anything more to say.

"Yeah." I shook my head and waved away his concern. "Dennis? Do you know...?" I couldn't bring myself to say any more.

Something flashed in Dan's eyes and the lines depended on his forehead.

"He doesn't have an alibi for the times of the murders, but equally, we have absolutely fuck-all to link him to anything." Even in the dimly lit room, I could see his jaw clench. "In fact, we just have fuck-all." His voice had turned into more of a growl as his fingers tightened and dug into mine. I realised how hard this must be on him.

The silence hung thick between us. He released his grip, standing and starting to undress.

"The woman, the last one... she was friends with some of the reception team at work." I bit hard on the inside of my lip, refusing to allow the simmering emotions spill over. I had no right to cry.

Dan closed his eyes for a few seconds and sighed. "Yeah, I know. We are having to interview a few of them, to piece together her last known movements, try to see if there's any connections."

Of course he knew. I felt the heat rise to my cheeks, conscious of how self-indulgent I was being, but I had to ask.

"Dan, do they really think it's coincidence? I don't want to try to make this about me, but these murders have only started since Dennis was released. The first one seemed close, but this last one, she was friends with people I knew." I swallowed hard, my throat suddenly too dry to speak.

"You haven't heard anything from him? He hasn't tried to contact you, has he?" He stared hard at me as he asked, almost challenging. There was no need to specify whom he was talking about.

My stomach clenched.

"No, nothing. I'd have told you." Fiddling with the corner of the bedsheet, I was unable to meet his glare.

Dan nodded, seemingly pacified by my assurances. "Good," he mumbled as he flicked off the light and fumbled his way back to the bed. He clambered in beside me, pulling me to him, and I snuggled in. We lay in silence for a few minutes. I was aware Dan hadn't actually answered my question, but I wasn't sure I had the energy to press him on it. It felt disgusting that women had been killed and my biggest concern was still for myself, but I couldn't shake the feeling that somehow, this was about me.

PUSHING my way through the heavy door and into the warm embrace of the shop, I let the aroma of coffee swamp my senses. Annie waved a hand frantically, springing from her seat, her face seeming to light up at the sight of me. Guilt gnawed at my insides with the knowledge that I had been avoiding my best friends.

"Hey." Annie beamed at me, throwing her arms open and drawing me in against her body. As always, she smelled like incense. "How are you?" She drew back, holding me at arm's length and studying me. Her brow creased as her eyes roamed all over my face, searching.

I shrugged, unable to meet her gaze. "I'm good. Just busy, you know?" I waved a hand around, attempting to force a smile and disguise my unease.

"Oh, put her down." Dalaja rose from her armchair, rolling her eyes dramatically and batting away Annie's arm playfully. "It's only been a couple of weeks. Maybe she just needed a break from your dramatics."

Annie turned to glare at her but was unable to hide her smile. "Shut up, ice queen." She finally released my arms and allowed Dalaja to step in, who pressed the side of her face against my own, the closest she came to an embrace.

It had always been a source of amusement to the three of us how mismatched we were. Annie and I had been dorm mates in college, and although we couldn't have been more different, we'd hit it off instantly. She had been the first person I had truly allowed myself to get close to, our natural friendship and living arrangement sweeping me up and making it impossible to keep her at a distance. Dalaja hadn't been so lucky with her dorm mates, living with a girl who liked to stay up all night listening to heavy rock, and another who smoked so much weed she constantly accused everyone of stealing her misplaced belongings. So when one of the other girls in our dorm had only lasted a week or two before dropping out, leaving a room free, Dalaja requested to be moved and had been offered the spare room with us.

It took me a little longer to warm to Dalaja. She had a cool exterior, the polar opposite to Annie, who would hug you as soon as look at you. I'd wanted to keep my circle small – reduce the chance of anyone discovering who I was – and although I hate to admit it now, I would never have opened myself up to her if it hadn't been for Annie. It had felt safe, with just the two of us. I had loved Annie instantly and had considered Dalaja a threat initially, but of course, Annie being Annie would never hear of anyone being made to feel unwelcome.

The three of us became the most unlikely trio.

Dalaja was fashionable, with a figure to die for and an unmatched ability to apply make-up to her already flawless complexion. Her expensive perfume would linger like an aura, intoxicating and drawing eyes which tracked her as she passed. She had legs that seemed impossibly long and a mane of ebony hair that she was able to fix into a limitless number of glossy styles. Her organisational skills were second to none and she came with absolutely no filter, always willing to tell you exactly how it was. That was part of what made her so good at her job as a paralegal for a major law firm.

It had been me that had introduced her to Phil after meeting him in a coffee shop near our university. He had been behind me in the long queue, and after finally retrieving my longed-for caffeine hit, I had accidentally knocked it off the side as I grabbed for the sugar. Cursing loudly, I'd watched, horrified, the contents of the cardboard cup spread across the floor. Embarrassed and close to tears, I apologised to the guy who came over with a mop, mortification turning to fury as he snubbed me, but was thankfully distracted by Phil, who nudged my arm and held out a fresh cup.

I'd been so grateful and touched by the gesture, I'd found myself agreeing to walk back with him, and had instantly warmed to him. My mind had warned me that I was allowing too many people to get too close, but I had shut out my fears, rebellion stirring inside me, the warmth of having people around me for the first time in my life more intoxicating than any drink or substance.

I had quickly introduced him to the girls, who enjoyed spending time with him as much as I did. It was impossible to miss the sparks between him and Dalaja, and when she had mumbled something after two shots of tequila about whether I would be mad if she told me she liked him, Annie and I had dissolved into fits of laughter at the idea that she had thought it possible we had missed it.

I had never been attracted to Phil. Already with Dan by

then, I saw Phil as more of a brother and best friend. I was delighted to see him and Dalaja together. Their relationship was as fiery as their personalities, and although they went through their share of turbulence, they had weathered it well.

Annie couldn't have been much more different to Dalaja. She was short, with mousy hair that sat on her shoulders. She wasn't overweight, but her rounded figure – especially next to Dalaja – and choice of baggy clothes always made her seem that way. She possessed a warmth that seemed to enter the room with her, and was able to engage with anyone and draw people to her. Annie's partner, Tim, was a timid man and we could never understand what Annie saw in him. He was undeniably more intelligent than the rest of us put together, but he was plain looking to say the least and as quiet and unassuming as Annie was vibrant.

Then there was me. I guess I fell somewhere in between, but there was only one thing I saw when I looked at myself beside my two best friends. The fake. The outsider. I guess that's what came when you could never fully open yourself up to people.

"We got you a latte." Annie gestured towards the huge bucket-like mug as I sank gratefully into the vacant chair and scooped up the mug.

"Hmm, thanks."

"So, how *have* you been? I know it's only been a couple of weeks." Annie shot Dalaja a look as she chuckled again. "But we never go this long without seeing each other."

It was true. The three of us rarely went more than a week without meeting, and we'd be in constant contact between times in our WhatsApp group. I had been acting strangely, avoiding my best friends, barely even able to bring myself to reply to their messages – I knew that. I had been all-consumed by my thoughts of Dennis and his intentions. How could I face two of the people who knew me best in the world and manage to keep everything hidden from them?

It had been a conscious decision not to tell them who I was at first. I had promised myself that I would never speak of my past again once I had become Rachel, but we formed a seemingly unbreakable bond, and I would have trusted them with my life. I faced a constant internal battle over the right thing to do, aware that I should tell them, that keeping from them something so huge would be detrimental to our friendship if they were to ever discover my awful secret. How could it not? I had just been waiting for the right time, and as of yet, all these years down the line, I had still never managed to slip it into conversation that I happened to be the daughter of a murderer. I used every excuse to justify it to myself, including that Dalaja would tell Phil. He had become an incredibly successful journalist, and despite how close we were, part of me wondered whether he would be willing – or able – to put his profession aside if a story of this magnitude was to fall into his lap. Granted, it wouldn't have been much of a story to write about the daughter of a killer, but I always knew the day would come for Dennis to be released, and I had always known that somehow, that would be the beginning of something. And I had been right.

Phil cared about me, no doubt, but I wasn't sure he was capable of turning off the predatory instincts when it came down to it. I could picture the conflict on his face – aware of the murderer's release, the start of another wave of killings, and the link one of his closest friends held to it all.

It would break his career to sit on something so big and allow someone else to yank it out from underneath him.

What would I even have said if he asked to interview me about it all? Promised he'd spin it so that I looked like the innocent victim I was? I didn't ever want to find myself in that situation.

Looking back, I knew I should have told them from the beginning, back when we were in college, allow them to make their judgement and hope that our friendship would be strong enough to withstand the confession. But I had been so afraid that they would freeze me out. I convinced myself at the time it was unfair to share it with Phil, who was working so hard to earn himself a name, and expect him to keep my secret. I couldn't take the risk of watching the life I had fought so hard for crumble around me.

They were the family I'd never had, and the thought of losing them, of them turning their backs on me, was too much to bear.

The more time that passed, the harder it became. Months became years and suddenly it was impossible to tell the people I shared everything with the truth of the most monumental event of my life. So I didn't.

"I know. I'm sorry. Everything's been crazy." I kept as much of my face as I could hidden behind my coffee mug. "Janet has been off sick again, so I've been picking up extra hours at work. I don't know where the weeks have gone." A heat flushed my cheeks as I allowed the lie to slip out.

Annie pulled a face, wrinkling her nose. "They can't expect you to drop everything and go cover every time she can't be arsed to go into work, Rach. Just because she's got kids." She shook her head, rolling her eyes.

Guilt prickled and I sent off a silent apology to my colleague for painting her out to be flaky after only a handful of times I'd actually had to cover her for sickness.

"It's fine." I shook my head, waving it off, keeping a tight grip on my mug with the other hand. "How's things with you?" I nodded towards Annie, widening my eyes, desperate to change the subject.

"Nothing yet but it's early days." She smiled but I didn't miss the slight droop of her shoulders. Annie and Tim had decided it was time to try for a baby. I don't know why I'd been so surprised when she had told us; it was what most people did.

Dan and I had discussed children early on in our relationship and I had almost withered with relief when he'd anxiously told me he didn't want to have any. I couldn't bear the idea of bringing a child into the world, all too aware of my resemblance to Dennis, petrified that if I created a life, it may also mirror our family. What kind of mother would I be if I resented my child every time I looked at them?

Dan had suffered his own traumatic childhood with a mother who was barely more than a child herself, pregnant at only seventeen. His father had sworn to be around for her, to stand by her and support her and their child, but had scarpered at the first sign of dirty nappies and sleepless nights.

Dan's mother had done exactly what I was afraid of and had resented Dan every time she looked at him. They'd never managed to fix their relationship. His father had contacted him a few years before, having tracked him down, keen to make amends for the years he had been absent. He hadn't gone on to have any more children, and they had barely had the chance to build any kind of relationship before he was moved into a nursing home, dementia eating away at what remained of his mind.

"I guess Dan is having to work all hours with… what's

going on?" Dalaja questioned, a hint of curiosity embedded in her tone. I couldn't disguise the heat that clawed its way up my body, leaving my face burning once more.

Whenever the girls asked about anything to do with Dan's work, my thoughts would instantly go to Phil.

He and Dan had shared more than the occasional awkward moment. They were respectful towards one another but we could always sense the battle for dominance between them. Their conflicting career paths made it almost impossible for them to be around one another. I couldn't help wondering if Dalaja would report back to Phil with anything I let slip.

"Hmm." I nodded uncommittedly, swallowing hard.

Dalaja eyed me, cocking her head. "Everything alright between you two?"

Relief flooded me at the shift in subject and that my best friend was making the assumption that there were issues within my marriage. I gave a small shrug and shamelessly allowed her to believe that was what was causing my discomfort.

"It's just tough when he's having to give so much time to the job." I pulled a face and sighed dramatically. "Nothing to worry about. Just squabbles because we are both overworked and underpaid." I huffed out a laugh as Dalaja offered a sympathetic smile.

"Hear, hear, sister. Story of my life." She rolled her eyes, raising her coffee mug. "On both counts. Phil seems more wrapped up in reporting on this case than he ever has been in me." She snorted.

"He's not worth having around the odd time he's actually home. Seriously though, it must be hard on both of you."

I turned to look at Annie, her features creased with

concern, frown lines running so deep they looked like they had been carved into her forehead.

"How is Dan coping with having to work such an awful case? It must be just horrendous having to witness first-hand the despicable things that monster has done." I wasn't sure I had ever seen Annie's eyes appear so dark.

The room seemed to lurch beneath me, and I gripped the arm of the chair for support, slamming my coffee cup down too hard and slopping its contents onto the wobbly table.

Annie's face cleared as she grabbed a wad of tissues and began soaking up the spillage.

"Sorry, Rach. It's probably the last thing you want to talk about, what with Dan living it at the moment. It's just all you hear about right now, isn't it?" She shook her head, mopping up my spilt drink. "To tell you the truth, the whole thing is freaking me out a bit and it makes me furious that because of a creature like that, preying on women, we are all afraid to be on our own, or walk the streets right now."

I cleared my throat, attempting to work out how best to respond.

"Disgusting, isn't it?" I turned to see Dalaja, eyes narrowed as she agreed with Annie's statement. "I hope when they find him, they throw away the key. Those kinds of animals deserve everything that's coming to them." She spat the words.

"Poor Dan, having to be so closely involved. No wonder you guys are feeling the strain. It can't be good for you, coming that close to a psychotic killer."

7

BEFORE

My mother wouldn't allow my father to take me to a doctor. She told him they would treat me like a lab rat. I heard him shouting at her that they couldn't continue on like nothing was happening, that they were sticking their heads in the sand and couldn't live with a psychopath under the same roof.

I'd heard the term mentioned before, but that was the first time it really piqued my interest. Cycling to the local library, I pored through books, devouring every snippet of information on psychopaths and who they were. It was incredible. I was utterly enthralled reading about others who shared my intelligence, my urges, understanding for the first time exactly who I was. The books taught me we held the ability to mimic those around us, and that so many before me had used this method to continue on, hiding in plain sight. It was never difficult; my memory had always been photographic, so I could recall exactly how to display every feeling I needed to conjure up with perfect accuracy.

I continued to visit the library, my mother insistent to my

father that I had found an outlet in books, that she had been right and it was nothing more than a phase that had fizzled out once I had found a way to channel my intelligence. I quickly learned the things to say, the ways to act that would have her in the palm of my hand. It was easier than I had even imagined it would be. My father on the other hand still didn't shift. I regularly caught him staring at me across the dinner table. As I got older, he would flinch if I got too close to him, avoid being in a room at the same time as me. I couldn't stifle my sniggers as I would watch him cower away from me if I turned my head quickly enough towards him. He would scamper off as if I had been about to bite him. I was smart enough to know never to allow my mother to witness those moments, always ensuring I was no less than charm itself while she was around.

I could see the decline in their relationship. The more perfect I became in the eyes of my mother, the more of a monster I became to my father. What started out as a splinter continued to fracture until their relationship disintegrated around them.

Up until then, I had never had a reason to be interested in how it might have affected my brother.

8

Dan and I had become like passing ships and I missed his company, the comfort of having him near, of not having to pretend. He was the only other person – apart from my aunty and uncle – who knew my true identity. With my mother dead and my father incarcerated, my maternal aunt, Alison, had been the only other relative I had left. With no others anywhere near local to us, social services had placed me with her, and somehow, I had been kept out of the media, allowed to live what would have appeared to anyone else a normal life.

My aunty had despised my father, of course, blaming him for not supporting my mother enough, for not being there when she needed him. She had insisted that my mother would have given up the drugs given the right support, and that he never gave her the chance, lumbering her with us kids the whole time while he went out and enjoyed his freedom. I could, of course, understand her fury towards him but struggled to see how she could believe that his working to keep a roof over our heads could be considered "freedom." Until I found out about Naomi Wells. Naomi was a work colleague of my father. They had seemingly gotten along well until, of course, he killed her.

She had been murdered in the same way as my mother and a local schoolteacher – strangled with their own scarf. Their deaths weren't connected straight away, the MO not conventionally obvious. It was only after my father had been locked up that friends and colleagues of the pair came forward with their belief that Dennis and Naomi may have been participating in an affair. My father's solicitor heavily denied his responsibility for her death, along with the death of the teacher whom he seemingly had no connection to. The lack of evidence made it impossible to charge him, but the public were convinced of his guilt.

My mother's sister, Alison, had dabbled in drugs herself but considered herself clean, seemingly blind or unwilling to see the endless bottles she drained. She said she drank to forget, but I always thought it was as much to block out the things that were going on right under her nose. I had seen the way my uncle looked at our neighbour's daughter when she came to visit her elderly mother, seen the way that he would always have an errand to run soon after her car had pulled up outside. Alison buried her head in the bottle.

As soon as I was old enough for social services not to give chase – and aware that my aunt and uncle would have no desire to – I had moved as far away as I could get. As I was legally considered an adult, and with the strong possibility of my identity being leaked now there was no obligation for me to remain anonymous, the legal system allowed me to leave behind my past identity, changing my name and helping me start over.

The guilt had tugged at me – that I had left, never telling

Alison where I was going or who I had become. She had never exactly become a mother figure to me, but she was the closest thing I had and she had done her best. But she was the last link to my past and if I truly wanted a clean break, I had to break that link. I didn't think of them much, but did occasionally wonder if she was still alive, or if her search for the bottom of the bottle had finally caught up with her. I doubted they thought of me.

I had promised myself, once I had cut all ties with my old identity, that I would never speak of it again, that I would become Rachel Johnson and forget that Joanna Raiker had ever existed. My father had sent letters to me while I had lived with my aunt, but naively, I had never expected to hear from my father or the prison again once I had left. I had even managed to keep it from my best friends.

And then I had met Dan.

I had been working as the manager at a sandwich bar whilst I put myself through university. I hated the job, but the pay was better than average, and I got to take home any leftovers. For someone as poor as I was, with no parents to siphon money from, the chance of a free meal was always too good to pass up, so I stuck it out.

I'd noticed Dan the second he had walked in. It was late afternoon and it was the lull after the lunchtime rush. There was no missing the way heads turned to appreciate him. I never considered for a second that he would so much as offer me a second glance – I was nothing more than the sandwich girl with the lank hair. I remember cursing myself for not making more of an effort for work as I'd watched him approach, all the same. He had studied the menu and I had used the opportunity to admire him. He'd been in his uniform but had the kind of air about him that meant even if he hadn't been, you'd have still known that, somehow, he was a figure to be respected.

I had dropped my gaze, fixating on the list I was making for the suppliers. My cheeks had started to flush as I had sensed him hovering in front of me, and I had been unable to meet his eye. I remember thinking that he had on just the perfect amount of aftershave. The guys at uni seemed to either slather it on, making it almost impossible to breathe around them, or they'd smell distinctly of body odour. There didn't seem to be a happy medium.

He was older than the boys I'd been with, but it only served to make him more desirable. He seemed distinguished, mature.

Dan had ordered his sandwich, chatting to me as I prepared it. I had enjoyed the conversation, reminding myself that he was just being polite and that he was only talking to me to pass the time while I made his food order. I had still been disappointed when he had left, a tiny part of me hoping that he had enjoyed my company as much as I had his.

I spent a little longer on my hair the following morning, applied a little make up. My head shot up every time the bell rang on the door, signalling a customer had entered, but Dan didn't appear. Then the following day, just as I had started to think he wouldn't be back, he had swept in through the door, bringing with him that wonderful fresh scent along with the clench of my belly as the sense of nerves and excitement fluttered inside me.

He had come in several more times, our conversation growing more familiar and verging on flirting. Again, I tried to tell myself that he probably flirted with everyone, that it didn't mean anything, but I couldn't stop myself from daydreaming about spending time with him outside of the bloody sandwich shop.

I had envisaged the perfect moment, where he would finally ask me out and I would be so cool about it, casually agreeing as though that kind of thing happened to me all the time. That had not been the reality. I had stood there gawping at him, replaying his words in my head and trying to figure out if there was a possibility I had misheard him.

Dan had begun to look uncomfortable, shifting from foot to foot and rubbing his stubble with the tips of his fingers. After way too long, I had agreed, with no sign of keeping my cool. I had practically fallen over myself to say yes, and he had visibly brightened at my reaction. His shoulders lifted and he seemed to become even taller.

We had exchanged numbers and Dan had promised to message me.

We had only gone out twice before I knew that I was falling for him. Dan was amazing, not only gorgeous to look at but kind, attentive and thoughtful. He had mentioned the age gap, a serious expression on his face as he'd questioned if it was a concern for me, which of course it wasn't. Men like Dan didn't come along every day, and a few years between us was hardly a reason to pass up the chance of being with him. The realisation had slammed into me that with Dan in his line of work, at some point there was a good chance he was going to find out who I really was. I considered breaking things off with him, cutting contact to save the heartache for us both. He spent his days working to put away filth like my father, vicious criminals who lived for the suffering of others. Would he ever be able to look at me in the same way if I told him?

I had decided to allow myself one last date with him. I

would forget everything, block it all out and enjoy the evening before telling him that I thought it was probably best if we cooled things off. But the end of the evening came, and I found myself allowing him to walk me home and kiss me goodnight at my dormitory entrance, and agreeing to see him again the following day.

More dates meant me falling further, and eventually, I was in too deep to just call it off without a decent explanation. Regardless of my promise to myself, I had no choice by that point but to be honest with him.

I'd prepared myself for the worst, expecting to witness his lip curl, his features crinkle with horror and disgust before walking out on me. We had been out to the most perfect little restaurant, a tiny place that felt cosy rather than cramped and had hit the perfect balance between being fancy and still welcoming. The place had a delicious buttery aroma and I had watched plates of food being delivered to neighbouring tables, my mouth watering, but when our food arrived, I had pushed it around my plate. I had felt his eyes on me as I had stared down at my barely touched meal.

"Rach, are you okay? Is there something wrong with the food?" He had dropped his head, attempting to move into my line of sight. My fork had slipped through my clammy fingers with a clatter, my hands trembling and my chest seeming to compress my lungs. I couldn't put it off any longer. I reached for my water glass, swallowing back a few gulps before I composed myself.

Tears had pricked the corners of my eyes, and I'd blinked rapidly in an attempt to disperse them before Dan noticed.

He lowered his own knife and fork, lining them up perfectly on his plate as he did every time.

"What is it? What's going on?" His voice was low, and I

wondered if I imagined the wobble that seemed to have entered it.

I cast a glance around at the occupants of the other tables. "Dan, there's something I need to tell you. I probably should have told you before, but... Well, I didn't know how things were going to progress between us and I didn't want to... I mean, I haven't told anyone this and I hadn't planned to, but with you being a police officer and everything..."

I risked stealing a glance at him. His eyes seemed to have turned a shade darker, his lips pressed together and his forehead almost forming a V. He searched my face, and I fumbled around for the best way to voice the awful truth.

"So, when I was younger, like a lot younger..." I cleared my throat, scanning the people around us once more to ensure that no one else was listening in. Everyone around us seemed to be lost in their own conversations, oblivious to the bomb I was about to drop on the man I had grown to love in just a few short weeks, along with my own life.

"Erm, my dad... he, erm... he committed a crime. A pretty terrible one." I avoided meeting his gaze, rubbing at the back of my neck as I felt my face flush.

"What kind of a crime?" Dan's voice was low, no hint of warmth to it.

Reaching for my water glass again, I lifted it, swirling its contents, absentminded. I still couldn't bring myself to look at him. Thinking back to my childhood therapy sessions, I focused on my breathing. In for four, out for six, my chest still feeling as though it may be about to burst with my impossibly fast heart rate.

"He... well, he... he killed some people. Including my mum and sister. I was young, really young. I don't remember any of it." I snapped my jaw shut, realising that I was blabbering.

There was a sharp intake of breath. The wall of stony silence I was met with after that somehow seemed worse than if he'd yelled at me. I was desperate for him to say something. I dropped the glass back onto the table, only avoiding spilling it due to the lack of water left in it. Reaching for my napkin, I gripped it in my fingertips just to give them something to do, fighting the urge to shred it.

"Were you there?" His words were barely more than a whisper.

It took me a few seconds to process his question. I had expected disgust, horror, fury even, but not that question.

"Yes. I don't remember anything about it, though. No one knows why he didn't hurt me too. There were theories that I'd been hiding or something, but when the police arrived, I was in his arms like nothing had happened. He was holding me and I showed no sign of being afraid. He had plenty of time to kill me too if that's what he'd wanted to do." I shrugged, shame burning at my admission.

I felt his hands before I saw them. They cupped mine, gripping them and giving a tight squeeze. His warm, dry skin felt so good against my clammy palms as I turned my hands, linking my fingers through his.

The tears overpowered me despite my efforts to fight them. Dan released my hands, reaching over and brushing one away.

"I am so, so sorry for what he did, Rach. For what he's put you through. Thank you for trusting me enough to tell me."

Snapping my head up, I met his eye for the first time all evening. His compassion was far more than I deserved, but surely it was about to be followed by his explanation of why we could no longer be together. His features were soft, no sign of the anguish or disgust I had expected to see.

"He's still locked up, right? You're safe from him?" I had witnessed his body visibly tense as he'd asked the question, leaning in closer towards me.

I nodded rapidly. "He's still in prison. His release date is years off. The prison are the only ones who know where I am and will inform me when the time comes." I paused. "That's not why I told you all of this, Dan. I'm not asking you for your protection if that's what you're thinking. I wasn't expecting to meet anyone, to feel... The way that I do. I'm telling you because you deserve to know... and what with your job and everything..." I trailed off, uncertain as to how to finish the sentence.

"I know you don't need my protection, Rach, but I would like to be there for you. You don't have to face the world on your own. Regardless of what your dad did or didn't do, it doesn't change my feelings for you. It doesn't change anything." He shrugged, sticking out his bottom lip.

"But your job? Doesn't it cause some sort of issue for you, being with the daughter of a convicted murderer? If anyone was ever to find out... And what if... what if I turn out to be like him?" I bit the inside of my lip, unwilling to allow the emotions to get the better of me again.

Dan had reached for my hands again, gripping both of them in his and giving a gentle squeeze.

"Oh, Rach. This was your father's crime. You are not your father. You aren't capable of those kinds of things. I *know* you," he repeated. "What kind of a police officer would I be if I didn't recognise traits like that in someone?" He tilted his head, his eyes softening with a warm smile.

I gawped at him, unable to accept his words, his perfect reaction to the bomb I had just dropped on him.

"But Dennis wasn't always bad, was he? My mum married him, and they had us before he..."

Dan held up a hand, his face turning serious again. He leaned in towards me.

"Evil isn't in the blood, Rach. Yes, it can be in your genetics, but not because of something your parents did. It's just part of someone's makeup, like if one of your parents can sing. It doesn't automatically mean their children will have the same talent. We're capable of breaking cycles, and even those who have the capability still have the ability to make the choice." His jaw clenched. "Trust me. I've seen enough to know what it looks like. You're not the same as him. If you were, I wouldn't be falling in love with you."

That night was the first we spent together.

9

I gave the treatment couch one last wipe-down, the overpowering smell of the antibacterial cleaner causing me to feel dizzy. The cleaners would be in, but I liked to make sure the room was neat, ready for Janet. I ran my hands under the tap, then wiped them on my trousers, satisfied.

I was more than ready to leave, always having hated being one of the last in the building in the evening. Flicking off the light, I pulled the door closed and turned the key in the lock. Making my way to the reception, I passed through the empty waiting room. There was no reason for the goosebumps to break out all over my skin, but something was making me feel uneasy about being in an area that was usually so full of life. Shoving my way through the door to the reception with my shoulder, I practically fell over myself to get inside as the door gave easily against my weight, and flinched as I saw the outline of someone standing beside the window.

"Oh Christ! Rachel, you just about gave me a heart attack

bursting in here like that." Lydia held her hand against her chest, her face flushed, eyes wide as they darted around.

"Sorry." My own heart hammered against my ribs and I attempted to regain some composure, aware that I sounded breathless. Lydia didn't seem to notice the state I had gotten myself into, having turned back towards the window. One hand was still hovering over her chest and she chewed on the thumb nail of her other, craning her neck, seeming to be searching for something. The blinds had been closed on all but the one window she stood in front of, where they remained partially open, just enough to see out of.

"I just came to see if there were any scripts for signing before we go." I paused, gesturing towards the prescription tray, aware she wasn't really listening to me. "Are you okay?" I turned to observe her odd behaviour, my own practically forgotten.

"It's just been a bit of a weird evening." She glanced round at me before slumping back down into the chair at her desk. "I'm sure we're all just a bit on edge, you know, with everything that's going on."

My skin prickled again as a cold ripple passed over me. "Weird in what way?" I questioned seriously, unwilling to shrug it off and leave if Lydia was feeling agitated by something.

She sighed, her forehead creasing as she looked up at me.

"The buzzer went a couple of times, and no one was there when we picked up."

After hours, the doors were locked and only patients with prebooked appointments could gain entry to the building. There was a buzzer system so the receptionist working the late shift could buzz the patient through, once they had confirmed their appointment.

"Could've just been kids?" I shrugged, uncertain as to whom I was trying to convince.

"Yeah, that's what we said at first." Lydia's eyes moved to the window again before returning to meet my own. "But then we thought we saw someone hanging around outside. Thomas was here then and he was certain he'd seen him too."

My skin turned from ice to fire in an instant, my stomach plummeting. "Him?" I fought to keep my tone even.

"Hmm." She nodded, subtly stealing another look out of the window. "It had to be a man; we could tell by the build." She lifted her shoulders and held out her elbows, signalling a larger frame.

"Then Thomas left. He promised to keep his phone in his hand and call me as soon as he got to his car. When he phoned, he said he'd seen the guy again. He was hanging around at the back of the building. Thomas said he was tall, wearing a long coat with a high collar. It was dark and he was fairly far away so he couldn't see what he looked like. He was pretty freaked out and asked if I wanted him to come back." She swallowed hard. "I didn't want him hanging around outside so told him I'd call the police if I heard anything, and of course, I've got the panic button on my computer." It was policy that the last doctor on shift always stayed in the building until the rest of the staff were ready to leave. "I promised we'd walk together to the cars."

Her hand moved back to her mouth, and she chewed on her thumb nail subconsciously once again.

I crossed the room towards the window, duplicating Lydia's earlier stance as I peered out into the darkness. It had gotten darker still in the short time I had been in the office, making it almost impossible to see out beyond my own reflection. The thought that I could barely see out and yet anyone outside could so easily see us, sitting targets in the illuminated office, unnerved me. I pulled the cord, closing the blind with a swooshing sound.

"Have you seen or heard anything since?" I turned back to Lydia. She shook her head. Dropping her hands onto the desk, she grabbed a pen, beginning to click it in and out repeatedly.

"No, nothing. If Thomas hadn't been here, I would have been certain I'd imagined the whole thing." The clicking of the pen increased in speed. "I think we're all just feeling so anxious at the moment, with everything you hear on the news and stuff. I don't like being on my own much right now."

I swallowed past the lump that seemed to have lodged in my throat.

"Well, that's understandable given the circumstances. I think we—"

Hammering on the window cut me off. Lydia jumped out of her seat, flying towards me and letting out something between a scream and a yelp as she grabbed hold of my arm. My knees threatened to buckle as I jumped at the sudden sound. Lydia clung to me, both of us facing the window that the banging had come from, yet neither of us making any move towards it. We remained frozen, the only sound that broke the silence that of our rapid breathing. Lydia let out a whimpering noise beside me.

Before I could decide on what we should do next, the sound of the buzzer blared out, breaking the silence once again and causing Lydia to dig her fingers into my arm as her body jerked. I winced at both the pain and the sudden blare of the buzzer.

Placing my hand over Lydia's, I attempted what I hoped would be a reassuring look as I squeezed. I gently prised my arm from her grip, lowering her hands back to her sides as she stared at me, wide eyed. "Rachel, please don't." She reached towards me, her hands trembling as I began to move towards the buzzer.

"It's okay," I soothed, holding up my hands. "I'm not going to let anyone in. I'm just going to—" The buzzer screamed out once again, unrelenting as whoever was outside held down the button. I dropped my hands, suddenly irritated. Crossing the room in a few long strides, I snatched the phone from its cradle.

"Can I help?" I snapped, fear, fury and tension bubbling inside the pit of my stomach.

There was a crackling sound through the phone. A few beats of silence passed before a shout almost burst my eardrum, leaving me flinching away from the phone.

"Can you hear me?" The yell seemed to reverberate around my skull, undoubtedly being heard as clearly by Lydia, who still remained the other side of the room.

Holding the phone away from my ear, I spoke into the mouthpiece.

"Yes, I can hear you, but I am afraid the practice is now closed for the day. If you have something that can't wait, you should call—"

"I need a prescription." The man on the other end of the phone had not lowered the volume of his voice, still feeling the need to yell.

"I'm going to need you to stop shouting, sir. I can hear you. I'm afraid, as I said, we are now closed for the day. If you want to come back in the morning, we can have a look into—"

"I can't wait till the fucking morning. I need my prescription now. Why the hell do you think I'm here? You can't not give me stuff I need. You've got a duty. I ain't going nowhere."

Lydia's shoulders had visibly relaxed, although she still looked tense. It wasn't common for this kind of situation to arise, but I guessed this was preferable to a serial murderer hanging around outside the building. I wondered if she had noticed the clear relief I was also feeling regardless of the torrent of abuse I was receiving.

The door to reception was shoved open and Ollie's head appeared around the door, his face clouded with concern.

"What's going on?" Oliver Maple was one of our other doctors.

Lydia turned towards him. "Someone's been hanging around outside. They started banging on the windows and holding down the buzzer. Rachel just answered and he's demanding a—"

She was cut off by the barrage of expletives bursting from the phone in my hand. I stared at it, listening to the vulgar threats and abuse that were being spouted as Ollie instructed Lydia to call the police. She nodded, returning to her desk and snatching up the phone with a sudden sense of purpose.

An hour and a half later, having finally made it home, I sank into a hot bath. The water was verging on too hot, but I welcomed the heat, desperate to feel clean, to wash away the unwelcome feelings the evening had brought.

The police had arrived at the surgery quickly, advising the man that he would be arrested if he didn't move along. It turned out that he was a patient, an addict who was on a controlled benzo regime to help him fight his addiction. He had collected his day's medication only a few hours before, but the urge had taken hold and he had been willing to do anything to gain himself another hit.

The officers had escorted us to our cars, assuring us that the situation would be dealt with. Ollie had returned to the building. The threat having been handed over, he wanted to finish what he had been working on and said he would lock up the building once he was done.

I was relieved when I had seen the officers, not because I had been particularly afraid of the patient, but because I had wondered if Dan would have been informed that I was involved in the callout and, although way below his pay grade, turned up to the scene.

Lydia had seemed much calmer as we had left, perhaps comforted by the presence of the police. I hadn't said anything, unwilling to cause her any further upset, but she hadn't seemed to notice that the patient was short and stocky, nothing like the build that she herself had described. Nor was he wearing a coat with a collar, but in fact, nothing more than a t-shirt, even in the cold chill of the winter evening.

As I lowered myself further under the bubbly water, my skin tingling with the heat as I did, a loud crash made me sit up abruptly, sloshing the water over the edge of the bath and leaving it slapping at the sides. I was certain it had come from the garden. Then a scraping noise left me in no doubt. I hadn't imagined it.

Images flashed through my mind. Had the patient gotten

away from the police? Followed me home? Or had whoever had been there before him, the stranger in the long coat, tracked me down, hanging around outside my house now?

I shivered in the cool air now that my damp skin was exposed, out of the warmth of the water. Already on edge from the events of the evening at work and aware that I would be unable to settle back into my bath, I hauled myself up, reaching for my towel and wrapping it tightly around my body.

Crossing the hall to the bedroom, I hastily dried myself and yanked on a t-shirt, oversized hoodie, and leggings. The logical part of my brain told me to stay inside the house, to make sure that the doors were locked and call Dan. Maybe even the police. But what would I say? I think I heard something in my garden that could be someone from work stalking me, or my psychotic father, or equally it could have been the wind, or an animal.

Everything that had happened, along with thoughts of my dad, were making me paranoid – that was all. Any other day I wouldn't have hesitated to walk outside and check what had caused the noise, and would have considered the idea of calling Dan ludicrous, let alone the police.

I shook my head, releasing my clenched jaw and berating myself for my stupidity. Irritated that I had allowed it all to get to me for the second time in a few hours, I descended the stairs and stalked through to the back door, turning the key and pulling the door back on its hinges.

The cause of the sound was immediately obvious when I flicked on the outside light and spotted the bin, lying on its side, bedside the fence.

My body sagged but the relief was quickly chased away. It was strange that the bin had been left beside the fence. It was something Dan had told me off for in the past, informing me that I was basically setting up a step for an intruder to use to gain entry – or make a quick escape. His warning had shocked me, unnerved me enough to ensure I always kept the bin away from the fence. I couldn't believe Dan would have left it there either, but one of us had to have.

I wrapped my arms across my chest, the wind ruffling my hair as I crossed the garden and battled with the bin like an old drunk to get it back upright.

Once I had dragged it back to its usual spot by the wall, I scurried inside, pulling the door closed behind me.

"Rach?" Dan suddenly appeared in the kitchen clutching a carrier bag of takeaway food, making me jump. "What were you doing in the garden?" Dan eyed the back door, his brows dipped.

"Nothing. The bin lid had blown open and was banging against the side. I just went out to close it up." I gave a forced smile, but my shoulders sagged with the relief of having him home.

Dan studied me for a few seconds before his face cleared and he gave a sharp nod.

"I got your text. I wanted to pop home and check in on you. I know I haven't been around enough and I'm sorry."

I gave a small shrug, unable to argue. I had sent him the message after I'd got home, playing down the events of the evening but aware I needed to tell him, just on the off chance a well-meaning officer mentioned it in passing.

"Are you okay? It must have been scary for you all." Dan's frown was back in place.

I waved it off. "Oh, I'm fine. It wasn't a big deal. Just a patient getting a bit demanding after hours. You have to feel for him, really. He was obviously pretty desperate."

Dan raised a brow. "My sympathy is running a little short for the guy who abused my wife earlier this evening." There was a beat of silence as his words hung between us. "Anyway, enough about him. I brought us Indian. I know it's getting late, but I guessed you wouldn't have eaten with everything that went on." He held up the prized bag of food and my stomach gurgled.

"Sounds perfect." I didn't have to force my smile this time. "I'll grab some plates."

I finished setting the table as Dan emptied the bag of takeaway. "It's so lovely to have you here." Stepping up behind him, I wrapped my arms around his waist and laid my head against his broad back.

Dan turned, drawing me in against his chest and holding me to him.

"Are you sure you're okay?" he mumbled into my hair. "Just... with the timing and all, it must have shaken you up a bit."

"I'm fine. I promise. It was totally unrelated to Dennis. It's just great to see you." I squeezed him tighter, breathing in his scent and wishing I never had to let go. "You're still coming to Dalaja's birthday, right?" I pulled back from him slightly, searching his face. "Annie's been messaging me about it and I've told them you're coming."

"I promised I would." He kissed the top of my head. "Let's eat before the food goes cold. I'm starving."

I took my seat at the table, going through the motions of dishing up and shovelling food into my mouth. But the food, which I knew should have been delicious, seemed bland and hard to swallow.

I couldn't think of a time where I had lied to Dan before. Not that it was really a lie – more an avoidance of telling him the whole truth. Things were crazy for him at work. I also knew that his whole team must believe that my father was responsible for the deaths. The last thing I wanted was to add to his workload, or give him another reason to feel concerned about me. I couldn't – wouldn't – be so selfish. Besides which, I wasn't even totally convinced myself that I wasn't just being crazy and letting my imagination get the better of me. Dennis had been on my mind a lot over the past few weeks, more than usual. It was bound to be leaving me feeling a little jumpy.

My mind crept back to Lydia as she described the man that Thomas had seen hanging around the surgery. Tall, with a long coat and a high collar. That couldn't have been much further from the man who had been outside when the police had arrived. I had all but managed to push that from my mind, convincing myself that Thomas had got it wrong, that he had been too far away to see the man properly, that they were one and the same. But what had left me spooked, what I had held off telling Dan, barely having had time to process it myself, was what I had seen in the garden.

Finding the bin on its side had, of course, struck me as slightly odd. It was a large bin; it would have taken some strength of wind to cause it to tip. But once again, denial had set in and I had assured myself that we had been having some pretty wild weather. It was possible that one strong gust of wind in the right direction *could* have caused it.

But what I couldn't explain, no matter which way I turned it over in my mind and however much I tried to find a reasonable explanation, was the dent in the lid of the bin. And on top of that, fresh enough that the rain had not had time to wash it away, the outline of a muddy footprint.

10

We cleared the kitchen while Dan chatted about office politics. I was only half listening, relieved when he told me he was going to go up and shower. He kissed me lightly on the cheek, peppering kisses down my neck as I pulled my hands free from the rubber gloves.

"You could join me." He raised his eyebrows, and I ached to accept his invitation, forget everything and lose myself to him. I smiled up at him as he ran his hands down my back.

"I had a bath earlier, when I got back." I shrugged, aware of the flimsy excuse.

"You can never be too clean." Dan wiggled his eyebrows, making his intentions clear as he cocked his head.

I batted his arm lightly and turned away, my body protesting at my rejection of him.

"Go have your shower."

Dan's shoulders sagged but he didn't push it, giving a tiny shrug and a sigh of self-sympathy as he trudged up the stairs.

The second I heard the bathroom door close, I was out of the back door, studying the bin lid. Any sign of a footprint had been washed away, replaced by a rapidly growing pool of water that now gathered in the fresh dent. I dipped my fingers into the freezing water, lowering them to feel the shape of the dent, trying to figure out another possible cause for it.

Taking a quick glance back at the house, ensuring that Dan hadn't reappeared, I hurried over to the back gate. The bolt had rusted and become stiff. I cursed as I wiggled it, trying to force it to open. If someone had been trying to make a quick getaway, they would never have been able to use the gate. The bolt squeaked with every wiggle, alerting anyone close to its squeals of protest, and it took all of my strength and effort to get it moving. Finally, the bolt gave with a loud thud as it cracked back against itself. Pulling the gate open, I thrust my head through the gap.

There, in the ally, perfectly in line with where our bin had been on the opposite side of the fence, a pallet rested, propped up against it.

The pallets had been there for weeks. Dan had assumed that Joyce next door had received something delivered on them, and had popped over and asked if she would like him to dispose of them for her. Joyce had looked at him horrified, and insisted they were only going to be there for a short time. She informed him proudly that she planned to make planters from them.

Joyce lived alone. Her husband had left her years before for a woman half their age. Her son and only child was in his twenties and had moved away, his visits a rarity. Joyce had become bitter with age, always seeing the worst in people, and had fallen out with most of our neighbours.

Dan and I both knew Joyce had a hoarding problem, and that those pallets would remain where they stood until they rotted. Dan had left, infuriated, insistent that they at best were an eyesore and at worst would be a way for kids to climb on and get into our gardens.

Admittedly, I had always thought Dan a little overcautious, although I would never have said as much to him. He was only concerned with keeping us safe – and with his job and the things he dealt with on a daily basis, who could blame him for that?

But looking at it now, Dan was right. The pallet would have made the perfect 'leg up' for someone to clamber over our fence. That, and with the dented bin the other side, it was hard to ignore the likelihood that someone had been in our garden.

"Bloody Joyce," I muttered as I scurried into the alley, grabbing the pallet and tossing it back towards the others. As I did so I felt a sharp pain in my finger and looked down to see a small screw sticking out of the wood. "Shit." Clutching my hand as it started to bleed, I hurried back towards my garden, slammed the gate behind me, and dashed back to the house.

"Rachel?" called Dan's voice. "Jesus Christ! What on earth is going on?"

Dan was across the kitchen in a few long strides, meeting me at the door and taking in the sight of me under the harsh lighting.

"What happened? Are you okay?"

My heart hammered against my chest and my finger throbbed painfully.

"I'm fine." I nodded, slumping against the worktop.

"Rach, you're bleeding. What the hell happened? Are you okay?"

His eyes darted between me and the back door. I glanced down, realising that the rain had caused the blood to spread, making it appear much worse than it was. The front of my grey top was slowly turning from pink to crimson as I held my wounded hand against it.

"Oh, this. No, no, it's fine. It's only a little cut. I caught my hand outside but the rain… It looks much worse than it is."

Dan's features visibly relaxed. I held out my hand to inspect the damage to my finger. A small flap of skin hung from it and more fresh blood ran down, dripping off my fingertip.

"Eugh." Dan turned his face away. It always amused me that in his line of work, Dan could be averse to the sight of a bit of blood. He had told me in our early days together that he had originally dreamed of becoming a surgeon, but that blood and gore had always made him feel a little light-headed. He'd gotten better and managed to deal with it now – he'd had little choice considering his profession – but in moments like this where he was unprepared, it would still cause him to feel a little queasy.

"Sorry." I wrapped my hand back in my jumper as I crossed the kitchen to retrieve a wad of paper towel. I rewrapped my hand in a makeshift bandage before pulling some more from the roll and crouching down to wipe the droplets from the floor.

"Rach, don't worry about the bloody floor." I glanced up at him and watched his lips twitch. "Excuse the terrible pun." He rolled his eyes, leaning on the countertop and shaking his head. I smiled, glad to feel the tension lift.

"It's fine." I shuffled along on my knees, wiping away the last smears of blood.

"I'm going to grab some plasters, a wipe or something to clean that out." He gestured towards my hand before turning towards the utility where I heard him rustling around in search of supplies. He returned a minute later clutching a makeshift first aid box.

"Here." He dropped it onto the table and pulled out a chair for me.

"Thank you." I manoeuvred myself awkwardly into the seat as Dan opened the box and carefully laid out what I needed.

I ripped open the packet of the alcohol wipe with my teeth, gritting them, aware of the pain I was about to self-inflict. Carefully, I removed the tissue, which had already begun to stick to the wound. Sucking air through my teeth, I pulled it away, fresh droplets forming instantly as I tore the skin open once again.

I pressed the wipe against my finger, cursing under my breath at the stinging sensation. Dan, who had been hovering, keeping his eyes averted, lowered himself into the seat beside me. He tore the plaster from its packaging and held it out as I offered up my finger. He wrapped it around the wound so gently, with such care, a surge of love for him made me want to reach out and pull him to me.

"What were you doing out there? In the pouring rain? You never actually told me what you did to your hand." Dan's face was creased with a mixture of concentration and concern as he focused on applying the plaster.

"I thought I heard something. I went out to check and it turns out it was one of Joyce's flippin' pallets." I rolled my eyes. "It must have blown over, and when I tried to stand it back up, I caught my finger on a nail."

"Fucking Joyce." His jaw clenched. "I am getting rid of those goddamned pallets tomorrow whether she likes it or not." He slammed his fist down onto the table, his eyes narrowed.

I fiddled with a loose strand of the fresh plaster, uncertain of how to reply.

"What were you thinking though, babe, going out into the dark by yourself when you thought you'd heard something? Why didn't you call me?"

I prickled at the thought that I had become so helpless. That I wasn't safe in my own garden.

"It was just a frigging pallet. It was the bin earlier. It's windy. Things blow around. Should I call you every time I hear a noise outside? I didn't need you rushing to my aid to save me from a splinter." I managed to bite my tongue in time to stop myself making an unnecessary dig about his dislike of blood.

He winced at my harsh tone and I instantly regretted my snotty response. My anger was misdirected at him, the fear having built to such an intensity that it seemed to have bubbled up, needing an outlet. Fury simmered under the surface, but it was preferable to the fear. If I allowed it to fizzle out, the emotion would overpower me.

"I know that. I'm not trying to patronise you, Rach. It's just, well, with everything going on right now... I thought I heard the bolt on the gate, then when I came downstairs and saw you stumble into the kitchen like that, with all the blood, I... I thought..."

I closed my eyes, taking a deep breath and seeing the scene through Dan's eyes, realising how it must have looked.

"Sorry. I shouldn't have snapped." I looked up at him. "I know you're just concerned about me. I'm just sick of feeling on edge. What with Dennis being out and someone killing women as a pastime walking the streets." I shook my head and blew out my breath. "I'm scared. Terrified, actually. My father is free, and it's very likely he'd like to see me dead. I'm petrified that everyone will find out who I really am and think I'm the same as him. I don't know which scares me more. And I'm pissed off that some creep is out there – maybe my own father, maybe not – and again, I don't know which is worse. But either way, he's free to walk the streets whilst he steals our freedom, leaving women afraid to be alone in case we turn out to be the next victim in his sick, twisted game." I snapped my jaw closed, shocked at my own outburst.

Dan hadn't moved. His face remained impassive although something flickered in his eyes. It was gone before I could decipher it. My body seemed to deflate, my rant having taken all of my remaining fight and leaving me burnt out. Pressing trembling fingertips against my forehead, I rested against them as I allowed my breathing to slow, the events of the evening to process. Dan had no idea that the real reason for me being so wound up was due to the very real concern that someone had been snooping around in our garden whilst I had been alone in our house. My finger throbbed as though reminding me I hadn't imagined it.

I desperately wanted to feel Dan's arms slip around my shoulders, to lose myself in the safety of his embrace, but I could sense without having to look that he was still in the same position. The image of Dan, that look in his eye that was gone as quickly as it has appeared, filled my mind. Why wasn't he comforting me? And then I realised.

"Oh God. Dan, I'm sorry. I didn't mean to... What I said wasn't aimed at you. I know you are all doing your absolute best to..."

Dan studied me for a second before his features softened.

"I know." He rubbed at the back of his neck, starting up at the celling and shaking his head. "But you're right, Rach. Whoever it is, this guy's out there doing... what he's doing, and we are running around like idiots chasing our fucking tails." He slammed his fist into the tabletop again, rising from his chair.

The impact made me jump. I pushed back in my chair instinctively, almost toppling off it backwards. Dan didn't seem to notice.

"He's always ahead," he murmured. "And not just by a step. He seems to know exactly what he's doing. I'm starting to wonder if we have any chance of ever catching up with him. I don't know what it will do to our department if we don't. I feel like everyone is starting to lose faith."

I stared at my husband, noticing for the first time how drained he looked. Dan had only ever seemed full of energy and passion for his job, but for the first time, he appeared defeated. I had been so busy worrying about myself and everything I had going on I had barely considered the effect this was having on him. I realised how hard it must be on him, to not only feel as though he was failing the women who had died but to also be unable to make me feel safe. Pushing back my chair, I moved around to him, wrapping my arms around his waist. He leaned into me.

"I know you guys will get him. He has to make a mistake at some point. He'll get cocky, or overlook something, and you guys won't miss a beat. The second he does, you'll be there and he'll wonder what the hell hit him." I gave him a gentle squeeze.

"I sure hope you're right." Dan sighed, detangling himself from me and pulling away. "I'm going to go to bed. I'm knackered."

He turned, crossing the kitchen and disappearing within an instant. The tension was obvious in his tightly drawn-up shoulders. I'd never seen Dan seem so uptight, like a coiled spring ready to fire off.

"Okay. I'll be right up," I called after him, but I was met with a stony silence.

My throat seemed to tighten as I listened to him plod up the stairs, and I forced myself to face the fear that was becoming a terrifying reality. If Dan didn't get to him soon, I had a horrible feeling that he might get to me first.

11

I pushed through my front door, shoving it closed behind me before pausing to listen.

"Dan?" I already knew he wasn't home; his Toyota wasn't on the drive, and it was the middle of the day. Guilt prickled my flushed skin. Dan hadn't been in contact since he had stalked off to bed the previous evening following our exchange. Why couldn't I have thought before I spoke, chosen my words more carefully. The last thing I had wanted was to seem like I was blaming Dan, pointing out his team's failure to catch the killer. I knew how hard they were all taking the lack of evidence, the leads that all came to dead ends. It had been a huge strain on them all, especially Dan as the lead investigator.

The press on the other hand were having a field day. They had named the murderer 'the creeper' thanks to his ability to seemingly creep in and out of anywhere he chose, undetected. That and the fact that he was walking among us day to day, potentially picking out his next victim as he queued behind her for his morning coffee, close enough to smell her shampoo, only served to add more excuses to not see the girls in my mind. I felt awkward about seeing Dalaja, aware Phil's career would be thriving on Dan's shortcomings. I wanted to be excited about us all getting together for the first time in so long, but instead I was filled with dread at the thought of anyone saying the wrong thing.

Shaking my head, I pulled off my boots and retrieved the shopping bag.

I lugged the bag into the kitchen and glanced out of the back window, scanning the garden to make sure everything was as I had left it. Dennis was getting into my head without even having to try. I needed to get a grip if I was going to keep it together for Dalaja's birthday meal.

The events at work had spooked me. I'd come home, heard a noise, put two and two together and come up with five. They weren't connected. There probably hadn't even been anyone in the garden. If these things had happened just a few short months ago, I would have dismissed them, not giving any of it another thought. Dan could well have left the bin by the fence. Granted, it was unlike him, but he did have a lot on his mind. And the pallet – that was likely a coincidence. They had been out there for weeks. That one could have been moved before yesterday. I wouldn't have noticed if I hadn't gone out to look. I pulled, absentminded, at the edge of the plaster on my injured finger.

But I had been so certain I had seen a footprint on that bin lid.

I began to empty the contents of the bag onto the worktop, another surge of shame tugging at me as I retrieved the anniversary card from the shopping bag. How could I have forgotten our anniversary. The card from Dan had been waiting for me on my bedside table and I had rushed straight out to get him one in the hope he didn't realise I'd forgotten.

Opening the fridge, I unloaded the ingredients for the meal I had hastily planned, leaving the red wine on the countertop. I had selected it especially, aware it was one of Dan's favourites. If he was home to spend the evening with me. I checked my phone again, already aware that he hadn't yet responded to my question about dinner. It seemed to mock me in its bid to remain silent.

The coffee date this morning with Annie had been unavoidable. We'd had it planned for weeks, a chance for the two of us to get together for the last-minute arrangements for Dalaja's birthday. Dalaja had organised the get-together herself, but we had arranged the cake and a few decorations, as well as the gift card for her local spa.

My hope had been that seeing a friendly face, having Annie there to distract me for an hour or so with our easy chatter, would make me feel better, allow me an escape for just a few stolen hours. But it had done nothing to lighten my mood.

We had gone over our plans, but I had struggled to keep focused and Annie had known without doubt that something was wrong. She had gently broached it once the birthday talk was done, but hadn't pressed when I made it clear it wasn't up for discussion. We had never kept secrets from one another and the unspoken awareness between us that I was doing exactly that was stifling.

I knew that I had, of course, kept a huge secret from both of my friends for as long as I had known them, but somehow, it felt different now. When I had become Rachel, I had done everything I could to shed my past self, cutting that rotten part of me away as though it never existed, but I knew now I had never truly escaped him. The last time he had killed, I had been a child, unable to do anything, not old enough to even understand. This time, I felt somehow responsible, as though there was something I should have been able to do. Hiding myself suddenly felt more cowardly than it ever had before.

In all the time I had known her, Annie and I had never struggled to make conversation; quite the opposite. But we had barely limped along, searching for topics that felt 'safe' to broach, neither knowing how to navigate this unchartered territory for our friendship. Annie had paused as she had pulled back from our brief embrace as we got ready to leave, searching my face, silently pleading with me to offer something up as she'd asked if I was really okay.

I had assured her I was fine before watching her deflate in front of me. Giving the tiniest shake of her head, she had shrugged, reminded me she was only a phone call away, and left. The distance I was forcing between us was becoming cavernous, and I ached to make it all go back to how it had been before.

Aware I was slipping into moping, I busied myself preparing our meal. I was humming to myself when the doorbell chimed. Wiping my hands on a towel, I went to answer it and came face to face with a bouquet of flowers.

"Mrs Thatcher?"

"Yes. Thank you." I beamed as I took them from the delivery man and stepped back inside the house. I put the flowers into a vase and carried them into the sitting room, still admiring them.

As soon as I stepped into the room, I froze. Something felt off. I placed the vase onto the table with more force than

I'd intended, wrapped my arms tightly across my chest and tried to figure out what.

Fighting my increasing paranoia, I noticed the anniversary card from Dan had fallen from the mantle. As I was retrieving it, the sense of a creeping feeling instantly clawed its way back up my body. The ink of some of the words inside was smudged. It hadn't been like that this morning when I'd read it. I was certain I would have noticed. Wouldn't I? It looked as though water droplets had landed on it and someone had attempted to wipe them away.

Closing the card, I was unable to find comfort in Dan's words now. I needed to focus on preparing our food, calm down, and think rationally. As I replaced the card on the mantle beside our wedding photo and turned to head out to the kitchen, I stopped again, distracted by the old cupboard behind the sofa.

The cupboard door had been temperamental for as long as I remembered. It stuck when you tried to open it, meaning you had to wiggle it gently free, otherwise you also pulled the screw loose from the hinge. Dan and I both knew how to open that cupboard door just right and we kept very little in there, aware of what a pain it was to get into. It had been a running joke between us that it had been like it so long we had gotten used to it.

I couldn't think of a reason why Dan would have opened it, and even if he had, I was sure he would have made sure to fix the door back in place. I was a tidy person but nothing in comparison to Dan. He was almost anal in how he liked things to be. I always thought it was one of the reasons he was so good at his job.

Crossing the room to the cupboard and swinging open

the door, I peered inside. It had been so long since I had opened it I had no idea if anything was out of place.

I closed the door, pushing the screw back in and lifting the door back into position. I opened the drawer above and froze. The papers in the drawer had been riffled through without question. Dan certainly wouldn't have left them that way and I hadn't been in there. Had I? I shook my head. I was jumping to conclusions, instantly thinking someone had broken into our house to read a card and rifle through some old papers. Wasn't it much more likely it had been me and I had just forgotten? After all, if someone had broken in, surely they would have searched through more places, made more mess, taken anything valuable.

I glanced up at the framed photographs that sat on the shelf. There was a photo of Dan and me, taken on a long weekend break to Scotland a few years ago, that sat alongside a group one of Annie, Tim, Dalaja, Phil, Dan, and me on a night out together. We all beamed at the camera, arms thrown around one another's shoulders, our glassy eyes giving away how much we'd been drinking. The photographs had switched places. The one of Dan and me had always been on the left, the group one on the right. I frowned, checking them again. They had definitely been switched. A heavy feeling was spreading across my chest, the hairs on the back of my neck rising as I got the sensation that someone had been in my house.

Crouching down, I went back to the drawer, searching for anything else that looked out of place – for anything that might have been missing to identify what whoever had been in here had been searching for. Nothing seemed amiss and I leaned back on my heels.

Perhaps it had been Dan. Maybe he had been through

the drawers looking for something. Even as the thought came to me, the vision of the bin, the footprint, the pallet came to mind. I slammed the drawer shut. What if whoever had broken in wasn't here to take my possessions? What if they were after something much worse?

Sucking back a deep breath, I glanced towards mine and Dan's wedding album that usually sat on display higher up on the unit. It had fallen down and now lay flat. I felt a strong urge to reach up and pluck it from its position on the shelf. Some bizarre desire to see everything whoever had been searching here might have seen. As I lifted it down, I felt a pang of sadness at the pure joy that radiated from Dan and me in the photo on the front. I couldn't remember that last time I had felt that kind of happiness, untainted by the rot that seemed to be infiltrating my life. Flicking open the first page, I froze instantly, unable to move. My breath caught in my throat. My body felt as if it was in freefall.

Scrawled across the first photograph of us, as we held hands in front of the registrar, were the words:

I KNOW WHO YOU ARE.

12

BEFORE

I had never considered my self-diagnoses as negative. My awareness only served to offer me an unmatched freedom to mould to my surroundings, becoming the character that worked best in each and every situation.

It made no sense to me that anyone would choose to suffer emotions, be satisfied to lack the intelligence I possessed. My teenage years were some of the best of my life. Whilst others suffered, falling in love and having their hearts broken, I found myself the centre of plenty of girls' affections, but they could never have the hold over me that they did over the other poor saps. It came almost too easily to talk anyone into what I wanted them to do.

I could never see their characterisation as an insult. They label it a disorder, but that only serves as an example of their ignorance. They simply feel better throwing names at things they aren't intelligent enough to understand, trying to wrap them in a neat little box, file us away and act as though we are the broken ones. They label us the villains, and yet, given the chance, they would lock us in cages and run their tests as if that's praiseworthy. The irony of their hypocrisy left me sickened.

I had seen the way my brother looked at me. His eyes didn't contain the fear that I had come to recognise in my father's, nor the adoration I now saw in my mother's. I knew how to reflect those emotions and how to use them to my advantage. There was something else contained inside my brother's mind as he watched me smirk at my father's cowering, studied me as I showered my mother with a false show of love. The watcher became the watched. My brother made no secret of his interest in me, openly observing me with a curiosity that I couldn't fathom, leaving me to witness what it must be like to be one of those I had observed so closely to gain my insights.

I didn't believe my brother was like me. Granted, he didn't lack intelligence, but he was nowhere near my level, and he didn't quite fit the profile. I could sense the shift in our relationship too. I didn't have any feelings of love or caring for him, but he had become a thing of interest to me.

I could manipulate most people into doing anything I wanted them to by that point. You just had to start small enough for them not to notice before they were too far gone. He was almost too easy; the look of petrified horror on his face when I threatened to tell our mother about the porn magazine I'd found in his science folder hilarious to me. He swore it wasn't his, and the funniest part is, I think that was actually true.

All it took was patience, plus the knowledge and ability to recognise if you were pushing too hard, too soon. It was all about the long game, allowing your prey to come to you as you waited in silence, avoiding the chaos of the chase.

By the time my brother entered my room, he was already

too far gone to realise how deeply I had burrowed inside his head. I couldn't wait to see what it would take to make him the next cat in the shed.

13

My hands still trembled as I placed the bottle of wine onto the table, checking that the cutlery was lined up and there weren't any smudges on the glasses. It had taken a long time to stop myself panicking after seeing the words scrawled across the photo of Dan and me. So when Dan's message had come through to say he would be home to spend the evening with me, I had wondered if this whole thing was a ridiculous idea. How could I pretend everything was normal? I would have to tell him what had happened. The front door slammed shut and I winced at the conversation I knew was inevitable.

I turned to stare at the door to the kitchen as the sound of Dan whistling filled the hallway. He appeared a few seconds later, his face spreading into a wide grin as he took in the sight of the set table and the effort I had made with my outfit.

"Wow, Rach." He let out another long whistle. "You look amazing. And the food smells so good." He crossed the room, no sign of the hunched shoulders or creased brow he had been crushed under the weight of less than twenty-four hours ago.

He held my face in his hands and kissed me deeply. I wondered if he could taste the alcohol on my breath from the wine I had already consumed. Forcing a smile, I gestured for him to sit down, wishing I could soak up his light mood.

Dan easily filled the silence, his vibrant chatter in such contrast to the previous evening I found myself studying him a couple of times, not taking in anything he was saying.

I was barely holding it together, aware that I had to tell Dan what had happened but desperate to have just a snippet of normality before our world inevitably imploded. I was petrified at the idea of being alone in my own home ever again.

Gulping back more wine, I felt the world was beginning to go fuzzy around the edges.

"Hey, have you been in the cupboard in the lounge recently?" I asked halfway through our meal in the most casual tone I could muster. I wanted to gauge Dan's reaction before I dropped the grenade.

Dan paused, his fork hovering in mid-air. A hunk of steak was jabbed onto the end of it, and I watched the peppercorn sauce drip onto his plate.

"What?"

"The cupboard at the back of the living room? You know, the one that sticks. Have you been in there at all?"

Dan searched my face for a second. "No. Why would I? That cupboard's a pain in the ass." He shovelled the steak into his mouth. "And I know – I know – I need to get around to fixing it." He spoke between chewing, rolling his eyes dramatically. His light tone let me know he was joking.

I forced a smile. "Why do you ask?" He swallowed his food, reaching for his wine glass and taking a gulp.

Pushing my own food around my plate, I attempted to make it look as though I had eaten at least some of the meal, barely having put my own glass down.

"It's just... this afternoon I... I..." I trailed off, unable to find a way to put the horrific events into words.

"Are you alright, Rach?" He cocked his head, lowering it in an attempt to force himself into my line of sight. "You've been quiet all evening, you've hardly touched your food and—"

The shrill sound of the doorbell cut him off mid-sentence and I jumped, my heart racing.

"I'll get it." I pushed my chair back from the table, grateful for the excuse to cut the tension. I was afraid if I didn't get hold of myself, Dan would think I was losing it. Or worse – that I wasn't.

I didn't miss the expression on Dan's face as he took in the sight of my trembling hands.

My legs felt unsteady beneath me as I flicked on the hallway light. I had skipped lunch, not feeling much like eating, and the lack of food mixed with wine was a bad combination. Dan had topped up my drink, unaware that I had already had a few glasses. I made the decision to lay off the wine and move on to water for the rest of the evening. Blinking, I shook my head, trying to clear my vision. Perhaps even a strong coffee.

I pulled back the front door.

"Joyce?" It was more of a question than a greeting, but our neighbour didn't seem to notice.

"Good evening, Rachel." She offered a bright smile, but it didn't reach her eyes. "I was wondering if you could offer any explanation as to where my crates have gone. They seem to be missing."

She cocked her head, raising her bushy eyebrows in question.

"Your...?" My head felt fuzzy, my vision swimming slightly as I attempted to focus on what she was saying.

"My crates. You know, the wooden things that were in the alleyway. The ones I had planned to make planters from, that your husband was so keen to dispose of." She narrowed her eyes at me and pursed her lips.

"Oh, the pallets." I held onto the front door to keep myself balanced, suddenly realising why Joyce was on my doorstep.

"Crates, pallets, it's all the same. Do you know where they have gone?"

"Erm..." I swallowed hard. "I think they might've gone mouldy or something. I think Dan was going to get rid of them for you." I fought not to slur my words. *What is wrong with me?*

"Is that right?" She pursed her lips again.

I lifted my eyes to meet hers, blinking rapidly as I struggled to bring her into focus.

"Are you okay, Rachel? You look a little..." She trailed off, reaching out a hand as though to steady me before thinking better of it and withdrawing, as though I might have been about to bite.

"Hmm? Oh, yes. Thank you. I'm just a little under the weather."

She drew back, as though afraid I may be contagious. She cocked her head, regarding me. "And Dan? Is everything alright between the two of you?"

The bluntness of her question snapped me out of the wine fog.

"I mean, I wouldn't usually ask, only I can't help but notice how much his car is gone at the moment." She gave a tiny shrug, her mouth pulled down at one side.

"He's working," I said bluntly.

"Of course." She held up her hands, her eyebrows rising to almost meet her hairline. "I'm sure he is incredibly busy, out all hours trying to catch the bad guys."

I searched for something to say, not sure if it was the wine or whether I was just finding it impossible to read what she was getting at.

"I actually thought it was him hanging around here earlier," she continued. There was an unmissable glint in her eyes now.

"What do you mean?" I didn't want to bite but I had to know.

"There was a man here. Wasn't he with you?" She blinked at me, all mock innocence.

"No. What man?" I knew I was indulging her, playing right into her hands, but I had no choice if I wanted to get to the bottom of what she was saying.

"Oh. It looked like he had come out of your house." She stuck out her bottom lip and gave a small shrug. "I assumed he'd been inside with you. At first, I thought it was Dan, but when I called out to him, he sped up and dashed off down the street. Then I realised he wasn't as tall as Dan, and that his car wasn't in your driveway." She gestured behind her to Dan's Toyota, eyeing me.

"No... I... I wasn't here either," I stuttered, shaking my head and causing the world to shift beneath my feet again. I gripped the door frame.

"Hmm, how strange." Joyce pulled a face. "Your car was here."

"Yes, I'd been out for coffee, with a friend. I got the train there, walked back." I swallowed hard, trying to disguise the tremble that seemed to have permanently entered my voice.

Joyce didn't react and I reminded myself it was the least of my concerns, justifying myself to her. She had caught me off-guard and thrown yet another grenade right into my lap, but not for any of the reasons she was imagining.

"Well, must have been a delivery guy or something." She smiled, her eyes narrowing again, and I fought the urge to shove her off my doorstep.

"Must have been." I returned her false smile. "Was there anything else, Joyce? Only I—"

"Joyce." The boom of Dan's voice caused me to flinch, and Joyce's eyes lifted to a point somewhere over my shoulder.

"I wondered why you were taking so long, babe." Dan appeared beside me and held his hand against the small of my back. I fought the urge to lean into him and bury my face in his chest. He turned his focus back on our neighbour, a bright smile fixed on his face. "What can we do for you?"

Joyce didn't appear concerned by Dan's comment.

"Joyce came over to see what had happened to her pallets." I looked up at Dan, trying to focus on him as my head spun with everything happening around me. Everything seemed to be moving in slow motion, the truth I had been withholding from Dan now intoxicating my mind almost as much as the wine. I was desperate to get my neighbour off my doorstep before she mentioned anything about the man to Dan. I didn't want him to believe I'd only told him thanks to Joyce forcing my hand.

I hoped that reminding her of the apparent reason for her visit would cause her to forget about our conversation.

"Ah, the pallets. I got rid of them," Dan didn't hesitate to tell her. "I'd heard some of the neighbours talking about fly-tipping and such. They assumed you'd dumped them out there and were threating to phone the council. I thought it would be best if I just moved them before it came to anything. They were soaked through anyway, not good for much by that point."

Joyce's nostrils flared, and something flashed in her eyes. "Well, how good of you." She offered a tight smile, eyes narrowing. "I'll be off, then." She paused, turning her glare on me, seeming to consider her next move for a second. "Perhaps you should consider getting some security measures put in place, maybe a camera or two. I mean, if you really don't know who that man was." She lifted one eyebrow, a smug look on her face as she glanced at Dan before spinning on her heel and sashaying off down our driveway.

I closed my eyes, sighing, not wanting to witness Dan's reaction, wishing I could sober myself up before I had to face the inevitable. Shoving the door closed behind her, I turned and ignored his questioning stare. I rolled my eyes and pulled a face at him that I hoped he would construe as my irritation towards Joyce and made my way back through to the kitchen on jelly legs. I silently pleaded that by me ignoring it, Dan would do the same. He appeared in the kitchen just as I collapsed back into my chair. He stood behind his own, glaring at me.

"What was she talking about? What man, Rach?" Dan's face was dark, his features pulled together in a tight frown.

My jaw was clenched so tight it was causing my head to

throb, the sound of my own heart rate thumping in my ears. I knew Joyce had delivered that parting blow on purpose. She assumed I was having an affair with the man in question and – left bitter by her own experience – hoped to punish me at the same time as stick it to Dan.

I reached for the wine bottle with trembling hands, missing my glass as I attempted to pour and the wine slopped over the edge. I righted it and continued to pour regardless of my struggle to focus on it. I knew I shouldn't, but I took another gulp, desperate to feel numb, to forget everything that was happening around me and lose myself in a drunken haze.

"Rach?" Dan's raised voice startled me, almost causing me to lose my grip on the wine glass. He couldn't hide his frustration at my clear reluctance to answer, and I had drunk too much to be able to think clearly enough to come up with a believable lie.

Placing the glass back onto the table, I laid my hands flat against its surface to steady myself and attempt to appear in control.

Lifting my face, I met Dan's dark expression.

"I don't know." I struggled not to slur my words as Dan arched an eyebrow. "She's just told me she'd seen someone at the house this morning."

"Seen who? You're not making any sense."

I sucked back a deep breath, aware that I probably wasn't.

"Joyce said she'd seen someone outside our house this morning. She thought they had come out from inside. She thought it was you, but when she called out, whoever it was ran off down the road." I paused, risking a glance at him, gauging his reaction.

His eyes had clouded. I watched him processing what I was saying.

"She thought I was here because my car was parked on the drive. I think she assumed I'd had a man here while you were out working." I snorted, attempting to lighten the oppressive atmosphere that was crushing us with how ridiculous that notion was, and masking the fear that was snaking its way around me.

"Where were you?" Dan questioned. I searched his face, wishing I was sober and able to decipher what he was questioning me on. My stomach plummeted and a heat rose to my cheeks.

"Having coffee with Annie," I snapped back. "You can check with her if you don't believe me." My heart pounded in my ears as I clenched my jaw, furious that my husband might be checking up on me after all he'd just heard.

He pulled his chair back from the table, lowering himself into it and reaching for my hand.

"Oh God, Rach, I wasn't *questioning* you." He held my hand between both of his. "I was concerned for whoever this arsehole is that's creeping around our bloody house so brazenly. I need to know you were safe. That at least he didn't come in here whilst you were home."

The fury drained from me as I slumped against the table, body seeming to deflate as my head swam.

"What else?" Dan's voice was low, gravelly, and almost challenging. I stared at him blankly. "First the weird questions about the cupboard in the living room, then that crap with Joyce that you clearly weren't going to tell me about. Plus, you seem to be determined to drink yourself into a stupor." He jabbed a finger towards my wine glass. "What else aren't you telling me, Rach?"

I pressed my thumb and forefingers into my eyes until all I could see was bright balls of light. I attempted to gather my thoughts, wishing that I was sober, that I could put this conversation off until I had my wits about me, knowing there was no way to pacify Dan. I was a terrible liar when it came to my husband even when I wasn't intoxicated, only able to keep so much from him lately as he hadn't asked, too distracted with his work to notice. There was no way I could lie whilst he looked me right in the face.

I drew in a breath, shaking my head and instantly regretting it as the floor seemed to lurch beneath me.

"I... I already knew someone had been in the house," I stammered.

Dan's frown loosened for a fraction of a second as his features slackened, then his face twisted into an expression of rage.

"What? Who? What did they do? For Christ's sake. I'm calling this in." Dan rose, shoving his chair back, which hit the floor with a crack as it fell. I staggered up, reaching out towards him.

"No, Dan, please don't."

"Our neighbour witnessed someone outside our house, Rach." Dan clenched his jaw, something flashing in his eyes as he jabbed his finger towards the adjoining wall. "Tell me what else."

"Someone had been through some of the things in the cupboard in the living room. And..." I gulped, feeling nauseous. "There was something written in our wedding album."

Unable to say it out loud, I lurched over and retrieved the album from where I had left it on the living room floor, returning to the kitchen. I held it away from my body, as though it might detonate at any given moment.

Dan's face creased with confusion as he watched me place it down. For a few seconds, neither of us moved. I couldn't bring myself to flip open the page again, to see the red writing across our faces. Dan leaned forward, tossing it open.

I kept my focus on Dan. Even in my alcohol-infused state, I didn't miss the flash in his eyes.

He let a few seconds pass before saying anything, the muscle in his jaw giving away his battle to regain his composure. He cleared his throat, opening his mouth to speak before clenching his jaw closed once again, repeating the action.

"I have to report this, Rach." There was an edge to his tone, something that had crept in and left my hands trembling harder than they had been previously. I tucked them under the table.

"It'll draw attention," I squeaked, fear and self-preservation tearing me apart from the inside.

He threw me a withering look. "I think we're past that. I'll do all I can to keep it under wraps, but the most important thing here is your safety. We cannot ignore this." He gestured towards our wedding album but didn't look at it.

"Do you think it's him?" I breathed, unable to say his name out loud, afraid it might summon him up.

"I don't know." Dan closed his eyes, shaking his head and pinching the bridge of his nose between his thumb and forefinger. "But whoever wrote it, they managed to get into our home. They wanted us to know they could get in here. I'm going to arrange to have officers drive by. I'll push and see if we can have one stationed here until I can arrange to have you moved somewhere safe." He seemed to be talking to himself more than me now, almost as though he had forgotten I was there.

"Moved?" I drew my head back. I had wanted Dan to reassure me it was nothing, to tell me they'd arrest Dennis and it would all be over.

Dan blinked at me, as though suddenly realising I could hear his thoughts.

"Of course. We can't leave you here if someone is breaking into our home, making threats." He glared at me as though it was obvious.

I swallowed hard. "It's not really a threat..." I started meekly, aware no amount of downplaying this would make it go away. "And how am I going to explain my sudden departure to everyone else? Do you not think my friends might question why I'd suddenly upped and left with no explanation?" Panic had begun to rise like water, threatening to submerge me.

"You could tell them we took a couple of days away." Dan's shoulders sagged, his head rested against his hand, his elbow resting on the table.

"But it wouldn't be *we*, would it, Dan? It would be *me*. You really think anyone's going to believe that you left in the middle of the biggest investigation of your career, left your team dealing with a serial killer on the loose to take a couple of days off and go on a mini-break? And what about my job? What do I tell them?"

Dan's jaw was flexing again as he stared at a point over my shoulder.

"This isn't keeping it under wraps," I almost pleaded. "Everyone will know."

"I am just trying to do whatever I can to keep you safe."

Dan met my eye, unblinking. "You have no idea what kinds of things I have to see in my job every day, so you'll excuse me if I want to do whatever I can to stop my wife becoming another fucking statistic."

I drew back, my lips parting but unable to find words. Rarely in all our years together had I heard Dan speak in such a tone.

"You're so worried about what everyone else thinks, but it won't matter if he gets to you, Rach. We aren't discussing the possibility of an absent father returning to your life. We're talking about a murdering psychopath, someone who thought nothing of murdering his own family, whose agenda we know nothing about." He jabbed his finger into the tabletop as he made his points. "Men like Dennis, men who've been in prison for the number of years he has, do you not think they make connections? You don't believe that if he really wants to find you, he could? Like that?" He snapped his fingers, cocking his head at me.

I wasn't sure if he was trying to scare me further, but if he was, it was working.

"I know you don't want your friends to find out the truth, don't want to have to put your life on hold or be apart from me. I don't want any of that either, but regardless of how deep you bury it, Rach, you're still his daughter, and if that means something to him, good or bad, what does he have to lose?" He shook his head, dropping his head into his hands. Seconds passed, the silence between us thick and heavy. We remained so still the ticking of the clock sounded too loud, the sound of Joyce's television audible through the wall.

Dan rubbed his temples, glancing up at me but unable to hold the contact. I couldn't be sure if it was the fog of alcohol or the shock of Dan's outburst that had left me unable to find a way to reply to all he had just said. I sat dumbly, staring at my husband, rooted to the spot.

He looked wretched, as though he had aged in the last half an hour. He dragged the skin of his face as he rubbed his hands down it. He knew he had gone too far. He sighed, shaking his head.

"I shouldn't have... What I meant... I didn't mean to..." he trailed off, still unable to look at me. "I'm sorry. I'm going to speak to the guys at work. Then I need to shower, get my head down for a bit. I'll arrange for uniformed officers to keep an eye on everything until something better can be arranged. There's no need for them to know why you're considered a possible target. Obviously, a small number of my team know about your connection to Dennis anyway, what with the investigation. I promise you it'll be kept strictly on a need-to-know basis. We can ensure it stays that way for your protection." He rose from the table, paused beside me as if he was going to say something else before releasing another deep sigh and continuing out of the room.

I made no attempt to move, afraid that if I did, I may crumple into a heap and never find the strength to clamber up again. I listened to the sound of Dan moving around upstairs, devastated that he could say such cruel, frightening things and then just go off to bed. Why wasn't he here, consoling me while he could be?

Reaching for my wine, I gulped back the remaining liquid, draining it in one.

14

The wind chased us in as we stepped through the door of the restaurant, and I used my free hand to hold down the skirt of my dress. My hair whipped around my face as the door slowly closed, but I chose my dignity over my appearance. As soon as I was able to let go of my dress without fear of exposing my underwear, I ran my hands through my tousled hair as best I could.

It was a new place in the centre of town that had recently opened. The owners had bought two places, converting them into one huge building. We had been invited for pre-dinner drinks at the cocktail bar, and would proceed to the connecting restaurant. The place was booked up for months and I could only imagine that Phil had had to pull more than a few strings to hold Dalaja's party there.

I kept my arm linked through Dan's, turning my head to glance at him. Usually, I would have been delighted, reminding myself to savour the rare time with him while we were here together. But tonight, I felt more like he had come with me as a chaperone than my husband. It had been three days since I had found the scrawl on our wedding photo, but the tension hadn't eased between Dan and me.

I'd gone to bed that night after far too much wine and practically passed out on our bed. I'd woken feeling as though I might be about to throw up, and found the bed beside me empty. I had crept out onto the landing, making my way to the bathroom, but had frozen at the sound of Dan, downstairs, in mid-conversation. I had only caught snippets of what he was saying and was aware from the pauses and one-sided nature of it that he must have been on the phone. But even with the tiny amount I had heard, I could hear the tension, the animosity in his voice.

The urge to vomit had cut me off from being able to listen for more than a few seconds, overwhelming my senses, and I had dashed into the bathroom, hugging the toilet bowl for the next twenty minutes. By the time I had crawled back across the landing, Dan was back in bed, seemingly asleep.

When I'd asked him about it, Dan had looked at me as if I were mad. He told me he'd taken a phone call from his boss about our situation, but assured me there had been no cross words, the type I was certain I'd heard. I decided I must have dreamt it; after all, I had been pretty drunk and Dan had no reason to lie.

Dan had arranged for officers to watch our house. He had argued with his superiors that I needed to be moved, but they had made the decision to hold off, blaming lack of resources and funding. They had countered that no threat had been made and, as it stood, my identity was still under wraps. It was only the top line of the investigation that knew of my connection to Dennis. For my protection, the superiors had decided it was best to keep it that way. We had no way to know for sure that it had been Dennis who had written the note. The idea of it being someone else didn't make me feel any better.

The time since had been uneventful, but that hadn't helped to put me at ease, instead leaving me feeling as though we were building up to an earth-shattering storm.

I plastered on a smile, trying to force myself to enjoy the evening. The pounding in my chest was a stark reminder that this wasn't a normal evening. Being around Phil and the girls still made me anxious, but if I kept my head and made sure to steer the conversation away from any touchy subjects, there was no reason I couldn't enjoy the company.

I figured it shouldn't be too difficult. No one wanted to discuss murder at a birthday celebration, and everyone was aware of the tension any discussion of work brought up between Dan and Phil, so it was perfectly reasonable to avoid it.

The mood felt light around mine and Dan's darkness. Loud chatter and barks of laughter mingling with the chink of glasses and the occasional pop of a cork filled my senses. I could feel the tension lifting from my shoulders, and I allowed myself to believe I was safe while surrounded by those I loved in the bubble I'd just entered.

"Rach!" Dalaja disentangled herself from Phil, whose arm had been wrapped around her waist as she perched on his knee. She broke through the group that had surrounded her at the bar, leaving Phil on the bar stool. He offered me a warm smile and a wink, raising his glass in silent greeting. It was so good to see them all.

"Dan! It's so good to see you guys," Dalaja echoed my thoughts, pulling us both in for tight hugs one by one. The drawn-out way she spoke and the full embrace let me know the glass of fizz in her hand wasn't her first. Others wouldn't have noticed; she wasn't slurring, but when you knew each other as well as we did, you just knew those kinds of things.

The thought caused my heart to contract as I was reminded of the things they didn't know about me.

My friends could tell you my drink of choice, what I'd order from every takeaway in a ten-mile radius, the things that Dan did that pissed me off most, and the way I fiddled with my hair when I was nervous. They knew every tiny detail about me, and yet I had managed to disguise the biggest part of who I was.

"Happy birthday," I called over the noise. She looked stunning in a fitted navy dress with sequins that sparkled under the light. "You look amazing."

"Thanks, Rach. So do you. Come and grab a glass, both of you," Dalaja enthused, gesturing behind her. "Phil's paid for a load of champagne. It needs drinking." She shrugged, feigning innocence.

"Thanks. I might just grab a coke or something first."

Despite the fact that Dan had insisted on getting a taxi in case I changed my mind, I had made the decision that I wouldn't be drinking. Even with the days that had passed, I still felt the ripples of the hangover after our anniversary evening. I wondered if I was actually coming down with something, certain no hangover should leave me feeling this groggy days afterwards.

"Are you joking? Don't be ridiculous. You can't drink coke; it's my birthday," Dalaja scoffed. She grabbed me by the hand, guiding me through the gathering of people. She plucked a glass of champagne from the tray with her free hand, turning and pressing it into mine that she was still holding. I took it with a tiny shrug as I rolled my eyes. Dalaja repeated the action, passing Dan a flute and retrieving herself a fresh one. Turning to face us both, she held hers up in front of her at eye level.

"Cheers." She thrust it forwards and we chinked glasses, all taking a gulp. Dalaja eyed me as I drank, the bubbles popping against my lips, the alcohol cool and refreshing. Licking my lips, I lowered my glass, crossing my arms over my chest.

"So, what did Phil get you?" I asked, tilting my head and raising my eyebrows. It was a running joke that Phil would instantly be dumped if he didn't spend a month's wage on her birthday gift.

She fought the smile that tugged at her lips and leaned in towards me.

"He's taking me to the Seychelles." She pinched her lips together and raised her eyebrows, a signal of her excitement. She leaned in further, holding her champagne flute to cover one side of her mouth as she whispered conspiratorially, "I'm hoping he might just bring a ring with him too. What more convincing does he need than seeing me in a bikini for an entire fortnight?" She wiggled her hips, giving me an exaggerated wink.

Dan had angled his body away from us, uncomfortable with the conversation, which made him feel even more like some kind of bodyguard.

I snorted out a laugh, taking another gulp of my champagne and relaxing slightly into the easy flow of the evening.

A woman I recognised as a work colleague of Dalaja's appeared behind her and placed her hand on the top of her arm.

"I'm so sorry to cut in. The staff want to ask you something about the table." She gestured behind her towards the archway that led from the bar area into the restaurant.

Dalaja apologised, telling us to grab some more champagne and that she'd catch up with us as soon as she could before dashing off. Spotting Annie and Tim chatting with another couple at the other end of the bar, I smiled and waved before turning back to Dan, whose face seemed to be fixed in a scowl.

"I'm going to go and say thanks to Phil for the champagne." I lifted my glass. "Then go say hi to Annie and Tim. Are you coming?"

"I'll thank Phil later," he muttered. "I'll go rescue Tim first. He looks like he's about to be bored to death." He didn't wait for me to respond, crossing the room and slapping Tim on the back by way of greeting.

I edged my way through the people, with no idea who was part of our party, and made my way over to Phil. The heat of so many bodies in such a small area was making it stifling, and I could feel my hair sticking to the sweat forming on my hairline.

"Hey." I nudged Phil's arm and he turned, his face creasing into a smile as he stood and opened his arms.

Leaning into his embrace, I felt his stubble rub against my cheek as he kissed it.

"Thanks for the champers." My words were muffled against his shoulder. He released me.

"It's so good to see you, Rach. You look amazing. It's been too long. How are you? Dan not with you?" He glanced over my shoulder although I was sure he must have spotted Dan when Dalaja had greeted us earlier.

"You too. I'm good. Thanks. Yeah, Dan's here somewhere. Over there, avoiding the crowd with Tim, I think." I smiled to disguise the awkwardness – we both knew Dan was actually avoiding Phil.

Phil nodded, saying nothing.

"Dala tells me you're off to the Seychelles." I pulled a face. "Very swanky." I nudged his arm again in a playful gesture and he let out a low chuckle. He wore a tailor-made suit that had probably been purchased for this occasion. His tie matched the fabric of Dalaja's dress. I felt frumpy in the old yellow dress that I had pulled from my wardrobe.

"You know what she's like." He rolled his eyes theatrically. "It was that or a ring, and I figured the holiday would be cheaper. Plus, I get to enjoy it too." I swiped at his arm this time, causing him to chuckle again.

"I think she might be hoping for both." I spoke through the side of my mouth with my eyebrows raised. Phil barked out a laugh this time, and I shook my head at their never-ending battle over marriage.

Before either of us could say anything more, the sound of metal tapping a glass broke through the noise and Dalaja shouted for her party to move into the restaurant.

Phil slung his arm around my shoulder, guiding me through the crowd with ease. I searched for Dan but noticed him ahead with Annie and Tim. Dalaja beamed as Phil and I made our way to the table, stepping towards us. Phil threw his other arm around her too.

"Not one, but two stunning women to escort to dinner. What did I do to become such a lucky guy?" Dalaja giggled but I made no reaction as I caught Dan's glare.

We took our seats, Dalaja to my left, with Phil beside her and Dan on my right, Annie and Tim opposite us, along with two other couples whom I recognised vaguely but whose names I couldn't recall. Phil told Dalaja how gorgeous she looked and I watched her throw her arms around his neck, drawing him to her and kissing him. Someone whistled and she giggled as she pulled away from him. I glanced at Dan, whose focus seemed to be fixed on the menu. I nudged him.

"You okay?" I whispered. His features softened as he looked around at me and sighed. "Yeah. Sorry, Rach. I don't mean to be a misery. I just have so much on my mind."

Placing my hand on his knee under the table I squeezed, feeling his hand on top of mine as he smiled at me. I leaned my head on his shoulder and relaxed.

We ate until we were stuffed, the food absolutely exquisite and almost worth the eyewatering prices they didn't even print in the menu. There had been no let-up in the flow of champagne, and Dalaja had ordered cocktails for us girls too. My head was beginning to feel woozy.

Even Dan seemed to have relaxed and was deep in conversation, laughing at a story Tim was animatedly sharing about a crazy client he'd worked for.

I excused myself, sliding my chair away from the table and placing my napkin down.

"Hold on. I'll come with you." Annie pushed back her own chair, standing too quickly and having to regain her balance with a giggle.

We stumbled through to the bar, making our way to the toilets, when a man stepped out in front of me, blocking my path. I had to pull back my head to stop it colliding with his chest.

"I know you." He narrowed his eyes at me, and I froze, seeing the red writing on the photo as my heart began to race. I started to tremble as he wiggled his finger at me, as though he was telling me off. I studied his face, trying to decipher if I knew him, if he might have been the man to have broken into my home and left a similar message scrawled in my wedding album.

The man clicked his thumb and middle finger with a snap.

"You're that GP. You see my mum. Mrs Gooding." Relief flooded my veins. I had no idea who his mother was, but I didn't care as long as he wasn't here to expose me in front of everyone. "She loves you. Said you were the only one who listened to her. Let me buy you girls a drink."

"Oh, that's very kind. There's no need, though. I'm so glad your mum—"

"I insist," he cut me off. "What are you drinking?" His tipsy gaze flicked from me to Annie and back.

"Pornstar martinis." Annie smiled. "But if you'll excuse us, we're just on the way to the bathroom."

"Of course. Sorry." He stood to one side to allow us to pass.

"Did you see his face when I told him what we were drinking?" Annie chuckled. "He looked like he was going to have a heart attack. Not exactly a cheap round." We pushed through the toilet door as I forced a laugh. The innocent encounter had left me shaken, reminding me of everything that was happening outside of the evening.

"Bet he does a runner while we're in here," Annie continued before she turned to look at me. "Are you okay? He seemed to make you a bit... Edgy. I know he was a bit overzealous, but I think he meant well."

I forced a smile and nodded. "Yeah. We just had some problems with a patient at the surgery this week making threats and stuff. He wanted extra meds. It wasn't very nice. Police were involved." I waved a hand around as if to dismiss it. "I guess it has left me a bit edgy."

"Oh, Rach. You never said," Annie gushed.

"There was nothing to tell." I shrugged.

We left the toilet and, as Annie had predicted, the man was nowhere to be seen. We made our way back to the table and Dalaja turned towards us, a wry smile fixed on her face.

"Who'd you two make an impression on?" She gestured towards the two cocktails which waited for us on the table.

"Bugger me, he actually bought them." Annie laughed, before beginning to explain it to the group.

"So, it's been freebies all round for us tonight," Annie finished, chuckling and sipping her fresh cocktail. "Cheers. Thanks, Dala, for being born. Thanks, Phil, for footing the bill for every one of her birthdays since uni."

Everyone laughed at Annie's tipsy speech as we all chinked glasses.

"She doesn't give me much choice," Phil muttered, and Dalaja elbowed him playfully.

"So, the Seychelles." The woman across the table sitting beside Annie, whom I now knew to be Miriam, stuck out her bottom lip and raised her eyes. Dalaja had re-introduced us earlier in the evening, reminding me that she was a work colleague and we had met once before at Dalaja's previous birthday celebration. "You'll have to tell me your secret." She gestured at the man sitting beside her. "I don't think I could get Rob to take me to Benidorm."

Rob shrugged and stuck out his lip as though his wife was right.

"When do you go?"

Dalaja leaned into Phil.

"We haven't officially booked anything yet. Phil is too tied up with work at the moment. But as soon as all this horrid to-do is over and Phil breaks the story, we'll be off."

I sensed Dan prickle beside me, sitting up straighter in his chair. Annie and Tim threw discreet glances in our direction.

"Hopefully sooner rather than later, then, for everyone's sakes." Miriam pursed her lips.

"Absolutely." Dalaja tilted her glass towards Miriam and nodded.

"I'm sure it won't be long," Phil added. "The police are working around the clock on this. But they can't be expected to work miracles, and with their funding being constantly cut and all. They can only do what they can."

Dan's hand curled into a fist on the table beside me.

"I suppose. But surely, they must at least have a lead. I mean, how does someone just get away with wandering in and out of houses, killing women while the police are working *'around the clock'?*" She made air quotes as she spoke.

Annie's cheeks had turned pink. I didn't dare look at Dan.

"He obviously knows what he's doing," Phil replied. "It's not an easy task for the police. It's like searching for a needle in a haystack."

Miriam scoffed. "Didn't they take a convicted murderer in for questioning who's just been released? That seems like a pretty big needle to me."

I felt the colour drain from my face, my hand freezing with my drink lifted halfway towards my lips.

The group fell silent for a few seconds, no one sure of what to say next – most painfully aware of Dan's profession.

Dalaja cleared her throat.

"Well, they must have had a reason to let him go. They obviously don't believe he's guilty." She was trying desperately to be diplomatic while I struggled to remember to keep breathing.

"Bullshit." Miriam screwed up her face. "Most of the police force these days don't know their arse from their elbows. They're so busy out with their speed guns and searching innocent people on the streets. It's all about making back money. Giving out fines to those who don't deserve it. Turning a blind eye to all the stuff that matters." She sat back in her seat, drink in hand, a look of smug satisfaction on her face.

"That's simply not true." We all turned out attention to Tim, the last person any of us would have expected to speak out.

Miriam leaned in again, looking around the others to see Tim.

"Oh?"

Even Tim seemed a little taken aback by his own intervention, but he lifted his chin and pushed back his shoulders, addressing no one in particular as he spoke.

"You cannot lump every police officer together. Of course, there are those who aren't as *diligent* as others, but that's the same in every profession. In my experience, the majority of officers devote a huge chunk of their lives to provide a service for the general public, whether we are deserving of it or not. They have to deal with and witness some truly harrowing things. They deserve the upmost respect and our gratitude for what they sacrifice. It isn't as easy as following a trail of crumbs to the bad guy. They have to prove it, beyond reasonable doubt, to a jury, people like you who aren't always the most supportive of their endless work. Can you even imagine what that must be like? Killers don't walk around with a sign on their heads announcing their misdemeanours. For the most part, they appear to be normal people. Hell, in the right – or wrong – circumstances, any one of us could find ourselves caught up in a murder." Tim snapped his jaw shut as if his words had tumbled out before he could stop them. He blinked, seeming to have forgotten where he was as the rest of the table watched him in stunned silence.

"I mean, I'm not sure I agree with that." Dalaja pulled a face. "There's no way I could ever be capable of murder. I don't have it in me. I think you have to be a certain type of person to be able to go through with something like that. You have to be wired wrong or something." She tapped the side of her head.

"I actually agree with Tim," Miriam's husband, Rob, cut in. I remembered he was a high-profile lawyer. "Of course you get *'the type'*." He made air quotes with his fingers. "But equally, any of us can be caught in a moment and things can happen beyond our control that we never could have imagined. I've had my share of clients – good, honest people – who found themselves in the wrong place, wrong time." He shrugged. "A husband who tells his wife he's having an affair with his secretary just as she's chopping the veg for their evening meal. She would never have meant to kill him, but in the moment, with all that rage, him seemingly not even sorry for what he's done, destroying her entire life for a few office hook-ups. She has to release that fury. It just so happens the knife was in her hand."

Miriam snorted again. "Typical defence attorney spiel." She scoffed, rolling her eyes. "And I guess the poor desperate housewife happened to slip in his blood and that's how she ended up cutting his balls off too?" She narrowed her eyes at her husband, a false smile in place as the rest of the table let out a low chuckle.

"I hear what you're saying, though." Phil shrugged and stuck out his lip. "Crimes of passion, that kind of thing. Do you remember that guy a few years ago who didn't know himself if he'd murdered his wife in his sleep. He had a condition – para-something or other. Press called him the sleepwalker. Weird things can happen. The people who murderer in the spur of the moment, instantly regretting their actions. You see it when men get into fights in pubs, how easily it can happen with one wrong punch. Anyone is capable of it; it just has to be the right set of circumstances."

"So, the guy they questioned." Miriam turned her gaze on Phil, raising her eyebrows. "Dennis something or other, wasn't it? You think that was a crime of passion? Didn't he kill his mistress, his wife, and his infant child?" Her lip curled.

I could barely breathe, their words coming in and out of focus, as though I was underwater. I tipped my glass to drain the last of my cocktail, and realised it was already empty. Slamming the glass down harder than I'd meant to, I snapped the stem. No one but Dan seemed to notice, too consumed with the conversation. I plucked the champagne flute from the table, Dalaja having recently refilled it for me. Dan's hand slid into my lap.

"Oh, yeah. There's no excuse for scum like him." Phil nodded, his lip curling. "He's one of the ones who has it in his genetic makeup. No hope for evil bastards like that."

"Do you think it runs in families?" Dalaja asked, her interest piqued.

"Absolutely." Phil nodded enthusiastically. "It takes a certain type of person to plot to kill. A whole different level to kill your own too." He shook his head. "Probably best for his littlun that she didn't make it. Imagine having to grow up with a dad like that."

I swallowed down the last gulp of champagne just as Phil delivered his parting words, aware all too late of my rising urge to vomit.

15

I tried to avoid looking at the headlines splashed over every newspaper as I made my way inside our local supermarket. It hurt to know that Phil was part of that, and seeing the faces of the women made it all too real. The thought of Phil brought with it the memories of the previous evening.

Thankfully, I had made it to the toilet in the restaurant before throwing up everything I had eaten and drunk over the course of the evening. I would have liked to have blamed it all on the trauma of the conversation I'd had the ordeal of sitting through, but the amount of alcohol I'd had, plus the hangover, told me that was only in part to blame.

It had taken me until late morning before I had felt able to attempt to leave my bed. My head had pounded as though someone was attempting to break out from inside my skull with a sledgehammer. I groaned as I attempted to roll over and wondered if I would make it to the bathroom before I threw up again.

It was becoming a struggle to remain rational. Every time

someone held my gaze too long, or looked away too quickly, my palms would become clammy and I had to talk myself down from hyperventilating at the idea that they might have worked it out, recognised me as Dennis Raiker's daughter. If it wasn't Dennis that had broken into my house, someone else knew who I was.

I grabbed a couple of microwave meals, dropping them into my shopping basket, and avoided the alcohol aisle on the way to the checkout. The thought of wine still made my stomach somersault.

What was wrong with me? After being so adamant that I wasn't going to have a drink at Dalaja's birthday, I had failed to say no to the first glass offered. Once again, I had lost control and relied on alcohol to blank everything out. It had been the second time within a matter of a week I had turned to drinking. I burned with shame as I pictured the way the girls had looked at me, then at each other, as Dan had helped me out of the restaurant. The concern mingling with shock at the state I had gotten myself into. The way Dan had hissed at me to walk as I had clung to his neck, him practically having to carry me out to the taxi. I needed to rein it in before it became any more of a problem.

I scanned my items, dreading the idea of returning to an empty house. It seemed pointless, cooking. After our night out, Dan would return to his erratic schedule, leaving me with no idea when – or even if – he would return home each night. I couldn't bring myself to cook for one, but it somehow made me feel worse being greeted by nothing but his untouched meal still waiting in the fridge the following morning, another plate of food I would scrape into the bin.

After the way I'd embarrassed us both the previous

evening, I wouldn't blame Dan if he would rather not come home at all.

Nothing more had come of the break into our home. I had ensured to leave things around the house a certain way, so that I could be sure to know if anyone had been inside. I had wedged small pieces of paper inside the living room and kitchen doors before pulling them closed, aware that an intruder wouldn't know to look for them but that it would leave me with undeniable proof that someone had been inside.

I had found the scrap of paper I had been using left on the kitchen worktop that morning, a note scribbled on it.

Sorry I missed you. I hope you're feeling better this morning. Hopefully see you tonight. Love you. D. xxx

I had read and reread the note, trying to hear it in my husband's voice, thankful that he didn't seem to be mad at me. I wondered if he had realised the significance of the scraps of paper. I had, in that moment, questioned my own sanity, but had once again wedged it in before leaving for the supermarket.

The memories of the discussion my friends had started at Dalaja's birthday swirled in a loop in my head.

Phil would clearly believe I was like him, by virtue of being his flesh and blood. But I wasn't my father. I had never even so much as laid a finger on another person, and the knowledge of what he had done weighed as heavily on me as anyone else.

I shook my head, trying to dislodge the memory of that conversation. I realised my mistake as the ground seemed to lurch underneath me. I stopped, taking some deep breaths. I shut the noxious thoughts down and forced them out instantly.

It didn't last, my mind stuck on a loop, unable to move around the memories that sat like road blocks. It found its way back to the same thoughts, the way your tongue continually searches out and prods the sore spot in your mouth.

The night had left things more than a little strained. I wondered if Dalaja regretted her comment to Dan about hurrying up with the case. She had been joking. I could only assume it was her unfiltered way of addressing the elephant in the room, but surely, she would have known what that would have been like for Dan.

The tension between Dan and Phil had been palpable. Of course, I understood Phil was only doing his job. It really wasn't personal. But the press seemed to be taking pleasure in ridiculing the police, labelling them as incompetent for enabling this person to brazenly continue with what he was doing.

They had reported on Dennis being 'invited in' for questioning, and on his release, pushing the point that they had no idea whom to look for and that they were either focusing on the wrong man, or were allowing a convicted murderer to run rings around them. The public were left feeling more vulnerable than ever in their blind unawareness of how he was choosing his victims. Those who didn't know about Dan – or weren't polite enough to spare me – seemed to have joined the witch hunt the press had stirred up.

The pressure of hiding who I was and seeing Dan under such scrutiny was becoming too much and I wondered how much longer I could continue before I broke.

Annie and Dalaja had sent texts during the morning, asking if I was okay, if I needed anything, but the need to keep them at arm's length was stronger than ever. They had been kind and skirted around mentioning the state I had gotten myself into – Dalaja claiming to barely remember the end of the evening – but I burned with shame every time I thought about it, wishing I could go back and redo it, or better yet, not go at all.

My phone buzzed with a message as I arrived at the front door to my house, weighed down with the shopping bags. I glanced around, wondering when the last drive-by had been, whether it would seem too pitiful to ask one of the officers to come and check the house for me. I closed my eyes, blowing out my breath. Hadn't I embarrassed myself enough? I imagined the officers telling Dan how I'd made them escort me inside.

As I slotted my key into the lock and pushed my way inside, I paused to listen. I flicked on the hallway light, aware that, with no Toyota in the driveway and the house in darkness, it was very unlikely Dan was home. I called out anyway, wanting to be sure. Or maybe to warn any intruder of my presence.

"Hello?" I remained still, waiting for any sound, but none came. I was jittery, unable to shake the thoughts of that writing on our wedding photo every time I entered my own home. Why would someone want to tell me they knew who I was if they didn't plan to use it against me? There had to be something brewing.

I slipped off my trainers and tiptoed down the hall, noting the paper still wedged between the kitchen door and its frame. I pushed it open, allowing the paper to flutter to the floor and heaving the bag onto the table. Pulling my phone from my back pocket, I dragged down the screen, previewing but being careful not to open the WhatsApp.

Hey, are you free tonight? I want to see you and hate thinking of you alone while Dan is working so much. We could go for a drink? Or grab something to eat? Or I could call over? Would be so nice to see you and catch up properly. Let me know. Xx

I could hear Annie's desperation through her message. I felt awful that I was shutting her out. She was just caught in the crossfire of the whole sorry mess. Dropping the phone onto the table beside the bag I gave a deep sigh. I couldn't see her now. After the previous night's mess and the constant charade I was having to hide behind just to get through work and my day-to-day life, I was exhausted. I wasn't strong enough to keep it up around my friends in a one-on-one setting. I would pretend not to have seen her message for another hour or two and then I could reply and make my excuses. It was the weekend but I could tell her I was the on-call GP for the evening and assure her I would see her soon. I would have to build up the strength to meet with my friends or I knew it wouldn't be long before they arrived on my doorstep, regardless of my protests.

Phil had messaged me separately, checking in after my embarrassing display too. I had sent a brief reply, thanking him for the concern and assuring him everything was fine. My response had felt oddly formal.

I grabbed the milk and ready meals from the bag and slotted them into the fridge. I didn't have much of an appetite and decided I would rather shower and get into my pyjamas before I ate, with the television for company. Folding up my bag, I carried it back towards the front door with me, planning to put it with my shoes so I would remember to put it back into my car.

As I crossed the hall, the living room door caught my eye. It was closed, as I had left it, but the little bit of paper I had wedged in it was on the floor just outside. I couldn't believe I'd missed it when I came in, too busy hauling my shopping bags in to check.

I froze, straining to listen for any sound, trying to remember if I had definitely put it back before I left.

There was no sound apart from the ticking of the clock and my own heavy breathing. My heart slammed hard against my chest, and I had to lean on the wall for support.

My brain screamed at me to go back to the kitchen, to call the police – or wait outside for them to come back to check the house. But how would I explain why I'd freaked out? Because a scrap of paper wasn't where I left it? The thought of saying that out loud seemed insane. I wasn't even totally sure I had put them all back in place thanks to my hung-over state. I might've run back inside to pick up my phone; I did that all the time.

It isn't Dennis. He wouldn't come here.

The voice in my head did nothing to ease my trembling, every hair on my body standing on end as I battled internally over what I should do. Hadn't I embarrassed myself enough? It was bad enough that I'd gotten wasted in front of all my friends, and for the second time in a week. What would it be like for Dan to have his colleagues discussing his unhinged wife who set up paper traps despite the presence of their units regularly checking the house?

I turned away from the door, returned to the kitchen and called Dan.

I listened to the ringing, waiting for it to connect, desperate to hear his voice and for him to tell me what to do, that I wasn't being stupid to call. He'd send in a unit to check. Eventually, his answerphone cut in and I dropped my head into my free hand, cursing under my breath as I waited for the beep.

"Dan, it's me. Can you give me a call when you get this. I'm... everything's fine but I..." I searched around for something to say, coming up blank and aware the silence was stretching too long. "I just wondered what time you'll be home. Love you." My shoulders sagged as I hung up, glancing towards the kitchen doorway. My fingers hovered over the phone screen, my mind going back and forth, debating the implications of calling the police.

The decision was taken out of my hands as the soft click of the living room door came from the hall. I held my breath, too afraid to release it until I had identified the cause of the door opening.

"Hello, JoJo."

I dropped my phone and it clattered to the floor. I froze. My body refusing to move, too afraid to run. Staring down at my phone, which lay face down on the floor where it had landed, I gripped the edge of the worktop for support.

I couldn't look up. Seeing him there would make it real. He couldn't be here – in my kitchen, in my home. He couldn't.

For a split second, I wondered if this was how his other victims had felt. Had they been paralysed with this same fear, or had they fought him?

"I think you'd better come through and sit down." He gestured towards my living room. The sound of his voice caused every hair on my body to stand on end as my muscles went rigid. There was an edge to his tone. It wasn't a request.

Glancing towards my phone again, I wondered if I could

move quickly enough to get to it before he could cross the kitchen.

"Leave that."

I jolted at his order and despite the resentment, the fury with myself that I wasn't strong enough to fight him, I followed him to the living room. How many times had I played this out, assured myself that I would be the one to stand up to him on behalf of every woman he had terrorised. I had imagined myself fighting him, attacking, and ripping any part of him I could get close enough to, but the harsh reality was that I was nothing more than another victim.

I edged into the living room and pressed my back against the wall as Dennis brushed past me.

He perched on the edge of my sofa, leaning forwards, his hands clasped together, elbows resting on his knees. He stared at me, his eyes hard and unblinking. I willed myself to do something, to flee from the room, to run at him and fight with everything I had. But my fight or flight instinct appeared to have failed me, and instead, I remained exactly where I was, rooted to the spot – unable to so much as meet his stare.

"It's been a long time, hasn't it? I'm sorry for that." His gruff voice was barely more than a mumble. My breath came in short, ragged bursts, almost gasps as I fought to gain control, pleading with myself not to have a panic attack. I wrapped my arms across my chest to disguise the trembling that had taken over my body. I didn't want to give him the satisfaction of seeing how terrified I was.

"I also apologise for..." he cleared his throat and lifted his hands, gesturing around himself, "the way we had to meet again." He rubbed his chin with his palm, his face impassive.

"I didn't want to turn up uninvited. But I had to see you, JoJo."

I couldn't speak, barely able to recall the last time I had been addressed by my old name, let alone a nickname. I didn't remember it, but the way he said it seemed to stir something within me, leaving my skin burning with a mixture of terror, shock, and rage. I could hear my heartbeat racing, the blood pumping so quickly it left me lightheaded.

I fought to keep my expression stony, refusing to let him know how badly he was scaring me, that he had the upper hand on me in my own home.

Swallowing hard, I scrambled around inside my mind for the best way to handle this, wondering what Dan would tell me to do. If I screamed and no one heard me, what might he do to me? My knees went weak at the memories of the other women whose homes he had broken into already. My best chance was to keep him talking.

"You shouldn't be here," I stammered, clenching my fists with the effort to hide the way my voice shook.

"No, probably not." He cocked his head, raising his eyebrows. "But there are some things you need to know. Some really important things. That's why I'm here. I needed to see you while I still could."

My breath caught and I found myself at a loss for how to respond. While he still could. What did he mean by that?

This wasn't how I had pictured this scene playing out, certain that if Dennis was going to turn up, he would be waiting, late at night, hiding somewhere in the shadows, to ambush me and torture me as he watched the life drain from my body. The Dennis that sat before me in my living room unnerved me more than the scenarios I had visualised, leaving me blindsided, with no idea what he was talking about and what his next move might be. Was this all some sort of game?

We both knew I was on the back foot. The daylight had barely been extinguished and yet Dennis had been here, having easily broken into my home, despite the police presence, and had been lying in wait for me. I had no idea why he had come or what his agenda might be.

I considered making a dash for the door, wondering if I could get through it and to the front, or to the kitchen to grab a knife. There was a possibility he was armed, but with nothing whatsoever to hand, I was completely defenceless. As I eyed Dennis for the first time, I noticed his physique. He was fit and lean, clearly having put his prison days to good use.

My eyes flicked towards the door but he didn't miss a beat, his mind clearly still as sharp as his body was capable.

"Do it if it would make you feel better."

I eyed him wearily.

"If that's what it takes for you to hear me out, I'll wait while you go and get yourself a weapon."

My lips parted and I gawped at him, thwarted by his apparent ability to read my thoughts. It only served to terrify me further that he was so sure of his ability to overpower me he would be willing to allow me to arm myself. Or was it some kind of trick? I didn't move, keeping my back pressed to the wall.

"I'm not armed." He held up his hands as though to surrender but I didn't feel any reassurance. This man was no more than a stranger to me; worse, in fact. I would have rather faced a stranger than him. His assurance meant nothing. He could easily have a knife or gun concealed, and even if he didn't, I knew just by looking at him that he could overpower me without breaking a sweat.

He's playing with you. The voice in my head screamed so loud I wondered for a second if I had spoken the words. Dennis allowed his hands to drop, but said nothing.

"The police are outside," I stammered, doing all I could to disguise how badly my voice shook. "They've been watching the house."

Dennis regarded me for a few seconds before lifting one eyebrow.

"If you are referring to that friend of your husband's…" His brow creased, and he clicked his fingers as though trying to recall. "Matthew – I think they call him Clarky." He pointed his finger at me as he said the name with satisfaction. "He did drive around the area a few times, but it's trailed off."

I stared at him blankly. Dan had told me they'd put units in place to watch the house, not that one guy would drive past every now and again. He left me winded, as though I'd taken a body blow. A few seconds passed while I regained my composure as best I could.

"My friend's due to arrive any time now." I glanced over at the clock, as if to confirm it. I stuck out my chin and shifted my weight from one leg to the other, spurred on by my quick thinking. "She texted me just before I got home."

I was desperate to steady my breathing, to sound more assertive and less like I was panting as I spoke.

He studied me once again, before pressing his lips together.

"You don't need to lie to me, JoJo. If you'll agree to listen to what I have to say, I'll go. I swear. And if you never want to see me again, you won't." He held up his hands again, wearing a serious expression as he nodded at me, unblinking.

Swallowing hard, I lifted my eyes to take him in properly for the first time. He had blindsided me once again with the way he'd steered the conversation. I had been prepared for threats, for him to detail every second of my mother and sister's suffering before inflicting the same fate onto me, but I was at a loss for how to react to this.

I debated if it was worthwhile attempting to keep up the charade that Annie was on her way. Eyeing Dennis once again, I searched his features, so similar to my own.

His expression was soft. I considered what he had said. He seemed to be genuine, but then, how far could you trust a convicted murderer who had brazenly broken the conditions of his release, as well as into my home?

This is what men like him do, I reminded myself. It's a game to him.

It was not a game I wanted to partake in, but what choice did I have? My phone was in another room, I had no idea when, or if, Dan would return home, I'd cut off all of my friends, and was facing a man who seemingly had nothing to lose. Would I even want Annie to turn up? Not only would it potentially put her in danger too, but if we did both make it out of the situation, I would be left with no choice but to tell her everything.

It struck me that the latter scared me in equal measure to the former.

"How did you find me?" I whispered, glaring at Dennis, desperate to disguise the fear that snaked its way around me when I looked at him. Despite my best efforts to leave every part of my old life behind me, it seemed it had been effortless for him to track me down. All the sacrifices I had made, and he had traced me within days.

Dennis's brow dipped, his face creasing.

"I received letters," he answered, shifting in his seat.

I stared at him blankly. He cleared his throat, avoiding my gaze.

"While I was in prison. They never said who they were from or why they were writing to me. Just gave some basic information about you, your new name, where to find you."

I drew back, suddenly feeling as if there wasn't enough air in the room.

"I don't want to bring you any trouble, JoJo. I just had to see you. I only planned to check in on you from a distance, but then..."

He trailed off. I snapped my head up.

"You *have* been following me. You were in here, weren't you?"

He dropped his head into his hands.

"This isn't how I wanted this to go." He shook his head, raising his face to meet my stare and seeming to register my fear for the first time.

"I would never hurt you." He held up his hands, his words barely more than a whisper.

"Then why leave that note?" I hissed. "If not to try to scare me, why would you do that?"

His expression went blank as he searched my face.

"I never left a note." His eyes didn't leave mine. "What did it say?"

I scoffed, refusing to enter into his game. I wouldn't be his puppet.

"I didn't leave any note, JoJo. I looked around, I admit,

but why would I have left a note? What would that have achieved?"

Once again, he was convincing, but I wasn't stupid. He'd admitted to breaking into my home, to stalking me. Who else would have written it?

His shoulders sagged when I didn't respond, and he stared at the ground in front of his feet, as though he couldn't bear to look at me. "I know what you think I am, what you think I did, but I loved your mother and Julia. I didn't... I would never have..."

Fury suffocated my fear.

"So, the police got it all wrong? Is that what you came here to tell me?" I screwed up my face. "The neighbours heard you fighting that morning. You never even tried to protest your innocence. Why would you be okay with everyone believing that you killed your wife and child? You stayed silent for all these years but decided now's the time to suddenly play innocent?"

His jaw clenched and he continued to stare at the floor. Something had changed in his demeanour. "There are things that you don't know, things you don't understand. I *did not* hurt your mother or sister, JoJo. I don't deny your mother wasn't always the easiest woman, but my God, I loved her. I would never have stuck around for so long if I didn't. I made mistakes, but I never laid a finger on them. Either of them."

He lifted his face to meet my hard stare. I struggled to disguise my shock at the tears that had formed in his eyes as he spoke of my family. He seemed so sincere, but I would not be taken for a fool.

"And you expect me to just take your word for that? Accept it as the truth and believe the police got it wrong? That you stayed silent when accused of murdering your wife and *child*? Just allowed everyone to believe you did it? Let the real murderer just get away with it and spent most of your life in prison? What possible reason could there ever be for that? I really struggle to see why would you ever—"

"For you, JoJo." The words seemed to burst from him, interrupting me mid-flow, and I flinched at both the volume and ferocity of them. He seemed to deflate before my eyes as what he had said infiltrated my resolve and began to extinguish my rage. The fear that I had felt earlier at the very sight of my father wrapped itself around me like a python, choking the air from me as he repeated himself.

"I did it for you."

16

BEFORE

He had crept around the door, eyeing me from his position against the wall whilst rubbing his foot backwards and forwards across the carpet. I had turned my head slowly to watch his movements, identifying them as an anxious trait.

I had said nothing, feeling no desire to set him at ease. The light from the hallway had illuminated one half of his face, which he seemed unable to hold one expression on.

"Why d'you do those things to Dad?" he asked, his leg beginning to jiggle.

I didn't respond other than by arching an eyebrow.

He had swallowed hard.

"You know what I mean. Why d'you like to freak him out when Mum's not around?"

Still, I had said nothing, but I pushed myself up onto my elbows from lying on my bed, swinging my legs around and lowering my feet to the ground so that I was sitting.

"D'you know, he says you're a psychopath?" He rubbed

his nose with the back of his index finger and sniffed. "He told me to keep away from you. Said you're dangerous."

I could feel the smirk that spread across my face.

"So why aren't you listening?" I cocked my head, my tone smooth compared the tremble he attempted to conceal in his.

He lifted one shoulder in a half shrug, screwed up his nose.

"I ain't scared of you." The muscle in his jaw that continuously worked told me different. He sniffed loudly again, and I sniggered.

"What're you gonna do about him?" He stuck out his chin.

"Who?" I asked cooly.

"Dad. He ain't gonna stop watching you. He told me it's a matter of time till you do somethin' and then he'll prove to Mum what you are."

As I stared at my brother, there was a flash in his eyes that – just for a second – made him look exactly like our father. His fate was sealed.

17

"You're not making any sense." I shook my head to try to dispel what he was saying. "Why would you hurt our family and think it was for me?" My voice was weak and my breath came in sharp bursts. I fought to keep hold of my composure. This was what his kind did. I had researched it. He was trying to rattle me. It was how he took control.

He dropped his head into his hands, his elbow resting on his knees, and let out a groan.

"I didn't want to tell you like this." He huffed, more to himself than to me. "I wasn't going to..."

"Tell me what?" My heart raced as I tried to convince myself this was all part of his game. Clenching my jaw, I realised my hands had formed such tight fists my fingernails were digging into the flesh of my palms.

"You have to understand, JoJo, this *was my* fault. Mine and your mother's, but I accept the majority of responsibility." He looked wretched as he lifted his head from his hands to look at me. I wanted him to stop speaking. I had no idea why, but I knew I didn't want to hear whatever he was about to tell me. The desperate urge to turn on my heel and sprint from the room was almost overwhelming. I was certain that the adrenaline that had begun to pump would be enough to allow me to leave Dennis standing. My feet remained rooted to the spot, betraying me.

"This isn't going to be easy for you to hear. But I do believe you have a right to the truth." He dragged his hands down his face, lifting his eyes towards the ceiling as if there was someone up there he could ask for help.

I both wanted to yell at him to get on with it, just tell me what he'd come to say, and stick my fingers in my ears, reverting back to the child that he had known and refusing to hear anything more from him – in equal measure. Once I knew what he was about to tell me, I had a feeling nothing would be the same. But if I refused to hear it, could I continue on, always wondering what he might have said? I'd drive myself insane conjuring up every possible scenario. What choice did I have but to hear him out?

"You should sit down." Dennis gestured to the armchair opposite where he sat. I did as he said, not giving consideration to the bizarre situation I found myself in, being treated as the guest in my own home by the stranger I'd once called Dad.

My body sagged. I was grateful to have taken the weight off my feet even if it suddenly seemed to hang over my head.

Dennis regarded me as though weighing up whether I was resilient enough to withstand whatever he was about to disclose. He closed his eyes for a few seconds, seeming to compose himself before blowing out his breath.

"I didn't hurt your mother, JoJo," he repeated what he'd already told me whilst looking at me straight in the eye. It was me who struggled to hold the contact. "I'm not going to lie to you and pretend we had an easy marriage. Ruth, well... she was... ill."

"I know Mum had a drug problem," I interrupted. "Alison never told me, of course, but I read everything I could find about it when I got old enough to look into it all for myself. The press believed that's why you killed her. They said you'd had enough of having to take care of her, pay for her addiction. That you finally cracked."

Dennis winced. He was either genuinely stung by the harshness of my words or truly the best actor I had ever met. Alison, my aunty, had hated Dennis, so it was no surprise she'd failed to mention my mother's issues.

"I hated what she was doing to herself. I tried so hard to help her clean herself up, but she just didn't have the strength." He stared over my left shoulder at nothing in particular, the pain of the memories etched into his features. "I loved her and just wanted her to get better."

"Did you kill her by accident?" I whispered, desperate hope rising, the thought never having occurred to me before thanks to the picture that had always been painted by everyone around me.

He shook his head slowly, bursting my bubble of hope. He was admitting that he murdered my mother intentionally. I gripped the arms of the chair, wondering how much more I could stomach.

"I didn't kill her, JoJo. It *was* my fault that she died, though." He sighed deeply. "She cared so much for you and Julia."

The mention of my sister's name caused my skin to prickle and the hairs to stand up on the back of my neck. I had never gotten the chance to speak of her to anyone other than Dan. My aunty had refused to talk about my family once I had gone to live with her, preferring to try to forget about their existence rather than relive the horror of it all. Hearing my sister's name on my father's lips caused my blood to course like lava through my veins. I swallowed down the bitterness, aware this may be the only chance I ever had to hear what he had to say. I needed to hear it, even if I was never going to get to leave. Dennis continued.

"It wasn't her fault. She'd been given painkillers years before due to a slipped disk in her back. When the doctors decided that she shouldn't need the pain relief anymore, Ruth found that she struggled to function without it." I leaned forwards in my seat, taking in every word. I had never been offered any information on my family and so drank in everything Dennis offered, pushing aside the little voice in my mind warning me that it could all be lies.

"She thought that taking that stuff helped her to be a better mother. She said it made her less tired, gave her the energy and ability to keep up with you and your sister. It meant a lot to her, to be a good mum to the two of you." He offered a watery half-smile. "She couldn't see that the poison she put into her body was the only thing stopping her. She would be wonderful with you girls, until she would start to come down from her highs. She wouldn't even feel as though she'd been high, by the end. She needed it just to function, to feel normal. I remember her trying to describe it to me, telling me that it started so small, like that itch on the bottom of your foot when you have your shoe on. To start with, you can ignore it, wiggle your foot a little to pacify the urge to scratch, but eventually, the itch takes over your whole body, leaving you feeling as though you have bugs crawling under your skin, trying to claw their way out, a noise inside your head that cannot be silenced, so loud it feels as though your skull might explode. The simultaneous feeling of wanting to tear at your own skin whilst breaking into your own skull just to relieve the pressure." His eyes had a faraway look as he stared off, unblinking.

"I cannot imagine the lengths you would be willing to go to when you are suffering so deeply that all you want is to end it all, and yet you know that you can get instant relief, be there for your family and live like a normal person, with just one hit. She told me she would feel so desperate for it, like an intense thirst, like you can almost taste and feel it on the tip of your tongue, making it so much harder to resist. She wanted to stop, JoJo, she really did. She tried but it was so hard for her, it caused her so much pain. I wanted her to go to rehab but she wouldn't leave you girls. That and she was so afraid of the stigma. She convinced herself if she went away, I would realise I could do better, replace her whilst she was gone, and that we wouldn't want her back." He shook his head, closing his eyes. "I would never have looked at anyone whilst I had her."

Tears pricked, swelling in the corners of my eyes. I had no idea of what had led to my mother's death, but I didn't doubt for a second the sincerity in Dennis's recalling of what she had been though leading up to it. As a doctor, I knew the pain of addiction. It was an illness not to be taken lightly, and back in the time when my mother had been suffering, it was even more of a taboo subject than it was now. I eyed Dennis, unable to believe that anyone could be this good at forging emotion. I wondered for the first time if he truly had loved her, questions racing through my mind. Psychopaths weren't capable of love. If he really had cared about her like he seemed to, it must have been an awful time for them both. I briefly wondered how I would feel about Dan if he managed to get himself into the condition my mother had. Would I care for him unconditionally? Or would the strain eventually become too much? The conversation from Dalaja's dinner party came flooding back to me.

Pushing the thoughts aside, I reminded myself that no matter what he did or whatever happened between us, I would never be able to hurt Dan, let alone murder him. Dennis was being extremely clever, manipulating me into feeling sorry for him despite knowing what he did. I gave myself a mental shake and reminded myself of who the person in front of me was.

"She promised me she was going to stop. I think I knew really that she never would, but I was so desperate to believe her. She managed to feed her habit herself for a short while, but that's where it all went so badly wrong." Dennis's eyes met mine and I couldn't miss the guilt and pain they still seemed to hold.

"She sold some things, managed to pay for a week or two, but when she ran out of money and resources, she asked them to give it to her in good faith, swore to them she was good for the money. She'd never had a problem paying before, so they gave it to her, but with an interest rate. They were not the type of people to be involved with, let alone to borrow from. She didn't tell me she'd gotten herself into debt, just begged me for money and I assumed she'd just fallen off the wagon. We had a huge fight before I left for work because I refused to give her any money, told her that she'd done so well I wouldn't allow her to just destroy all that she'd worked for." He pinched the bridge of his nose between his thumb and forefinger, closing his eyes and blowing out a long breath. "It's the biggest regret of my life that I didn't help her. But you have to believe me, JoJo, I thought that's what I *was* doing."

A few seconds passed as I allowed all that he had just shared to sink in. I had studied him as he had recalled his version of events and had not managed to find a single sign that he was being anything other than honest, but psychopaths could be incredibly good at acting out and mimicking emotions. I needed to be wary, not gullible.

"So how did she die?" I questioned deadpan, refusing to allow him to know he had gotten under my skin.

Dennis's eyes dropped to the floor. He seemed to be aging in front of my eyes, his recollection of the past robbing him of his future.

"I'll never know that for certain." He shook his head slowly, his jaw tightening. I allowed him the time to get himself together. Regardless of whether this was an act, I had little choice but to hear it on his terms. "That's the truth. I can only assume it was the vermin who had been dealing her drugs, the ones who she owed all of the money to. I have no idea whether they planned to kill her, but during our fight, she said, *they will come for me.* I didn't know. I would've given her the money – I planned to – I was just so bloody furious that she'd gone back to it after I thought she'd come so far. I've never forgiven myself for storming out on her, leaving her to face the consequences of it all on her own."

A few beats of silence passed, and I watched Dennis as he swallowed hard, pressing his lips together, unable to look at me.

"But if all of that is true, why didn't you just call the police as soon as you got home and found her? Why would you go to prison for murdering your wife if you genuinely were innocent? You never even tried to protest – or explain your side of things. It makes no sense." The questions tumbled from me, more arising by the second. I felt as though I was trying to fight my way out of a dense fog that was thicker now than before he had begun his explanation.

Dennis shook his head, dropping it into his hands and kneading his eyes. I studied him, unease causing my stomach to drop and tumble as though sailing over crests of the roughest waves. What wasn't he telling me? Goosepimples broke out over my skin as another question slammed into my mind.

"What about Julia? Are you saying they killed her too? Why would they have killed her and not me? She was just a child. They had no reason to involve her, but if that's the kind of people they were, why not me too?" My thoughts spilled from me, my breath coming in sharp bursts as though I had just run uphill. There was a piece of the puzzle that I was missing. I needed it to slot the whole thing together, but everything in me screamed that I wasn't ready to hear it.

Dennis groaned. "I'm so sorry, JoJo," he whispered, his forehead pressed against his fingertips, his eyes betraying the agony he was desperately trying to supress.

I shook my head, the chill on my skin turning to fire as the heat clawed its way up my body.

"Why?" I breathed, trembling.

He looked up at me, meeting my eye, and I could almost see the internal battle that was raging inside his head.

"If there was any other way... If I could spare you... I never wanted to..."

"Tell me." My voice was raised but I couldn't disguise the quiver.

"When I got home, I found your mother and sister. I

phoned the police without hesitating. While I was on the line, I asked you what had happened. You were so young, you seemed so oblivious to it all. I didn't expect you to know anything." His voice broke and he cleared his throat, blinking rapidly.

"You told me that a man had been to the house, that Ruth had asked you to sit in the living room with Julia while she spoke with him. She said you could watch the television and play with anything you wanted." He gave a weak smile that didn't reach his eyes, remembering the words of an innocent three-year-old. "You said they had gone into the bedroom and Mummy had closed the door, but you heard noises. You said you were scared, but that the man came out of the bedroom and ran away." Tears brimmed in Dennis's eyes and he lifted his face to the ceiling to contain them. My body was frozen, my hands resting on the arm rests of my chair, fingers gripping them. I was unable to move and having to remind myself to continue breathing. My chest rose and fell too rapidly.

"You said you'd waited for Ruth to come out, but you got hungry. She had told you that you weren't allowed to go into the bedroom, and you were too afraid to disobey her. It wasn't the first time you'd had to witness something like that. The times she had faced withdrawal before, or taken a little more than she'd meant to, she wasn't always in a fit state to care for the two of you." He gave the tiniest shrug, the corners of his mouth turned down as his chin quivered.

"I should have taken better care of you. I wanted to be there for you more. I hated leaving you when she was so unwell. It wasn't her fault. But we had to keep a roof over our heads. If I hadn't gone out to work, I'd have lost my job. We'd have lost the house. Being homeless seemed like the worst possible scenario at the time." He gave a humourless laugh to cover the emotion fighting to burst from him. I remained motionless.

"Julia had started to cry. You were afraid she would wake up your mother if she was sleeping. You were scared that she would be angry with you for disturbing her."

I shook my head, desperate for him to stop speaking. He needed to stop. I wanted to yell at him to leave, to get out of my house and never come near me again.

"No. No, no, no. Don't say it. Don't you try to pin this on me. I was three years old." I jabbed my finger towards him, aware that my voice was rising, becoming hysterical.

He fell silent, his gaze on me, unfaltering. His features seemed to have crumpled with the weight of his admissions. He looked worse now than in any of the photos I had seen of him in the media in all of the time since his arrest. That scared me more than anything.

"You didn't mean to hurt her, JoJo," he whispered. "You should never have been left in that position. It was not your fault. You were failed by us all."

I shook my head harder, screwing up my face and balling my hands into tight fists as I attempted to close myself off from him.

"You were just trying to stop her crying. You wrapped her up, just pulled the blanket a little too high around her face and..."

"Stop. Just stop it," I screamed at him, a numbness spreading over me. He snapped his jaw closed, pressing his lips together and allowing his eyes to drop back to the floor. His shoulders sagged and his complexion had drained of colour. The skin seemed to hang from his cheekbones, like his mask had slipped, no longer fitting.

My own face burned, my cheeks so hot I questioned if I could be feverish, the whole thing just a hideous nightmare as a result of some illness that ravaged my body. I replayed his admission repeatedly, despite desperately fighting against it. His words left my head spinning and a nausea rising. Practically panting, I attempted to push it back down.

It wasn't true. It couldn't be. I wasn't capable of something so awful.

So why did so much of what he was saying make sense? Dropping my head into my hands I counted my breaths, sucking them in and out, trying to regain control before I lost myself to a panic attack. Dalaja's question came back to me, "Do you think it runs in families?"

"I'm sorry, JoJo," Dennis whispered again. "I never wanted to have to tell you. I... I..."

"Well, then why did you?" I hissed at him, despising him for dropping this on me. "Why would you want to come shoving your way into my life and try to destroy everything by saying something so... so..."

I screwed up my face, unable to find the words. It couldn't be true. I wouldn't believe it. He was a psychopath and a liar. He knew exactly what he was doing.

I glowered at him, the pair of us locked in a stalemate, neither one of us knowing what else to say.

Eventually he cleared his throat. "I know this is a hell of a lot to take in. And part of me wishes I could have just carried on, never telling you the truth, because of course I knew how much it was going to hurt you, JoJo. You're a good person and you would never intentionally harm anyone. I need you to know that regardless of who did what that day, this was my fault. I was the adult and I should have been there to protect all of you. I let you down, and for that, I will never forgive myself. I am so sorry." He paused, sniffing and wiping his nose with the back of his hand. "I had to tell you the truth because if I hadn't, you would never have believed anything else I said. You said it yourself, what other possible reason would there have ever been for me to go to prison – allow the world to see me as a wife and child killer?" His voice broke as he spoke and he cleared his throat, taking a minute to compose himself. I fought not to drown in my rising panic. If what he was saying was true, wasn't that what I was? A child killer?

It couldn't be true.

"I love you with everything I have, and I would do it all again in a heartbeat if it meant protecting any one of the three of you."

I couldn't meet his eye, my breath coming in short, sharp gasps. If what he was saying *was* true, then the man I had believed to be evil had, in fact, been protecting me.

"Why didn't you just tell the truth?" I gasped out. "If what you say is the truth of what happened, why didn't you tell the police that? I was three. They wouldn't have arrested me." My lips remained parted, hot, ragged breaths causing them to feel dry as I stared at him, pleading with my eyes for him to admit he had made it all up. I wondered if it would have been better if he had just come here to kill me. Death seemed a preferable concept to discovering that it was in fact me who was the monster.

"I just froze. I was on hold to the police while you were telling me what had happened. I don't even remember it all, but the phone must have dropped from my hand because the next thing I remember is the police bursting through the front door. We were sat together on the sofa and I was holding on to you so tightly. The phone was on the floor by my feet, the call still connected. I hadn't even considered that they might think I'd done it at that point. They searched the house, found Ruth and Julia and came in shouting at me to lie on the ground. I couldn't let go of you. They had to prise me away from you and drag you out. You were screaming and they arrested me. I didn't have time to think it through. I had no idea what they might do if they knew the truth, what might happen to you, but I *did* know it would ruin your life. So I said nothing. I assumed that because I was innocent, I'd be proven that way. There wouldn't be any evidence that I had done anything wrong because I hadn't. That's not how it turned out."

My jaw hung slack as I took in what he was saying. I wanted to pick apart his story, find every hole and use it to tear the entire thing to shreds, but I couldn't silence my brain to be able to think straight. The silent stillness of the room was a direct contrast to the relentless noise inside my head.

"They don't look too hard for evidence to help someone they want to believe is guilty. You didn't deserve to suffer for what we had done to you, JoJo. And believe me, I have battled with myself over whether to come here and tell you any of this. I am so sorry to just turn up here and do this to you but..." He studied me for a few seconds, seeming to weigh something up before placing both of his palms flat on his thighs.

"Look, I can only imagine how much this is for you to take in. I know I am probably the last person you want to be with right now, and I have to get back." He glanced down at his ankle, to where the tag must have remained a constant reminder that he still wasn't quite free. "So I'm going to leave, give you some time to process everything I've just told you. If and when you are ready to speak to me, or if you have anything you want to ask, you can call or text me on this number." He pulled a crumpled piece of paper from the pocket of his jacket and placed it on the coffee table beside him.

"I'll leave it here." He patted it with his fingertips. "I know what I've said is a lot, but you must understand that you are no more to blame than you've ever believed. You were no more than an infant. This isn't on you, JoJo." He leaned forwards, allowing a few seconds to pass before he pushed himself upright.

I remained where I was, unable to look at him, unable to find any sort of response.

"I really, really hope to hear from you soon. Please take care of yourself." He walked towards me, placing a hand on my shoulder and giving it a gentle squeeze. I expected my impulse to be to pull away, recoil from his touch, but I was too numb to feel anything. I couldn't allow the grief in, aware that once it pierced the surface, I would never be able to recover from the agony and shame for what he said I'd done. I physically ached as I considered all I had been, and all that I had once again – thanks to him – lost.

18

The front door slammed so hard it seemed to shake the house. I jumped, blinking and taking in my surroundings, not even certain if I had been awake. I had remained in the same armchair, motionless since Dennis had left, pulling the door gently closed behind him.

With no sense of time, I had no idea how long I had remained in the chair, but it had to have been a while as my backside had gone numb and one of my legs tingled with the sensation of pins and needles.

"Rach?" I registered Dan calling to me, an edge of panic to his tone, but still felt too groggy to respond.

Dragging my hands through my hair, I swiped my bottom eyelids with the backs of my finger, hoping to remove any remnants of mascara residue, wishing I had come to consciousness before now and gotten myself to bed before Dan had arrived home.

What was I going to tell my husband? For the first time

in the entirety of our marriage, I didn't want to have to face Dan.

I listened to the sounds of him moving around in the hallway, dropping his keys onto the shelf. I pictured him unlacing his shoes and slipping his feet out of them. Dennis had closed the door to the living room as he had left. Perhaps Dan wouldn't come in here and I could slip up the stairs and into bed whilst he was in the bathroom, pretend I was sleeping.

Straining to listen, I heard him walk along the hall and into the kitchen.

His footsteps instantly moved back along the hall, pausing as he came to the door of the living room. It seemed ridiculous that I could be so anxious at the idea of seeing my own husband, but I couldn't bear to witness the expression on his face when he found out the truth about me.

The door swung open and Dan's face appeared around it. He visibly jumped at the sight of me.

"Shit, Rach. You scared the living daylights out of me. Is everything okay? I just got your message. You sounded…" He shook his head. "I've been trying to call you back, but your phone kept going to the answering machine. I just found it on the kitchen floor. I panicked. What the hell are you doing sat down here at this time of night? Is everything okay?" He glanced at the phone he clutched in his hand as though he had forgotten he was holding it, and then at the television, obviously confused as to why I was sat in silence. I stared at him blankly, my overwrought brain unable to come up with a feasible excuse whilst it still worked so hard to process everything, from Dennis being in our home to the horrific version of events he had shared. My stomach rolled at the memory of it all and I could feel tiny beads of sweat forming on my top lip and along my hairline.

"Everything's fine," I muttered, unable to look at him. "I just wanted to know if I'd see you. After last night I felt a bit... I dropped my phone while I was getting a drink. Forgot to pick it back up. I must have dozed off." I shrugged, aware that I was a terrible liar and that it was likely Dan could see right through me.

"Not watching anything?" He gestured towards the television, and I thought I saw a flicker of doubt cross his face.

"I just switched it off when I heard you come in." I forced a smile. "I was just going to come and say hi. I didn't think you knew I was in here." I tried to keep my tone casual, barely able to remember how to have a conversation.

"I saw the light under the door." He shrugged one shoulder.

Was I being paranoid or did Dan seem a little off too? Surely there was no way he could know that Dennis had been here. Of course, if Joyce had seen him, she would have been desperate to tell Dan, but there was no way she would have been waiting up to ambush him, surely.

"What time is it?" I rubbed my eyes with the heels of my hands.

"Erm, around three." Dan stifled a yawn as if I had reminded him of the ungodly hour.

I let out a groan, aware I needed to react but knowing the time offered up no more knowledge of how long I had been sitting there. It must have been hours. Dennis had left in time for his curfew, but I had no idea when that was, or how far he'd have to travel.

"Have you been at work?" I looked up at Dan from under

heavy lids, my eyes gritty. I wasn't sure if it was a result of exhaustion, or if I had been crying.

"Of course," Dan snapped. "Where else would I have been?"

I spun my head to look at him, a little startled by his unjustified attitude. I had been so caught up in what I must look like, so concerned that Dan would notice that something was off, that I had failed to notice how awful he looked. I took in the sight of him. His neatly trimmed hair had grown longer than he would usually have allowed it, sticking up at odd angles as if he had run his hands through it countless times. His eyes had dark circles underneath them, highlighting the fact that his skin was a shade paler than it should be. The lack of sleep and overuse of caffeine gave his eyes a wild look, although they seemed to be almost sunken, and the designer stubble he usually sported had become more of an unkept look, like he had just forgotten to shave.

A pang of concern for him chased away any irritation I had felt at his fractious manner, so I just nodded. I wanted to ask him if he was okay, to offer to be a listening ear if he wanted to unload, but I couldn't take anything more, aware I would crack under the weight of one more blow.

The thought of Dennis brought with it the reminder of him dropping the bit of paper with his phone number onto the coffee table. I glanced down at it, panicking that Dan might spot it and question me on what it was. I was not ready to unburden myself of the events of the evening, needing to process it myself and have some time to decide how to go about explaining to Dan that Dennis had not only been here, in our home, but that I had allowed him to leave again and had told no one.

There was no doubt as to how Dan would react. He

wouldn't have taken it well at any time, but judging by his mood, he would be livid.

Propelling myself from the armchair, my legs weak beneath me after being in the same position for so long, I edged over to the table. Keeping my back to it, I bent my knees and feigned a stretch, which allowed me to reach behind me and pick up the paper, sliding it into the waistband of my trousers.

"I'm going to head up." I jerked my head in the direction of the stairs.

Dan glanced at me. "Sorry, babe, I didn't mean to bite your head off." He puffed out his cheeks and blew out his breath. "Last night was awful for us both and I'm just knackered." He dragged his hands down his pale face, his eyes still darting around, giving him the appearance that he had taken some kind of stimulant. The thought of my conversation with Dennis slammed back into my mind as I recalled his version of events – and wondered if this was how she had looked. My mother. I shook my head, physically attempting to jolt the thoughts out of it.

Dan offered a half-smile, assuming that I was dismissing his need for an apology. I was just grateful that he seemed as distracted as I felt and hadn't noticed my odd behaviour and skittish actions.

"We both just need to get some sleep." I forced a smile that I was certain appeared as more of a grimace. "Let's go to bed."

Dan sighed deeply, nodding and standing to one side, gesturing for me to go ahead. I fingered the paper that I had slotted into my waistband, ensuring it wasn't going to slip free and land right at my husband's feet.

THE SOUND of Dan's Toyota starting up echoed around the empty house, but I remained in my bed until I had heard him pull away and drive off down the street. Unable to pretended to sleep through his morning routine as he clattered his way around at gone eight, I feigned a headache as my reason for avoiding conversation with him. He had mumbled something about falling asleep in front of the television and the effects of blue light before leaving the bedroom and returning a few minutes later to place a pint glass of water and some paracetamol on my bedside table.

I TURNED the shower up hot enough to make my skin turn red. My stomach felt as though a rock had been dropped into it. The steaming jets were my best hope of somehow cleansing me of the sordid things that seemed to be scorched into my brain, leaving me feeling dirty. Screwing up my eyes, I allowed the water to blast directly into my face, attempting to stop the thoughts from ricocheting around in my head. I needed to make sense of it all, to process everything Dennis had told me and decide what I should do.

How could I even be certain that it was the truth? What if it was just lies, made up to lure me in, confuse me and leave me feeling guilty and as though I owed him something? What could his motives be for telling me all of this now? He had done the time already. Did he want to destroy my life? Have some kind of revenge? Was he bitter that I had cut him out after what he had sacrificed for me? But I'd had no knowledge of any of it. Was it to do with blackmail? My thoughts seemed to come in a figure of eight, winding themselves tighter around my brain, squeezing, tightening until it felt as though it might burst. Releasing something between a scream and a roar, I desperately wished that I could clear my mind, blank it all out and forget everything. Didn't that happen to people sometimes, when they were under massive stress? Their brain just blocked out the events that were causing it?

For a second or two, I frantically clung to the idea that I could have imagined it all, that I had somehow conjured it up as a result of my overwrought brain, so anxious about Dennis's release. I dismissed it, not willing to indulge in such a ridiculous theory. Jabbing the button to cut the power to the shower, I realised my jaw was aching from how tightly I had it clamped together. I wrapped the towel across my chest, not bothering to dry myself before I crossed the landing to my bedroom. Walking around the bed, I dropped down onto the edge of it, not caring that I was likely leaving a damp patch, and pulled open the drawer of my bedside table. The paper that Dennis had left sat impassive where I had slipped it, between the two books. Retrieving it, fingers still warm and damp, I opened it up and stared at the number as though it might hold the answers if I just looked at it for long enough. The number had been written using a red pen. Red. Like the message on our wedding photo. It felt like a threat, a warning of danger.

My hands trembled and I considered screwing it up and throwing it away – or better yet, burning it. But once I got dressed I slipped it into my pocket, aware none of those things were options.

I trudged down the stairs and into my kitchen. The scrap of paper that I had been using to wedge into the kitchen doorway lay discarded on the floor, mocking me in its uselessness. Kicking it to one side, I crossed to the worktop where my phone lay abandoned.

I tapped the screen, which did nothing. When I held down the button to switch it on, it just flashed a warning that the battery was low before the screen went blank again. Plugging it into the charger we kept in the kitchen drawer, I made myself a coffee while I waited for it to suck in enough power to switch on. As soon as it did, it beeped with numerous messages and missed calls.

I cursed under my breath at the multiple messages from Annie, soon joined by Dalaja, and both becoming increasingly more frantic thanks to my lack of response.

There was also a message from Dan that had come through fifteen minutes before. I tapped to open it.

> Babe, can you give Dalaja and Annie a call or something. Annie called me when I was on my way to work saying she's been trying to contact you since yesterday and can't get an answer. I told them you're okay, but they are in full meltdown, panic mode. They said they tried calling at the house last night but you didn't answer the door. I don't know what's going on, but can you call them, please, so they don't start to think I have you tied up in the bedroom or something. ;0D That'd give Phil something else to report on at least! xxx

Unable to find any humour in Dan's message, I swallowed hard, wondering how the hell I was going to face them all. A hazy memory of the sound of knocking not long after Dennis had left floated in. Heat rose to my cheeks and I hoped that my friends had not crossed paths with my father as he left my house.

Leaning my elbows on the worktop, I pulled Dennis's number from my pocket, and questioned how quickly I should contact him, aware that I had little choice. I could report him for breaching the condition of his release, but if he was lying, that gave me even more reason to be afraid of him and what he might do next. If he was telling the truth, it just made me more of a monster to send him back to a cell he would never have found himself in had it not been for me.

I typed out a joint message to Annie and Dalaja, sending it to our group chat, letting them know that I was fine and had just been asleep early thanks to a headache. I also replied to Dan, confirming that I had contacted my friends.

Dropping the phone back onto the countertop, I picked up the tatty slip of paper once again, staring hard at the numbers written in red, as though they may hold some clue to just what the hell was going on around me.

Sucking in a breath as I tried to steady my pounding heart, I reached for the phone again, carefully tapping in the numbers and lifting the phone to my ear before I had time to change my mind.

19

Cutting the engine of my car, I pulled up the handbrake. My body was trembling so hard I had no idea how I had managed to make the drive, almost stalling the car multiple times when my legs shook so badly it became an almost impossible task to hold down the clutch. I gripped the bunch of keys too tightly in the palm of my hand, only realising it when my house key began to bite into the flesh of my palm.

Dropping them into my lap, I gripped the steering wheel instead, as though if I weren't clutching on to something, I may float away.

The heavy feeling that seemed to have permanently lodged itself in my stomach reminded me that I was not likely to float anywhere.

My breathing was coming in short bursts, and I counted as I sucked in air, forcing myself to even it out. Glancing at my watch, aware that I was early, I counted eight minutes before we were due to meet.

Aware of the ache intensifying in my jaw, I unclenched it,

relieving the pressure that had been building in my head. Clenching my jaw until I caused myself a tension headache had always been a sign that I was stressed. Absentmindedly, I rubbed at my temples, then twisted and pulled at my hair. My fingertips tingled and I prayed I wasn't about to succumb to a full-blown panic attack.

It had been so difficult to decide where to meet. Still so anxious about being seen with Dennis, petrified that someone would see us or make the connection, I hadn't wanted to be anywhere too public. I had thought about claiming to be a journalist if push came to shove, but that wouldn't hold out for long. If anyone realised who he was, saw me with him, they would assume that I condoned what he had done. Or hadn't done, as he now claimed.

The whole thing scrambled my brain every time I thought about it. I had trained every fibre of my being to despise my father, to counter every single positive thought or feeling I had towards him with the reminder of the monster he was, the despicable things he had done to both my family and others'. Last night he had caught me off-guard, blindsiding me in every sense. I hadn't had enough time to overthink anything or decide what I felt towards him. Today was different. I knew I was about to face my father head-on, and the torrent of emotion I felt threatened to suffocate me. That actually might be preferable to having to subject myself to any more of my family history.

I dragged my hand down my face, aware that I looked wretched but unable to bring myself to care. My phone buzzed with a new message, which I planned to ignore until I realised it could be Dennis. I tapped the screen and saw one of the girls had sent a message to our group chat. I turned the screen off again, somehow feeling sick with guilt at the thought of being connected in any way to Dalaja and Annie whilst waiting at a prearranged meeting spot for one of the country's most hated men. I slammed my hands against the steering wheel, feeling the hot spring of fury form tears in the corners of my eyes.

How could things get any worse? I had rebuilt my life, started from scratch, and yet become involved with both a police officer and a high-profile journalist. Two of the closest people to me would be some of the worst possible professionals to discover where I was and what I was doing. What would people think of me if Dennis decided to tell the world his side of the story? It would fly off the shelves, the story of the convicted murderer, wrongfully accused, who'd held his silence for so many years. The daughter he had given up his freedom to protect, who had probably been born evil. After all, look at what I had done. What would I think if Annie or Dalaja told me they had been responsible for a death when they were only children? I tried to convince myself it wouldn't change how I felt about them, but I wasn't sure that was the truth.

I stared at my knuckles, wondering once again if Phil would give me up for a story this big. Would Dalaja forgive him if he did?

I swallowed back the urge to scream, to yell and pound my fists into anything within striking distance until my voice gave out and the chaos around me mirrored the chaos inside my head.

The light taps on my passenger window made me jump. My heart pounded so hard I wondered if it might give up on me before I'd had the chance to have this dreaded conversation. That might be preferable.

Reaching over, I pulled the door handle before I could

change my mind, and it struck me that I hadn't considered how vulnerable I had allowed myself to be in meeting him here. Shaking off the thought, I reminded myself that he'd had every opportunity to hurt me – or worse – the night before if that was what he wanted to do. My mind wouldn't let it go, though, and countered that thought with the realisation I had just voluntarily walked blindly into the perfect, secluded situation for him.

Did I subconsciously trust him more than I wanted to know, or admit? Did I believe his story? But why had he broken into my home? Left the message on my wedding photo?

The rush of cold air engulfed me as he opened the door, the warmth from inside the car dashed to escape its confines. Shivering, I wrapped my arms across my chest as the car shifted with Dennis's weight when he lowered himself into the passenger seat and pulled the door closed with a clunk.

The silence hung thick and syrupy between us as I was struck by a hail of feelings, completely overwhelmed.

I had convinced myself for as many years as I could remember that I felt nothing but hate for the man that now sat beside me, so the feelings that bombarded me, threatening to overcome me, left me muddled. A jumbled ball of chaotic emotions that I couldn't detangle.

I didn't turn to greet him. I had no idea how to. My focus remained on my window as my body continued to shake. Instead of looking through it, I gazed at my own transparent reflection.

"Hi, JoJo," Dennis's deep voice filled my car. Although he spoke quietly, it seemed too loud in the silence.

It had been a brief conversation when I had called him,

with Dennis unwilling to discuss anything over the phone and insisting that we met in person. He assured me that I could choose the place for our meeting, only requesting that it not be somewhere we could be easily overheard – or listened in to.

"I'm so glad you called. I was worried that you wouldn't." Dennis spoke softly, almost as though afraid to break the silence.

"It wasn't like I had much choice, was it?" I bit back. Did he deserve me to be so hostile? Whatever his reasons for tracking me down, the selfish part of me still wished he had stayed away, left me to live my life, ignorant to it all. Now I would spend the remainder of it under the heavy weight of his confession. I might never know the truth for certain.

"Can we talk about why we're here?" I turned slightly, angling my body towards him but keeping my face slightly averted, unable to meet his gaze. "I can't believe you've done this – after all of this time – just to be back into my life, so what is it that you want?"

It had crossed my mind that he was here to ask me for money, that his plan had been to blackmail me into funding his life now that he was free. Freedom came at a price, I guess.

He would be disappointed. My wage would never be enough to offer him any sort of lump sum, and I could hardly ask Dan to sub me in paying him off.

How would he react when I told him I couldn't pay? Would he threaten me? Or worse? I glanced around at my surroundings, regretting my decision to meet on an abandoned industrial site. Phil had told us that he occasionally met sources here, people for interviews if they wanted to remain anonymous. I imagined his reaction as he tried to get the scoop on the body that had been found on his territory, before discovering that it belonged to his girlfriend's best friend.

Dennis huffed out a deep sigh.

"I know you're angry with me, JoJo. I don't blame you." He sighed again, turning and looking out of his own window.

I chewed the inside of my lip. If what he'd said was true, shouldn't he be blaming me? Yes, I had only been a child, but if it hadn't been for me, for my actions, Dennis would never have taken the blame for a murder he didn't commit, my sister would still be alive, and my mother's real killer might well be behind bars. Would he really have done so much to protect a child? Surely, he could have told the truth and made them understand.

It seemed incredibly convenient that the man whom I'd spent my life focused on despising deserved nothing but my gratitude. It was plausible, but equally, it could be a very clever move from a psychopathic criminal. Besides, it didn't explain the coincidence of other women who had been killed at the same time, or since his release. Plus what he'd written in my wedding album.

The complex dance of intermingling emotions along with severe lack of sleep was giving me the warning signs of a migraine.

"I don't understand how you could just allow my mum's real killer to get away with it while you took the punishment, though." I frowned. "I can see your logic in wanting to cover for your child, but at the cost of allowing your wife's murderer to walk free while you served his sentence as well as mine?"

Dennis sighed deeply, closing his eyes and clenching his jaw.

"It was one of the hardest things I ever had to do, to allow that scum to get away with what he had done to your mother, JoJo. To all of us. But I could never have risked going after him as long as you were alive and safe. That man would have been nothing more than a tiny cog in a huge machine. Going after someone like that, all I would have done would be to have opened us up to being targeted by a drug gang. Leaving you having to spend the rest of your life looking over your shoulder. I was terrified that by standing up, speaking out against those kinds of people, I would put you in danger, JoJo. You have no idea what men like that are capable of, what they might have done to you in retaliation if I had testified against any of them. If it had just been me, I would have taken him down with my bare hands if I'd gotten the chance, but I would never have taken a risk like that while I had you to think of."

"And the others? What about the woman at your work? The one you were having an affair with? Plus the school teacher? Are you going to try to tell me they were on drugs too? Or better still, was I responsible for those too?" I hissed, the anger exploding out of me from nowhere.

He shook his head slowly.

"There was no affair, JoJo." His tone was soft and it only served to infuriate me further. Was he actually even capable of telling the truth? "She was a colleague, nothing more. I liked her and we got on well. I was shocked when she was killed, just like everyone else. It was easy for them to push the blame onto me. They linked the deaths because they were similar. It made everyone feel better, being able to tie it up in a neat little package and lock it away in a cell." He spoke through clenched teeth, a bitterness entering his tone for the first time.

"I didn't even know the teacher. But it was a witch hunt by then, the police and press desperate to pin it on me, regardless of the lack of evidence. The evil bastard who'd killed his family. They all wanted to believe it. The deaths weren't even the same. The others were killed with garments of their own. There was nothing... used on your mother. My defence argued that, but they just said my wife was a crime of passion, that it was different because of our connection." He spat the last word. "Maybe they did it that way so the police would think all of the deaths were connected. Huh. It certainly worked."

We didn't look at one another. The sincerity of his words had left me questioning everything once again, the continuous wheel I seemed to be on leaving me lost and unable to decipher which way was up. Dennis continued.

"I didn't plan to come crashing into your life. I never intended to hurt you. The whole reason I did this in the first place was to try to protect you. I realise I have royally screwed that up, but I promise you that was all I was trying to do. After what happened to your mother and sister, I couldn't bear the idea of anything bad happening to you. So I did what I thought was best in the moment. There hasn't been a day that I haven't questioned that decision, whether what I did was the best for you. I didn't get time to consider the idea they might believe I was guilty, let alone accuse me of anything more. Or the fact that it meant I would never be able to be there for you. Or that you might grow to hate me. But I always knew if it meant I had protected you from any further pain, or from people judging you, making unfair assumptions, I would do it all again in a heartbeat." He paused, his breathing heavy. I glanced towards him. He was focusing on a point beyond the windscreen, his chest rising and falling rapidly, and his lips quivered.

His words seemed to be winding themselves around my body, squeezing until it ached. A few beats of silence passed as he caught his breath.

"Why now?" I whispered the question, almost afraid to ask as Dennis lowered his gaze. "After not breathing a word of this for all these years, why are you telling me all of this now?"

He considered his answer for a few seconds before he spoke again.

"I can't deny there has always been a selfish part of me that wanted to tell you everything. You're my daughter, the only part of our family that I have left, and it chipped away at my heart every single day that you were missing from my life and that I couldn't be there for you. But in the end, JoJo, I had no choice. Someone is killing women. They are trying to make it seem as though it's me, and as much as I don't want to go back to prison, more than anything, I need to see that this monster is stopped. To know that you're safe too. No one else believes that I'm not a killer, JoJo. Why would they? You were the only person I had a chance of making believe me. I couldn't tell anyone else without telling them the full truth about you – and I would never have done that to you. If they pin this on me, I needed to know that someone out there knows the truth, that you wouldn't allow whoever really is guilty of this to walk away and continue this vile game. They sent the wrong man to prison before. None of those women have had true justice for what was done to them. I can't see that happen again."

His words hung between us as I processed all he had shared.

"And what about what you did? When you broke into my house?" I threw him a slideways glare, keeping my face as neutral as I could manage.

He turned his full focus on me, questions clouding his features.

"Why would you have written that in my wedding album?" I pushed.

"I didn't write that message, JoJo. I swear."

Pursing my lips, I raised my eyebrows and regarded him.

"I swear to you I didn't," he repeated, and the integrity with which he spoke caused me to falter.

"So you're trying to tell me someone else broke into my house?" I scoffed with a bravado that was fading fast. My stomach was plummeting with the possibility that Dennis might not have been the one to write the message.

"I'm not trying to tell you anything. Just that I didn't write any message."

A look of discomfort crossed his face. "I admit, I looked at the photos – all of them. I did see the message, but it wasn't me who wrote it."

He spoke seriously. I regarded him for a few seconds, unsure if I wanted to enter into this game, to potentially humour his fun.

"Who else would have written something like that? In red pen? Like the one you used to write your phone number," I bit back, his denial causing me a sick feeling of dread. It had to be him. The alternative was more than I could take. How could anyone else possibly know?

"Was it aimed at you?" he breathed.

I whipped my head around to glare at him.

"Of course it was. Being related to a convicted murderer wouldn't leave me particularly popular either, believe it or not."

"Who knows? Who would have done something like that?" His forehead was creased as he leaned in with a sense of urgency.

"Well, obviously you were the most likely candidate. My real identity isn't exactly something I usually broadcast." I shot him a look.

"I didn't write it. And if you don't know who did, you need to be careful, JoJo, because whoever did, they wrote it for a reason. They wanted you to know they'd been there. That they have something over you."

I had never felt so conflicted, completely unable to decide if I found myself with an innocent man who had as good as given his life for me, or in the web of a predator who knew exactly how to entice me in, convincing me it was safe just before I found myself too entangled to escape.

If he had been the one to write that message, he was playing some kind of sick game, enjoying inflicting fear, feeding it. If he really hadn't – I didn't even have the headspace to try to consider where that left me.

Either I had completely misjudged my father for my entire life, or he was even more intelligent and dangerous than I had ever given him credit for.

By the time I got home, I had gone over his version of events until my head was spinning. Questions and answers spiralled, twisting together, weaving themselves into and tightening the ball of anxiety that seemed to have lodged itself inside my head. No amount of processing it all would unravel the truth.

Why would he lie?

To convince me to speak to him. To make me feel guilty. To have some sort of hold over me. Weren't these the kinds of games his type played?

Why would he not have reached out to me before?

Because he never wanted to hurt me, he had no reason to tell me. Now he had no choice.

Would he really have sacrificed himself to cover for me, even though it meant allowing his wife's killer to remain free while he spent his life incarcerated?

He was being a dad; he would have been willing to sacrifice anything to keep me safe and protected.

I had lost track of time as we had spoken, Dennis allowing me to ask my questions, and I had been somewhat more compassionate with the delivery of them.

I agonised over the details. Parts of it did seem plausible. It was hard for me to be certain of how any of it must have been for him. I had no children of my own so couldn't imagine the lengths I would go to protect them. But how far would I go to protect Dan? Or Annie, Dalaja, Phil or Tim? The people that I cared about most in the world. In his position, could I honestly say that I wouldn't have done the same things to keep the people I loved safe? The truth was, I couldn't say for certain.

Doubt had crept in, once again taking its stance against Dennis's story and my own sanity. I had met – in secret – with a convicted murderer, at his request. He had told me things about my past that had left me in such a spin that I no longer knew which way was up, had left me feeling physically sick with the guilt of it, all while playing the doting father who had been backed into a corner at every attempt to move. Even now, his reasoning for telling me everything was seemingly selfless.

I couldn't allow myself to be blind to his ability to masterfully manipulate. Even if he wasn't lying now, he had spent the majority of his life spinning a web of lies to cover for me. Either way, he was a master of illusion.

I had listened to more than I had capacity to process. When I had quietly asked Dennis if he wished to be dropped anywhere, he seemed to sense the shift in my mood, declining my offer, thanking me for hearing him out and reminding me that I could contact him any time.

No matter which way I tried to turn things in my mind, I seemed to be met by a barrier of reasons to believe and disbelieve every part of what Dennis had told me.

It felt as though I had become trapped in a web. The more I twisted and turned, thrashing my body and desperately trying to disentangle myself, the more caught up in it I became, the web tightening itself around my limbs, stretching me so far I felt like I would be torn apart.

I glanced, absentminded, at my phone in time to see Dan's photo filling the screen as it silently rang. I hadn't taken it off silent since I had gone to meet Dennis. I tossed it aside, not yet ready to speak to anyone. I lay in silence for a few minutes before the guilt began to seep in for ignoring Dan. I sat up, reaching for the phone again just in time to see it stop ringing. The screen flashed up with eight missed calls – five from Dan and three from Annie – and my skin prickled as the hot anxiety crept over me that something was wrong.

I pressed the phone to my ear. It barely had time to ring before Dan's voice boomed through the tinny speaker.

"Rach? Are you home?" My stomach lurched at his tone.

"Yeah. Why? What's wrong?"

"Have you seen the news?"

"No. I've been... No. Why? What is it? What's happened?"

I searched around for the TV remote, unable to think logically whilst my mind raced.

"Don't put it on, okay? I'm on my way now. Don't go anywhere, just wait for me to get back."

I froze in my search.

"Why? What d'you mean? What is it, Dan?" Panic was rising and I leapt from the bed, crossing to the window, no idea what I was expecting to see.

"I'll be there in two minutes. I'm just round the corner. I'll explain everything."

"Tell me what the hell's—"

The line went dead and, true to his word, Dan's Toyota screeched its way onto our street. He was out of the car and at our front door before I'd had time to move away from the window. Racing to the top of the stairs as he pushed his way through the door, I stopped dead at the sight of him. He was breathless, almost panting, and his hair stuck up as though he had been raking his hands through it. We stared at each other, the anguish carved into his features only exacerbating my anxious state.

He threw his keys aside, kicking off his shoes and ascending the stairs like a man sentenced to death. He reached me but made no attempt to touch me, simply gesturing for me to go back into our bedroom.

A strange look crossed his face, the lines across it deepening and making me feel nauseous. I wanted to scream at him to tell me what was going on, but I knew I wasn't ready to hear whatever it was he was about to say. Could I possibly endure anything else?

He lifted his eyes to meet mine and I could hear the pounding of my heart in my ears.

Dan's eyes were wide, almost wild, as he stared at me, a sheen across them. His jaw clenched and unclenched as we stood in silence, facing each other, both searching for something to say.

"Rach, there's something I need to tell you. Can we sit down?" He gestured towards our bed, and I glanced behind me.

I lowered myself onto it, the sheets still warm from where I had vacated this exact spot only moments before. Despite his request, Dan didn't sit down. He began pacing the room, raking his hands through his hair again as he walked. My body had begun to tremble. The whoosh of blood pounding filled my head. I envisaged a car wreck, some kind of accident. He was going to tell me someone was dead.

"Dan?" I cocked my head, unsure as to whether I should interrupt whatever was going on for him, petrified of what could have left my usually level-headed husband in such a state.

He snapped his head round to look at me as though he had forgotten I was there, staring hard at me with a look on his face like I had never seen in all our years together.

"Rach, something's happened. I need to tell you… This morning, we had a break in the case."

I studied his face, baffled by the pain that seemed to be etched into the lines of it. All my mind could process was that no one was hurt.

"But that's great," I started before it dawned on me. My heart raced so hard throwing itself against my ribs, it left me feeling dizzy. "Oh." I breathed out, feeling the contrast of my colour draining whilst the most excruciating heat clawed its way through my body, almost choking me.

I had been with him that morning. He had been in my car. I had willingly met him on an abandoned industrial estate and swallowed all the lies. I had been so stupid. How would I tell Dan?

Does this mean I haven't killed Julia?

The tiniest sliver of hope ignited, a pinprick of light in the darkness that threatened to engulf me.

After the blow he had just delivered, I hadn't realised that Dan was still talking. I blinked, bringing him into focus and trying to make sense of what he was saying.

"What?" I mumbled, screwing up my face and squinting at him as though that might make his rambling clearer.

"The girl is alive. She's being treated in hospital. I didn't want to be the one to have to tell you. I know how hard this must be on you, especially with me having been so involved with his arrest." He broke off, running his hands down his face. Beads of sweat had gathered on his forehead and along his top lip.

"You've arrested Dennis already?" I gasped, shocked at how quickly they must have gotten to him after he had left me. I wondered if he had told them we had been together, if we'd been seen. Did Dan know?

Dan snapped his head up to look at me, his face crumpling into deep lines, his brows dipped and his eyes searching mine.

"Dennis?" He screwed up his nose and shook his head. "Rach, haven't you been listening to what I've been saying? It's Phil. We've arrested Phil."

20

BEFORE

My brother had been right, of course. There was no way my father would have ever let it go. He had seen something in me, a darkness that would have made him willing to sacrifice his own child. One son for another.

I was certain it was only his desperation to cling onto his relationship with my mother that had stopped him acting before. We both knew the balance beam we walked. If he attempted to topple me, he ran the risk of my mother turning her back on him – my father taking the fall with me. If that happened, it would all backfire on him, meaning he had no choice but to see my brother and mother left alone with me.

I couldn't just allow him to him to lie in wait, always loitering there in the background, waiting for me to slip up. Of course, I had no intention of giving him anything to use against me, but it would only take him to grow enough of a backbone to set something up. I had no option but to beat him to it.

My brother had been like an insect, unwittingly tangling himself up in my perfect web when he had come into my bedroom that evening. I couldn't grasp whether it was his fear of me – self-preservation making him smart enough to know to side with me and not my enemy – or if he genuinely wanted to see what would happen when my father and I locked horns. Either way, he had as good as delivered himself to me. Once I'd pushed him far enough – so far that he believed he was better off doing anything I asked of him than being found out for the things he had done – the rest came easily.

It hadn't been difficult. I had taken Dad's camera – his pride and joy – easily, without anyone noticing. I had enough girls sniffing around me to make it almost too easy. It didn't take a lot to convince a couple of them to allow me to take some photographs, only too willing to do whatever I asked to gain approval.

It had been my brother who had made the anonymous tip-off to the police about what he believed to be going on. He'd agreed when I had told him how easily I could move my attention to him if he didn't help me stop Dad from doing such awful things to those poor girls.

Aware of their impending arrival, I had ensured that my father hadn't been able to miss the way I was looking at him all evening. The smirks I offered as I fixated on him across the table. Even I couldn't mistake the nervous glances he shot me as I stared at him from under my lashes.

He had no idea what was about to hit him.

21

I didn't move, waiting for him to laugh or correct himself.

"Phil?" I breathed. "Dalaja's Phil?"

He nodded, holding his hands to the sides of his face as though he was hearing the news for the first time himself.

"What for?" Anger was seeping into my tone. I had no idea whom it was aimed at.

Dan's hands dropped from his face and his lips parted slightly. His skin seemed to sag from his cheekbones and his shoulders slumped.

"For attempted murder, Rach," he whispered.

"What?" I scoffed, screwing up my face and shaking my head as though to dislodge the ridiculous statement my husband had just made. "That's absurd. Phil? Dalaja's Phil? Are you actually serious?" My voice rose in pitch as well as volume.

Dan stared hard at a patch on the carpet. He had stopped pacing but made no move to sit beside me.

A horrific thought slammed into me, leaving me winded.

"Dalaja? Is she okay? Oh my God..." Spots peppered my vision as I gripped the bed sheets.

Dan realised my misunderstanding.

"No, no. It wasn't Dalaja. She's fine." He held up his hands, waving them around, and a surge of relief left my body weak.

"There was another victim, another woman. But she survived. We think he was interrupted. We found evidence at the scene. A strand of his hair. I'm so sorry, Rach."

Dan didn't look at me.

"Phil?" I shook my head, glaring at Dan, who nodded miserably.

"We ran it through the system. Phil's DNA was on record. He's been picked up a few times – not for anything big; comes with the territory of being a journalist." Dan gave a tiny shrug of one shoulder as if the explanation was important, the twitch of his eye the only giveaway of his distaste towards Phil's job, a subject he was usually so vocal about. "It was a match, Rach. We found his DNA at the crime scene."

He spoke the words as though they were only just beginning to sink in for him too, as though hearing it out loud was as big a shock to him as it was to me.

"Well, you got it wrong," I spat. Dan's head shot up, his eyes wide, shock and hurt swirling and intermingling.

"You need to *run it* again," I shouted.

His lips were parted, and I could hear the sound of his breath as we locked eyes. Neither of us spoke as the tension crackled between us.

Dan lifted his hands. "Rach, I know you're upset..." The calm, patronising way that he spoke in caused something to ignite inside my belly, fire spewing from inside me as I erupted.

"Upset?" I choked. "Upset is when you scratch the car, spill a drink, chip a fucking nail. You're standing here telling me that my husband arrested my best friend's boyfriend for attempted murder this morning? A guy that I have known since college, and you think I'm *upset*?"

Dan turned his head, gripping his hair in his fists and walking towards the window as he let out something between a yell and a growl.

"You've got it wrong, Dan," I continued. "Phil wouldn't… I *know* him. He just wouldn't."

He turned, glaring at me. "Oh, and you don't believe people are capable of keeping secrets, Rach? Really?"

I was thankful that I had remained sitting up until that point, as the pain inflicted by his cheap shot made my legs go weak. I was completely floored by the harshness of his words and for a minute, I couldn't speak.

Dan regained control of himself first, moving towards me, his hands held up in front of him, falling into a crouch in front of me.

"I didn't mean that. I'm so sorry. I'm in shock too. This has been…" He broke off, puffing out his lips and blowing out air. "I shouldn't have said that," he muttered again, resting his hand on my thighs.

His touch, which would usually have calmed me, shot bolts of electricity through my body and I stood up hastily, almost knocking him off balance. He stared up at me, our roles reversed.

"I need to see Dalaja. She's going to need our support until this is cleared up." I tensed my jaw, aware I was teetering on the edge, losing control. "Where is she?" My tone was void of emotion.

Dan cleared his throat. "She's been taken in for questioning," he mumbled, unable to look at me. He made no attempt to move from the floor.

"Jesus Christ," I hissed, incensed that they could do this to her. "Could you not have given her a second? Can you even imagine what she's going through?"

"It's the nature of it. With a case like this, we—"

I held out a hand to stop him.

"Don't. I need to go and be with my friend."

I turned on my heel and bolted down the stairs, not wanting to be in the same room as Dan for a second longer. I grabbed my car keys from where I had discarded them only a couple of hours ago. How could so much have happened in such a short space of time? As I pulled open the front door, a thunderous crash, followed by an animalistic roar, came from above me. My stomach dropped and for a second I hesitated, considering turning back, climbing the stairs and comforting Dan. I had never known him to lose control to this extent, and it felt so wrong to be abandoning him at a time when he needed me so badly. But his words were still fresh in my mind.

And you don't believe people are capable of keeping secrets, Rach?

I sucked in a breath and slammed the door, jabbing the remote to unlock my car before my emotions boiled over. My head simmered like a pressure cooker. Much more and it would simply implode.

"Everything alright, Rachel?"

I looked up to see Joyce hovering outside her front door, her arms wrapped tightly across her chest.

"Yes, thank you, Joyce." I gave her nothing, still moving towards my car.

"Just... I thought I heard a lot of shouting just now.

Sounded like someone was very distressed." She arched an eyebrow at me.

"Must have been the TV," I muttered.

"Then there was a huge crash. Sounded like someone was trying to break through my wall." She moved her head as she spoke like a nodding dog. I clenched my fists, gritting my teeth, forcing myself to keep it under control.

"Surround sound?" I shrugged, offering a forced smile and narrowing my eyes.

Joyce raised both of her eyebrows and wiggled her shoulders. "*Surround sound*? You're telling me it was surround sound that just shook my house?"

I shrugged again, reaching my car and pulling open the door.

"I can't live next door to this kind of disruption," Joyce called. "If you can't keep the noise down, I'll have to report it, and I'm sure that wouldn't go down well for a man of your husband's profession." She sniffed.

"Why don't you report it, Joyce?" I snapped. "Ask them to send someone round. While they're over here, we could ask them to wade through the crap in the hoarder's house next door. You might find your husband never left you at all, but was just lost in the piles of junk you keep stacked up in there."

I didn't hang around to watch her reaction, dropping into the driver's seat of my car and starting the engine before I had time to think about what I had just done.

Pushing my way through the doors of the police station, I cursed as my bag caught on the door handle. I had wasted ten minutes trying to figure out the new parking system, reading and rereading the board, my brain seeming to have shut down so I could no longer navigate the simplest of tasks.

In the end, I had given up, deciding that a parking ticket was the least of my concerns and hoping, if it came to it, that Dan could get me off the hook.

I had only been here a handful of times before. Dan's rank meant that he didn't often work in this building, but an office building further out of town.

The waiting room was cool but still smelled of sweat and stale bodies. Before I had a chance to get my bearings, Annie appeared in front of me.

"Rachel. Christ." She embraced me. "Why don't you ever answer your phone these days?"

"Sorry. I left it in my bag. I came as soon as I found out." My reply was muffled, my face pressed against her shoulder. I couldn't tell her that I hadn't wanted to hear from anyone after my meeting with Dennis that morning. How could it possibly still be the same day?

Annie drew back, holding me at arm's length and studying me.

"Are you okay? You look terrible."

Huffing out a humourless laugh, I rolled my eyes. "Gee, thanks."

"I'm serious, Rach. You don't look well." Concern flooded her features. She didn't look so great herself, her usually warm face drawn and devoid of colour.

"I'm okay." I waved her off. "Just shocked, that's all. And worried about Phil and Dalaja, obviously. What's happening?"

Annie heaved a deep sigh. "To be honest, I don't know

very much. Dalaja phoned me, hysterical. I could barely make out what she was saying. I went straight over to hers, but by the time I got there, they were already bundling her into a squad car. Wouldn't let me near." She shook her head and kept her voice low. "They were crawling all over the house too. I don't know why they're treating her like she knows something. It's obvious they've got it all wrong anyway. This is some kind of mistake. Phil would never…" She pressed her lips together, unable to voice any more. I nodded, reaching for her hands.

"I know."

She gave a nod, sniffing as she pulled one of her hands free and swiped at a stray tear.

"Come and sit with us." She gestured behind her and, still holding my hand, led me towards the corner where Tim was sitting.

He stood as we approached, his face grave with the same expression everyone wears at a funeral. He wrapped his slim arms around me, and I leaned into his embrace.

"It's good to see you, Rachel." He gave me a gentle squeeze before stepping back and dropping back into his chair, staring at nothing, lost in thought.

Forcing a smile, I moved to sit on the other side of Annie, painfully aware of Dan's absence.

Annie shifted in the seat beside mine, angling her body towards me and fixing her stare onto me.

"So, is Dan working on this? I assumed you'd know more than I did and be able to fill me in on more of the details." She searched my face, looking desperate.

Swallowing hard, I cleared my throat, not sure how to respond.

"Erm, I'm not sure how involved Dan is." I could feel the

colour rising to my cheeks. "He was the one who told me what was going on, but I dashed off to get here as fast as I could, so didn't get to speak to him too much." I stopped, praying Annie would stop asking questions yet knowing she wouldn't.

Her brows dipped. "So, he's not here?"

I shook my head with no idea what else to say.

"Oh." Annie sat back, blinking rapidly. "I thought he'd be trying to get it all cleared up." She waved her hands around as though cleaning an invisible surface.

I shrugged. "It's hard. He's limited to how much he's allowed to be involved in when it's a case involving someone he knows."

Annie nodded thoughtfully. "But he could have at least come to support you. Help us interpret what the hell's going on. He has told them this is all a mistake? That they've fucked up, right?"

"Annie," Tim scalded her.

Unable to look at her, I busied myself in my handbag, searching for a tissue.

"Sorry, Rach. I didn't mean to go on at you." She offered a watery smile before rubbing my shoulder.

"Do you know why they arrested him? I mean, we know they've got it wrong, but what the hell has made them consider him a suspect anyway?" She kept her voice at no more than a whisper.

"They found DNA at the scene," I blurted out, relieved to move off the subject of Dan for a second. My hand flew to my mouth as soon as the words had left it, wondering if I should be disclosing anything before checking with Dan.

This is Annie, I reminded myself.

Annie turned to gawp at me, her eyes wide.

"What? What DNA? How the hell did it end up at a murder scene?"

I shook my head and pressed my lips together.

"A hair, I think. He's a journalist." I lifted one shoulder. "He travels around all the time. It'll have been from something else. It has to be." I sounded more confident than I felt.

Annie nodded rapidly but her eyes were still wild.

"That's circumstantial, surely. She could have just brushed past him on the train or something. It's fair enough they would want to question him, but it can't be enough to charge him."

"Exactly." I nodded, buoyed up by Annie's point.

"Why did they have his DNA on the system?" Tim whispered, leaning around Annie. Annie whipped her head around to stare at him as though she was going to scald him for asking such a question, but she must have thought better of it as she slowly turned back to look at me.

"Dan said it was probably because of his job. You can't do that kind of work without getting yourself into a few scrapes." I fiddled with the tissue, folding it over and over.

"Yeah, that makes sense." Annie nodded again and we all fell silent.

A moment later the row of seats creaked as Tim lurched forwards. "I'm going to grab a coffee from the machine. Do either of you want anything?"

"Could you grab me a bottle of water?"

"Water would be great, thanks, Tim." I offered him a weak smile.

We watched him cross the drab waiting area and jab at buttons as he figured out how to work the machines. The silence that hung between Annie and me was awkward. I wanted to say something, break the tension, but I couldn't think of anything to say that didn't involve the events of the previous few days.

Turning my face away from hers, I studied the posters peeling away from the walls, offering grim statistics on crime rate and where victims could reach out for help.

One of the posters contained a photo of a haunted-looking man with a black eye and scratches to his face. The look in his eyes seemed to reflect my own pain and I blinked back tears, feeling incredibly lonely beside my best friend. I wondered if the man in the poster was an actual victim of crime, not quite believing that someone could be that good at acting.

Annie's hand on my arm broke me out of my thoughts and I turned to her, startled.

"Rach, I'm not saying... I mean of course I know he wouldn't..." She paused, throwing a glance at Tim, who was staring blankly at the vending machine.

"How could Phil's DNA possibly have ended up there?" The questions tumbled from her in a rush now that she'd started. "I mean, is it possible it could be coincidence? Could it have been transferred if he'd... I don't know, bumped into her or something? What did Dan say? He doesn't... He doesn't believe he did it, does he?"

Her eyes searched mine, desperate for me to reassure her, to offer answers that would make it all make sense. Unable to hold her gaze, I shot a look towards Tim, praying he was on his way back over and would cut the conversation short. He was waving his bank card around in front of the vending machine with exasperated gestures. I cursed myself for requesting water, making him take longer.

"What aren't you telling me?" she whispered. Fear laced her tone, and her eyes had that wild look again.

I sighed, dropping my head into my hand, and swore under my breath. Would Annie ever be able to even look at me again if she knew just how much I wasn't telling her?

"Rach, you're scaring me," she hissed, her stare burning into me.

Lifting my face, I nodded, searching for the words. Wringing my hands together, I glanced over at the poster of the man on the wall again, wishing we could trade places, regardless of what was haunting him.

"Okay." Sucking in air, I focused on her hands, unable to meet her eye. "Honestly, I don't know what Dan thinks, or how Phil's DNA ended up there." I swallowed hard. "But Dan was the one who made the arrest. He came home and told me he had arrested Phil."

As soon as I lifted my gaze, wondering if she'd heard me, I instantly wished I hadn't. Annie's face had completely drained of what little colour it had held and she stared at me with eyes like saucers, her jaw having fallen slack.

"What?" She looked as though I had physically struck her.

"Shhhhh." I gestured with my hands for her to lower her voice. "I know. I fucking know. Why do you think I didn't want to tell you?"

She snapped her jaw closed, the creases on her face giving away everything she was feeling.

"He just turned up at the house and told me. I stormed out and came straight here." I kneaded my temples as Tim finally retrieved the final bottle of water.

"Shit. So he must think... Does Dalaja know?"

"I don't know." My stomach contracted, anxiety clutching my insides. "But either way, she's going to find out."

Tim appeared in front of us, the water bottles wedged under his arm.

"Bloody machine. Took my money and the first bottle got stuck, then kept declining my card." He handed us our drinks and I had just begun to unscrew the lid when Annie's sharp intake of breath stopped me. Dalaja had appeared. She was in a hushed conversation with a police officer, and she nodded, wiping her eyes. I had never seen her so dishevelled, even after our uni nights out. Her mascara had left streaks down her face, her foundation rubbed away with her tears. Her hair was scraped back from her face, and she wore and oversized jumper that couldn't have belonged to her, continuously tugging the cuffs down over her hands.

Annie and I sprang from our seats, rushing at her and throwing our arms around her. Dalaja trembled.

"Are you okay? We're going to get this sorted out, Dala. Let's get you out of here and then we can work out what to do next. Please don't cry. We are going to clear up this mess. The police have it wrong and we just have to work out the way to show them that."

Annie threw the officer a look as she spoke with such conviction I almost believed her myself.

Dalaja's watery, bloodshot eyes fixed onto me, and I froze, terrified that she was about to challenge me on Dan's involvement.

"Rach, where's Dan?" she asked, her face wet with tears and snot. "Can't he help? He must be able to sort this out. We all know it's total bullshit."

Annie glanced at me, swallowing hard before reaching into her bag and retrieving a tissue. She wiped at Dalaja's face as though she were a child. Dalaja searched my face, desperation gripping hers.

I opened my mouth to reply, closed it again at a loss. I couldn't stand in front of her and lie to her face, but was now really the time to throw another grenade into her already imploding world?

"Let's talk about this back at mine," Annie broke the tension. "Let's get out of here and we can talk in private." She shot me a look before taking Dalaja's hands and leading her towards the doors.

"Rach, we'll take Dala in our car. You follow along and meet back at ours, okay?" Tim pulled open the door and a blast of cold air hit me. Wrapping my arms across my chest, I wished I was wearing more layers, dreading what was to come.

22

We filed into Annie and Tim's house, Tim bustling us in from behind in a bid to shut the cold out. There had never been a time I had felt so reluctant to enter my best friend's house.

Annie guided Dalaja to her kitchen table and sat her down as though she wouldn't have been able to find her own way. I felt as though I had been hollowed out watching them, wishing I didn't feel like such an outsider with a bomb to drop on one of the people I loved most.

I hovered awkwardly, leaning against the worktop and chewing my thumb nail as Annie moved to put the kettle on. No amount of tea would dilute any of this.

"It's all just got totally out of hand. The neighbours have told the police they've heard Phil yelling at me, that they think he could be violent. It's bullshit. It's those fucking video games he plays. He shouts at the screen with his headphones on. He doesn't even realise he's doing it. I've told him so many times he needs to stop."

Dalaja took a minute to compose herself while Annie

and I remained quiet. She turned to me, and it struck me again how awful she looked.

"So where is Dan? I didn't see him at the station. Is he trying to sort this out? He must have told them they've fucked up. I hope he gives whoever made such a pig's ear of all this a bollocking. It's *such* a waste of police time too." She stared at me expectantly, her tear-stained face a mess, with more streaks of mascara replacing mottled foundation.

Annie's eyes were on me and I swallowed hard.

"Erm. I don't know where Dan is..." I trailed off, the unjustness that I was having to break this to my friend whilst my husband hid away leaving me nauseous.

"What d'you mean?" She frowned before a look of understanding crossed her face. "Is he not allowed to tell you what's happening?"

"I guess he's got to be aware of the conduct." Annie shrugged, without looking at me. "Maybe it's best we don't blur the lines. You know, keep his work separate from this situation." I was grateful for what she was trying to do for both me and Dalaja.

"Separate? How can we possibly do that?" Dalaja glared at Annie as though she'd sworn at her.

"I know this is really hard but..."

"Dalaja, there's something I have to tell you and you're going to be furious," I cut Annie off, aware it was unfair leaving her in the middle of my shitstorm.

"Okay..." Dalaja stared at me. I could see her chest heaving with the rising panic at what she was about to hear. My insides turned cold.

"I'm so, so sorry. Please know, I had no idea about any of this until Dan came home just this afternoon." I ran my hand down my face, desperate to calm myself down before I lost it completely. I had no right to be the one to break down now. Dalaja remained silent, waiting for me to continue.

"Dan made the arrest, Dala. I don't know any more than that because I walked out on him when he told me. I'm so sorry."

The room seemed to freeze for a second, all the air sucked out of it. No one moved as my words sank in.

Without warning, Dalaja shot up from the table, scraping her chair back across the floor and storming across the kitchen towards me. For a second I thought she was going to hit me, but instead she ran straight past me and out of the room.

"Dala!" Annie yelled after her, abandoning her tea making and bolting across the kitchen to catch up with her. I remained where I was, rooted to the spot.

Feeling not only like the outsider of our friendship, but also the one who had blown it apart.

I'D NOT MOVED from where I had been stood in the kitchen, making no attempt to hear what they were saying. Dalaja ranged from low, angry tones to sounding almost hysterical as her voice rose in volume. Annie's tone was calm, her voice too low for me to make out attempts at soothing Dalaja. I had no desire to hear it, not needing to know what Dalaja was saying to guess what she felt towards me.

It seemed so unfair that I was taking the rap for Dan's actions. I'd had no involvement in his work. And if Phil's DNA really had been found at that scene, it wasn't me who should be the one having to fight my corner.

I shook my head, physically dismissing the thought. Phil hadn't done this. He wasn't capable. We *knew* him.

Thoughts of Dennis danced around in my mind, mocking my certainty. The sound of approaching footsteps dragged me out of my thoughts and I snapped my head up to see Annie appear. Her cheeks were pink and strands of her hair had fallen loose from her ponytail. She looked completely drained.

My mouth opened with the need to say something to her, but I drew a blank.

"She just needs a few minutes."

I nodded, unable to miss the conflict in Annie's eyes. This would be so hard on her too, being caught in the middle of her two best friends. She returned to the kettle, busying herself making the drinks.

"Is she... okay?" I knew it was a stupid question, but I had to say something.

"Well, her boyfriend's been arrested on suspicion of multiple murders, she's just been questioned by the police as if she's been covering for him, and now, she's discovered her best mate's husband was the one who started the ball rolling on it all. So... I guess she's had better days."

Biting the inside of my lip, I refused to allow myself to cry. This wasn't about me.

"Shit. I'm sorry, Rach. That was unfair. I just don't even know how to deal with any of this. Or what to think."

"And what does that mean?" We both flinched, not having heard her coming. Dalaja's tone was icy, laced with challenge. Annie's face flushed. She knocked a mug with the back of her hand, fumbling as she set it back upright.

"Nothing. It didn't mean anything. I just—"

"Just what?" Dalaja cut her off. "Wondering if my

boyfriend's a serial killer? Are you also wondering if I'm his accomplice, Annie?" She glared at Annie, her tone venomous.

"Of course not. I never thought for a second—"

"And what about you?" Dalaja rounded on me. "Are you the one dripping poison into her head?" She jabbed a thumb in Annie's direction. "Has good old Dan managed to convince you his lot are not capable of making a mistake, so Phil must've killed all those women?"

"Dala..." Annie pleaded.

"I shouldn't have called you. I should have dealt with this on my own. For all I know, you're only here to report back to—"

"Enough." Annie looked as shocked as we were at her uncharacteristic outburst. "Look, Dala, I'm so sorry for what's happened today. Neither I nor Rach believe that Phil did this. Don't you think it says something that Rach is here and not with Dan? I get that I can't begin to understand how hard this is for you, but we want to support you. Please don't push us away. We need to work out how to get Phil out of this. Together." Her chest rose and fell rapidly, and she held onto the work surface for support.

A few beats of silence passed while none of us moved and Dalaja considered what Annie had said.

She sniffed loudly before turning to me once again.

"I want to hear it from you. And you're one of my best friends so don't even think about lying to me, Rach. I want the honest truth. Do you think Phil is guilty?" She searched my face, a swirl of emotions building on her own.

"No." I didn't miss a beat, with no reason to hesitate. "I don't."

Dalaja's shoulders visibly lowered, and her face

smoothed out, almost as though she'd needed to hear this before she could fully believe it herself.

"But we do need to find out how the hell his DNA ended up at the scene of an attempted murder. I believe Dan's team have got the wrong man, Dalaja, I really do, but the evidence doesn't lie, so we need to work out *how* they've got it wrong."

Dalaja opened her mouth to reply to me but was interrupted by the chime of the doorbell. We all stared at one another, eyes wide. I prayed it wasn't Dan. Could it be the press? How would they treat one of their own in this kind of situation? I dreaded to think.

We listened as Tim called out to say he'd get it, and I strained to hear the sound of muffled voices from the hall.

"Oh God." Dalaja's face crumpled as the voices grew closer. I heard Tim explaining that we were in the kitchen and directing the visitor to where we stood. Although Dalaja had clearly worked out who had arrived, I was still none the wiser.

The older women's face appeared around the door first. Her dark hair was greying at the roots, giving away her age. The skin on her face was baggy, as though she was wearing a size too big for her frame, and there was a dullness to her eyes as she took in the sight of us, as though she'd seen enough of the world. She was closely followed by a man of around the same age, his attempt at a combover so bad it made me feel awkward for him just to look at it. The woman wore ill-fitting clothes that looked as though they had been going through the washing machine since before we were born. I watched them, recognising them from the only time I could remember meeting them previously. They had both aged badly since Dalaja's graduation.

"Dalaja. What in God's name is going on?" her mum

screeched at her. "I've been hearing all sorts of ridiculous things, and you weren't answering your phone. I ended up going to the police station myself. Vile place that was. They said we'd find you here."

Dalaja squirmed.

"I'm sorry, Mum. I only just left myself. I was going to call you." She shifted from foot to foot. "You remember Annie and Rachel, my best friends." She gestured towards us as she made the introductions.

"My parents, Deepa and Ravindra." She gestured towards them and shot me and Annie a look. Dalaja's relationship with her parents had always been strained. The didn't approve of her lifestyle and the way she refused to conform to her culture. At the beginning, they had been far from supportive of her and Phil's relationship, but they had come around and Dalaja joked that she thought her mother actually preferred Phil to her. Phil laughed along but we all knew how much it must have meant to him having their approval. His own parents had been killed in an accident a few years before we met, although he would never talk about what had happened.

It struck me as I observed them how much Dalaja resembled her mother.

Before I or Annie had been given a chance to greet them, Deepa's head snapped around to focus on me, eyeing me intently.

"Isn't your husband a police officer or something? Can't he do something about this?" She looked at me expectantly.

I froze, waiting for Dalaja to tell them everything.

Would they throw me out? That was probably the best I could hope for.

Annie shot me a look, the silence hanging thick.

"Erm... he... I..."

"He's not allowed to be involved. Too close to us," Dalaja grunted, not meeting my eye.

My legs went weak with gratitude as Deepa pursed her lips.

"Well, a fat lot of good that is." She turned her nose up. "Well, it's no good sitting around here drinking tea. We have to figure out what we can do to actually help Phil. They'll be targeting him because of his job." Her tone was shrill.

Dalaja glared at her. I was left giving silent thanks that the heat had shifted off me, Deepa giving her a new focus for her frustration. My hands trembled and I crossed my arms tightly over my chest to hide it.

I half-listened to them throwing around theories and discussing how to find him the best possible representation, all the while avoiding the obvious question that no one was willing to voice. Could we really be so certain that he wasn't guilty?

23

Dan and I had barely spoken a word to each other since I had been home. I hated the awkwardness that had lodged itself between us. Our relationship, which had always felt so strong, now felt as though something poisonous had seeped in and was turning us rotten from the inside. It was an impossible situation. Even though I wanted to remain furious with him, I understood Dan's position, but equally, he had just driven a wedge between me and my friends.

The atmosphere must have gotten too much for Dan because, eventually, he poked his head around the living room door where I was staring blankly at the TV.

"I'm going to head back to work for a bit," he mumbled.

I just managed to stop myself from making a sarcastic remark about him not arresting any more of my friends. Regardless of how mad I was, I wanted our relationship back.

"Okay," was the best I could offer.

"Look, Rach, I know how hard this must be on you. It

isn't easy for me either, despite what you may think." He sighed, massaging his forehead with his fingertips. "All I want is for the right person to pay for what he's done to these women. If that's not Phil, I'll prove it. I'm only going by the evidence that's presented to me, and I wouldn't be doing my job if I didn't take it seriously. What would you be saying to me if this was anyone other than Phil I'd arrested and their family and friends were coming at us, adamant that they were innocent?"

He had a point, but that only riled me further.

"But it's not *anyone other than Phil,* Dan. It *is* Phil, and we know him. I've known him since university. *You* know him. Do you really think he could have been doing this under all our noses, under *your* nose, while we had no idea?" Something flashed in his eyes, and I knew I was pushing him. This was exactly what I had been trying to avoid.

"People surprise you, Rach. It's shocking what someone can be capable of, with no one assuming a thing. I have no more idea than you do right now whether Phil is guilty, but I can only go by the evidence. It's my job to find out, and that's what I have to do. If he is innocent, it's also my job to prove that too, and then maybe you'll all stop hating me quite so much."

There was an edge to his voice. I knew I needed to stop but the words were out of my mouth before I could stop them.

"That depends on who you lot point the finger at next I guess. Dalaja? Tim? Annie maybe? Or could I have been slipping out, murdering women while you weren't looking?"

"What did Phil say at that party, Rach? Everyone is capable. It just has to be the right set of circumstances."

I tore my gaze from him, unable to look at him. He knew

what those comments had done to me. I ached with desperation to erase it all, to go back and somehow stop the whole sorry mess from happening.

"Jesus Christ," he hissed from between clenched teeth. In my peripheral vision, I saw him drop his head into one of his hands, gripping his temples between his thumb and middle finger. "I didn't mean anything by that... I'm just... I know you would never..."

I gave a sharp nod, unable to speak, aware I wouldn't hold it together. Somehow, I knew opening my mouth would also open the floodgates to every emotion I had held in over the past few days.

"I'm going to go. The sooner we can get to the bottom of this shitshow and find out the truth, the sooner we can get our lives back." He didn't wait for me to respond, instead just turned and left, slamming the front door behind him.

Eventually, unable to take the sound of my own thoughts any longer, I grabbed the remote, jabbing it towards the television before casting it to one side. I didn't care what came on, just needing to drown out the deafening silence.

The instant the news reader's sombre tones filled my living room, I scowled, pouncing for the remote, wanting to shut her up before I had to endure any more of the story.

I froze, remote clutched in my grip as I listened to what the reporter was saying. She continued on and I cursed, grabbing my phone and searching for the news headlines. I needed to confirm what I had just heard.

Skim-reading the first article I came to, I quickly located the information I was looking for. My breath caught as I gripped the phone tighter, rereading the date to be sure I had got it right.

The last girl who had been attacked, the girl whose

attempted murder Phil had been arrested for – it had all happened last night. They hadn't said if the girl was conscious, only that she was in a stable condition in hospital.

But what had caught my attention, what had once again turned my world on its axis and was shaking it around as though I were stuck in a snow globe watching the tatters fall around me, was the date and time of the incident.

Last night, estimated between six and eight p.m.

I lowered the phone, staring blankly at the news report that continued to play out on the television, no longer seeing or hearing anything she was saying.

Phil couldn't possibly be capable of murder – but the only other suspect in the case, the man whom the nation had believed had been guilty, had been here, in my living room, with me at the time of the last attack.

As I waited for the kettle to boil, I drummed my fingers against the worktop. It had only been a couple of hours since Dan had left but the house felt emptier than ever. Should I be contacting the police? Dennis's name hadn't been brought up since Phil's arrest, but the fact that he had been here, with me, could rule him out as a suspect. He wouldn't have had time to go anywhere but straight home once he'd left my house thanks to his tag, but if he didn't tell them he had been here with me, he would also have no alibi for the actual time of the attack. But what would my admission do to Phil? And how would I explain it all to Dan?

The voice in my head nagged at me to send a text to Dalaja, checking in to see if there was anything she needed, but I wasn't sure I had the strength to face her.

My mobile ringing made me jump, the sound too loud in the otherwise silent house as I hurried through to the living room to retrieve it.

Expecting it to be Dennis revelling in the proof of his innocence, I prepared to tell him to back off, to insist that I needed some breathing space. Seeing Annie's name threw me. I had only left them a couple of hours ago and my instinct had already become to avoid contact with my friends.

But I couldn't ignore her now, not with everything going on, so before I could change my mind, I accepted her call.

"Hi, Annie." I tried not to let it slip into my tone just how wiped out I felt.

"Rach, there's something going on... I don't know... Dalaja, she..."

My heart began to hammer against my chest and my stomach dropped.

"What? What's happened? Is she okay?" Images of my friend in a hospital bed flashed through my mind. Had everything that was going on with Phil pushed her into doing something to herself? Had she had some sort of breakdown?

"I don't know. She just called me and said Phil's solicitor contacted her. Phil is refusing to speak to her. He has requested that she doesn't try to make any form of contact with him. He said she needed to prepare herself."

"For what?" My stomach, which had only just stopped its plummet, twisted and my legs trembled.

"I don't know but it freaked her out. She's in bits. I'm getting in my car now and heading over to hers. Will you come?"

I paused, completely torn.

"Please, Rach. She really needs our support right now."

"Do you think she'll want me there? Even with what happened with Dan?" I mumbled. My stomach clenched at the memory of the look Dalaja had given me when I had told her.

"Of course. It was a shock to her, just the same as it was to you, but you are her best friend. She'll be way more hurt if you avoid her."

Annie was right.

"Sure. I'll head right over too."

ANNIE PULLED open Dalaja's front door within seconds of me knocking on it. Her face was pale, and her eyes darted around, taking in the mob of photographers that had set up camp outside the house. I hadn't been prepared as I had driven onto the street, feeling myself recoil at the sight of the countless journalists that lined it. I'd had to do a three-point turn and park on the next street over. I'd sat behind the wheel, contemplating driving away again. The last thing I needed was to get myself caught up in this circus. But Dalaja was my best friend, and I couldn't abandon her now.

"Come in." Annie grabbed me by the wrist and yanked me through the gap, keeping the door as close to closed as she could. Cameras flashed behind me, and questions were fired at the back of my head.

We shoved the door closed as though we were having to physically fight to keep someone out. We exchanged a look and Annie leaned in to hug me.

"Thanks for coming, Rach. She was hysterical when I got here. She sent her parents away. The police had turned the place upside down and then with Phil saying he wouldn't speak to her..." She trailed off. I couldn't imagine what Dalaja was feeling.

I nodded, squeezing her tighter to me, wishing I could tell her how much I needed them too.

"She's through here." Annie released me and gestured towards the living room. Following her into the room, I had to allow a minute for my eyes to adjust. The curtains had been drawn, I assumed to stop the press being able to see inside.

Dalaja paced the room like a caged animal, seeming not to notice my and Annie's appearance. Annie threw me a look, pressing her lips together. The concern was etched into her features, causing frown lines to run deeper than I had ever seen.

I took a deep breath and stepped further into the room.

"Hey, Dala." I kept my tone soft, apprehension for how she might react at the sight of me mingling with sympathy and pain at seeing her suffering.

The sound of my voice seemed to snap her out of her trance. She whipped her head around and blinked, as if bringing me into focus.

"Rach? What's going on? Do you know what's happening? Why won't Phil speak to me? What's Dan said?"

Stepping towards her I placed my hands on her upper arms, gripping her gently and meeting her gaze. My usually flawless friend was so pale her skin seemed almost translucent. Her hair was greasy, hanging in clumps where she had raked her hands back through it so many times, and her eyes were bloodshot and swollen. A sour smell radiated from her, and I couldn't believe how she had deteriorated in such a short amount of time. In all of the years I had known her, I had never seen Dalaja look less than perfect. Even when the three of us were dying of a hangover, Dalaja would still show up beautifully made-up, while Annie and I resembled something from a horror film. Annie was right; she did need us.

"I haven't spoken to Dan yet, Dala, but I will. I am going to get him to tell me exactly what's going on and we are going to sort all of this out, okay?" Her eyes had begun to wander, and I moved my head to force her to look at me.

"Dala, listen. We all know there has been some kind of major fuck-up here. We know Phil. *You* know Phil. There has to be an explanation for all of this. There just has to be. In a few days' time this is all going to be over. Nothing more than a horrendous memory. Hell, imagine the story Phil will have to write. Until then, we are going to be right here with you." I wasn't sure whom I was trying hardest to convince. I shook her arms gently, aware she was zoning out again.

"I think you should lie down. Try to get some rest for a while. I'm going to call Dan. Annie will be here with you." I led her to the sofa and lowered her onto it as she stared right through me. She didn't try to resist.

I turned to Annie, who was chewing her thumb nail, and mouthed the words, "She's in shock."

Annie nodded, looking as though she may be about to burst into tears. Somehow, I felt like I had become the one in charge of the situation that I had no control over and no idea how to handle. Before I had time to dwell on it, Dalaja's ring tone broke the silence.

She was off the sofa like a shot and across the room to where her phone had been on the mantelpiece. She grabbed it and swiped the screen without looking at the caller ID.

"Phil?" Her voice was shrill. Her features seemed to crumple as someone spoke on the other end of the line.

"Richard? Can I please speak to Phil? I don't understand why he won't—" She stopped speaking and I could just about make out the tinny sound of a male voice on the other end of the phone.

"What? What do you need to tell me? What do you mean?" There was a pause. "Yes, yes, I have someone with me... My friends are here. Why does it matter who I'm with?"

Nausea rose in my throat along with the anxiety. I did not like the sound of this conversation.

Annie and I watched on as Dalaja seemed to turn a shade paler than she had already been, something which I would have deemed impossible only the second before. Her face fell slack and she allowed her hand to drop to her side, opening and leaving the phone to fall with a soft thud onto the carpet.

We dashed forward in unison, just in time to support her as she fell to her knees.

I ensured Annie had hold of Dalaja before I released my hold. She was whimpering and dropped onto all fours as I let her go.

I scrambled across the floor to retrieve the phone from where it had landed. The male voice on the other end repeatedly called out Dalaja's name. Scooping it up, I glanced around at Annie, who was stroking Dalaja's hair and whispering soothing words to try to calm her whilst throwing wide-eyed glances in my direction. I pressed the phone to my ear.

"Hello? Who is this?" I tried to disguise the tremble of my voice, shaken by the state of my best friend.

"My name is Richard Bullard. I am a solicitor. May I ask, with whom am I speaking now?"

I swallowed hard. "My name is Rachel Thatcher. I'm

Dalaja's best friend and a good friend of Phil's." Dalaja had mentioned his name in the past, to do with cases her firm had worked on.

"Is Dalaja okay?" he asked, seeming genuinely concerned.

"To tell you the truth, I'm not sure. It's been a lot. What did you say to her?"

Richard cleared his throat on the other end of the line. I glanced over at Annie, who was focused on Dalaja. She had lain down on the floor and was sobbing hysterically.

"I shouldn't really share any information with you before confirming with my clients that they give their consent," he reeled off the well-practiced line.

"Oh, come on. You can hear the state of her. How are we supposed to support her if we don't even know what's going on?" I snapped, aware of the edge to my voice.

"I'm sorry. I understand it's frustrating, but I'd need Dalaja's permission to discuss anything with you. I have a duty to protect both hers and Phillip's confidentiality."

"Fine," I bit back, aware I was being unfair. He was only doing his job, but I'd had almost as much as I could take.

Stepping towards Dalaja, I crouched beside her, having to raise my voice over her crying and gasping for air.

I put the phone onto loudspeaker.

"Dala, I need you to tell your solicitor that it's okay for him to speak to me. He needs your consent to tell me anything."

She didn't react, continuing to wail. Something bubbled under my skin.

"Dalaja!" I said clearly. "If you want any sort of chance at sorting this bloody mess out, I need to know what the hell is going on. I can't help you or Phil while you're hysterical and we are in the dark. You need to give Richard the okay to discuss this with me, please. Now." My tone was firm, a little harsher than I'd intended, but it seemed to work. She released a sound that resembled a yes.

"Dalaja, can you confirm that it's okay for me to converse with Ms Thatcher about Phillip's current situation? I need you to say yes if you're happy for me to discuss it with her."

Dalaja let out another strained noise, a sound that more closely resembled a wounded animal.

"Okay. Thank you for your permission, Dalaja. I'll speak to Ms Thatcher now."

Grateful to him for accepting the questionable response from Dalaja, I turned off the speaker and pressed the phone to my ear again.

"Please call me Rachel. What's going on?" I turned away from Annie's questioning stare as she continued to comfort Dalaja. I stepped into the hallway, moving further from them, despite the fact that Dalaja had now fallen practically silent.

"I am sorry, Rachel. I wasn't trying to be difficult. I'm glad you're there with her. She is certainly going to need her friends." He released a loud sigh and my stomach seemed to drop into freefall again as I anticipated what I was about to hear. I leaned back against the wall, needing to feel something solid.

"You'll have worked out for yourself that it isn't good news. Unfortunately, Phil has been further arrested for the murders of three other women."

"What?" I breathed, feeling as though I had just taken a blow to the stomach. "Why? Based on what? DNA evidence at one scene doesn't mean they can just pin everything on him." My head spun as I wondered what Dan's involvement with all of this was.

"No, you're right, that wouldn't have been enough." He sighed again. "But they didn't need further evidence when Phil has just confessed to everything."

24

My legs went weak. I pictured Phil as clearly as if he was standing before me, wrapping his arms around me in greeting, talking animatedly about the latest juicy story he was chasing, his arm slung loosely around Dalaja's shoulders. Granted, he and Dan had never got on brilliantly, but that was only down to the clash of their careers. They were both fundamentally good people. I had been friends with Phil for almost as long as the girls. I had introduced him to them. How could I have read him so wrong?

Was there more to Dan and Phil's occasional digs at one another? We all laughed off the gibes they made, but Dan and I had admittedly had conversations about the media and how they could behave. I knew Dan was less than a fan of Phil's choice of job, but could he have picked up on something more than that? Something the rest of us had all missed?

"What?" I repeated my earlier question, praying I had somehow misinterpreted what he was telling me. "I don't understand. Why would he confess to that?" I tried to keep my voice low, fighting the hysteria that was threatening to overcome me. Dalaja needed us to keep our heads. This was going to be horrendous for her.

"Well, people don't usually confess to these types of crimes if they aren't guilty," Richard replied. My mind instantly went to Dennis. I pushed him aside; I didn't have the headspace to think of him right now. "With his DNA at the last scene and now his confession..." He trailed off.

"Is this why he was refusing to speak to Dalaja?" I whispered.

"Yes. He knows this is going to break her heart, and he couldn't face her."

I clenched my teeth, suddenly filled with a venomous rage. How could Phil do something like this and then hide away, leaving Dalaja to pick up the pieces of their shattered lives? The least he owed her was some sort of explanation.

"So why has he suddenly decided to confess?" I demanded. "He's clearly had no conscience about any of it up to now. What's suddenly changed?"

"He was very likely to go down for the attempted murder of the latest victim, Hayley Larkin. Especially if she is able to identify him. That plus his DNA was pretty damning. The police believe he was disturbed, or something went wrong. That's why he didn't manage to clean up after himself properly. I assume he felt it was better to confess to everything than have them build the case against him, aware they were likely to find proof now they have him. I can't tell you much more than that as he hadn't informed me of any of this before he made his confession. It came as just as much of a shock to me as anyone. He then requested we take a short break and asked me to come and call Dalaja. He wanted her to hear it from me."

"Well, how big of him," I snapped.

"Indeed," Richard agreed. "I have to get back now. The police are going to want to continue with the interview. I truly am sorry to have to be the one to break all of this to you. In all honesty, I actually liked Phil."

"Yeah. Me too." I sighed. "Thank you for calling."

"Take care of Dalaja, Rachel. She's got a shitstorm heading her way, I'm afraid." It sounded odd to hear someone so well spoken curse.

"I will. Thanks again." The call ended and I dropped my face into my hands. There was still an occasional anguished cry coming from the living room, although during my phone conversation, they had mainly dulled down to muffled sobs. I couldn't imagine what must be going through Dalaja's head. What could we possibly say to her?

Gripping her phone in both hands against my chest, I realised that my palms were sweating. I wondered if I had the same stale smell about me as I had been so shocked to detect on Dalaja earlier. I certainly felt grimy but wasn't sure that had anything to do with being physically clean.

I crept back into the room, at a loss as to how to broach the situation. Should I pull Annie from the room? Could we leave Dalaja alone in the state she was in?

It felt as though the air was too thick as I entered. The same heavy feeling lodged in my stomach as when someone had died, leaving behind an oppressive sense of loss along with a sense of failure at knowing what to say or do. I felt useless, and all too aware that my husband was on the opposing side. A sense of dread seemed to constrict me, tightening itself around my chest.

Annie's head snapped up, her hand continuing its rhythmic stroking of Dalaja's greasy hair. She lifted her shoulders in question, her eyes searching mine. Glancing down at our friend, I fought the urge to turn and run from it all. What would this do to us? Phil had been a part of us, one of us. What would this do to the dynamics of our group? To our friendships? Would Dalaja stand by Phil? How could I choose between them and Dan? Dots appeared at the edges of my vision as the pressure inside my head began to build, the early warning signs of a migraine.

I placed the phone down on the coffee table and made a decision. Crossing the room and crouching down beside them, I placed my hand on Dalaja's back.

"I cannot begin to imagine what you are going through, Dala, but I think you have a right to hear everything. I'm going to fill Annie in on what Richard has just told me. If you'd rather we left the room for me to do that, we will, but I don't want you to feel that we will be saying anything that we wouldn't say in front of you. We are in this together, okay?"

She continued to whimper, snivelling and gasping through the tears. I wondered if she had heard me and thought she had chosen to ignore me for a few seconds, until she reached out and grasped my hand in hers, looking up at me through red-rimmed eyes and giving a tiny nod.

I squeezed her hand and offered her a sympathetic smile.

When I looked up at Annie, her face had turned pale, and I could see her chest rising and falling too rapidly.

"Has something happened to Phil?" she squeaked. "He hasn't... is he..." Her eyes filled and I shook my head.

"No, no. It's nothing like that," I assured her, realising how it must look to her. "Phil's okay."

A look of relief passed across her features but was chased

away almost instantly by panicked confusion. "What is it, then? If Phil isn't hurt, what's happened?" She fixed me with an intense stare.

"It would be better if he was hurt. Phil isn't the one who's hurt. He's a piece of shit, that's what he is." Dalaja let out a string of curse words aimed at her partner and Annie flinched, her lips parting in shock at the outburst.

"Richard – Phil's solicitor – called to let us know that Phil's confessed to the attempted murder of Hayley Larkin." I delivered the news as gently as I could, aware there was still more to share. Annie's jaw dropped, her mouth unashamedly hanging open as she gawped at me.

Dalaja had screwed her eyes tightly shut as her breaths came in short bursts.

"Not only that, but he's also confessed to the other murders too." I still had hold of Dalaja's hand and could feel her nails beginning to bite into the skin of mine.

"What?" Annie's voice sounded far too loud, and I nodded towards Dalaja, hoping that she would get my meaning and pull herself together before reacting. It seemed to work as she snapped her jaw shut, blinking rapidly as she took a minute to gather herself.

"I don't understand it. Why would he do that?" He tone was less shrill, but instead sounded thick with emotion.

I shook my head and shrugged, at a loss for what to say. Dalaja startled us both as she broke the silence, her tone venomous.

"All those times he told me he was working, chasing up leads on stories or finishing writing stuff up. He was out there, and he was... He was... And then he was coming home – to our home, getting into our bed. Those same hands he'd just used to suffocate those poor, poor women, who'd done nothing to deserve it... I let him touch me with them."

"Dala, you didn't know. None of us did. This isn't your—"

"But no one will believe that," she cut me off. "Would you if you didn't know me? Would you honestly believe that someone could live with a murderer and be none the wiser? Really, Rach? Everyone will think I was in on it. Enabling it all. I'll probably be arrested now, won't I? Oh, Christ. I feel sick."

She closed her eyes and sucked air through her nose, covering her mouth with her hand.

"But we *do* know you, Dala." I placed my hand on the top of her arm, rubbing it gently, desperate to offer her some sense of comfort or reassurance. "The people that matter know you, and they'll know that you would never have been involved."

"Wouldn't you have said the same about Phil?" She cocked her head, eyes flashing, as I opened my mouth but, finding nothing to say, closed it again.

"Exactly," she snarled.

I HAD NEVER BEEN SO relieved to push my own front door closed behind me. It was one forty in the morning and I had finally left Dalaja and Annie at Dalaja's house. Annie and I had agreed that we needed to rest, and she had insisted on staying with Dalaja. Half-heartedly I'd protested, offering to stay too, insisting that we were all in it together. Annie had gently steered me towards the front door, quietly insisting that one of us needed to get some sleep. She asked that I bring some supplies with me the following morning and gestured towards the press who had seemingly set up camp in the street outside.

"To think they're his colleagues." Annie shook her head, a crestfallen look on her face.

"Hmm," I agreed, peering out into the darkness and preparing for the onslaught I was about to be met with.

"I'm very happy to stay here too, you know?" I offered again, guilt gnawing at me for the sense of abandonment.

"There's no need. I'll be here with her tonight, and we need at least one of us to be able to think straight." She attempted a smile before leaning into me and lowering her voice.

"Can you try to speak to Dan? I know this is really difficult for you and you're caught in the middle of it all, but maybe he can... I don't know, find out if Phil's in his right mind or something." She shook her head, drawing in a deep, shuddering breath.

"I will," I promised as I pulled her into an embrace.

NOW I WAS HOME, the anxiety swirled in my gut, and I felt at a loss as to how to approach my own husband. I had been hoping he might still be out at work, but when I had arrived home his Toyota had been parked on our driveway and our bedroom light was on. There was an ache in the pit of my stomach at the knowledge that Dan had been home and hadn't checked in to see where – or how – I was.

Shuffling into the kitchen I filled a glass with water, gulping it down as though it may offer me some Dutch courage. My body sagged with exhaustion and I was aware that I must've looked like hell, in need of a shower before I saw Dan. Even after all the years we had spent together, I still hated the idea of looking so repulsive around him. Dalaja's house had felt like some kind of infirmary, like there was something infecting us all while we were cooped up inside. I had been so relieved to step over the threshold and into the night air, even if that had meant battling my way through the press. The urge to wash the stale feeling that lingered on my skin from being there was almost physical.

I trudged up the stairs, my eyes stinging with the desperation to close. The idea of a shower suddenly dulled in exchange for just being able to lay my head on my own pillow and blank the whole nightmare of the last few weeks from my mind.

Reaching the top of the stairs I drew in a breath, my heart fluttering at the thought of facing Dan and the things we were going to have to discuss.

"Oh, Rach, hey. I was starting to think you weren't coming home. I wanted to wait up. Where have you been? Have you spoken to Dalaja?" He sat upright in bed, the duvet falling away and revealing his bare chest. I stared at him, feeling a desperate urge to cry and wanting nothing more than to lay my head against it. I instantly thought of Dalaja, in her home that had become her prison by Phil's doing, and my body went cold. Perching on the end of the bed I kneaded my temples.

"Yes. I've been with her and Annie all evening. It's been horrendous." My tone held a sharp edge.

Dan's face crumpled. "So you know Phil confessed, then?" he mumbled, his eyes dropping to stare at the bed sheet.

I huffed out a deep sigh. "Yeah. His solicitor spoke to me when Dalaja fell to pieces. Phil wouldn't speak to her and then she gets a call out of the blue from his bloody solicitor to tell her the man she lives with – that she loves – has just admitted to being a murderer." I couldn't take in the magnitude of what I was speaking aloud. "We were drinking champagne together only a few nights ago."

"I know. Poor Dalaja. I can't imagine what this must be doing to her."

We both fell silent, lost in our own thoughts.

"I just don't understand it, Dan. I still just can't believe Phil would do something like that. We all knew him. It just doesn't feel right."

"It's shock." Dan offered me a sympathetic look. "How many families and friends of people who do things like this do you think had any idea? If they weren't so good at hiding it, they wouldn't get away with it. How often have you seen it on the news – people all standing around and telling you how he was just an ordinary guy, how he always seemed so nice." Dan shook his head and rolled his eyes. "If they made it obvious enough for any of us to notice, we wouldn't have to have an entire department dedicated to it at work."

My shoulders slumped as I took in what he was saying. He was trying to make me feel better, but I hated that, even with my history, I had somehow allowed a serial killer into my life completely undetected. I had become one of those fools who blindly told the world what a great guy Phil had always seemed.

"Besides, why would he confess to it if he was innocent, babe? I know how hard this is to take in, but no one admits to something this huge if they didn't do it. You'd have to be mad."

I was pulled back, lost in the memories of the conversation that I had had with Dennis, where he had explained exactly why he'd admitted to something he hadn't done. Was he also making a fool of me, deceiving me, and using cruel and twisted lies to manipulate my actions?

My head was spinning with the jumble of thoughts that seemed to be ricocheting off one another.

"I can't talk about this anymore. I just need to stop thinking about it and get some sleep. I promised Annie I'd go back first thing tomorrow and I need to just get it out of my head for a couple of hours before I have to be neck-deep in it all again." My voice had risen, and I knew I was verging on losing it completely. Spots had begun to pepper my vision again and I knew the migraine that had been threatening all day was closing in on me.

Dan said nothing as he watched me strip off my clothes down to my underwear. I couldn't even summon up the energy to cross the hall to the bathroom and brush my teeth. Crawling into bed, I wrapped myself up as though it could protect me from the world.

Dan flicked off the lamp, plunging us into darkness.

25

Setting my alarm had been optimistic. I had sobbed myself into a fitful sleep, plagued by nightmares. Dennis and Phil's faces had appeared everywhere, taunting me one minute, then pleading with me to believe they were innocent the next. They merged together until I could barely tell them apart, seeing only a hideous grin of someone I barely recognised as it closed in on me, engulfing me, choking me. Dan had shaken me awake, gently informing me that I was yelling out in my sleep.

That had been around four thirty and I knew sleep had outrun me, too far for me to clutch it back.

Dan's phone had rung at around six, startling us both and causing him to launch himself from his light sleep and almost rolling me off the side of the bed. He was perched on the side in just his boxers, leaning forward as though ready to pounce. By the look of him, he hadn't managed to get much more sleep than I had, which only caused the knot in my stomach to tighten further. Dan never struggled to sleep, regardless of the case he was on. I had watched through gritty eyes, only able to hear his side of the conversation and gauge his reaction to it, despite straining to listen to who the caller was and what was so urgent.

"Right. Well, that's great. Has she said anything yet?" Dan's voice was gruff, still thick with sleep as the muffled sound of a tinny voice on the other end of the line answered his question.

"Okay... No, no, don't pressure her. Follow the guidance from her doctor. We need to do this by the book. If we allow her some time, hopefully she'll remember something. How is she?" There was another long pause.

"That's great. Really great. Does she have people with her?" He rubbed sleep from his eyes with his thumb and middle finger. "Okay. She needs to feel she can trust us. Don't overwhelm her. Give her some space and let the poor girl recover a bit. I know we are all chomping at the bit, but she's a person – one who has just been through one hell of an ordeal. We need to make sure she isn't treated like evidence. What are the gaffers saying?" Propping myself up onto one elbow, I watched him as he glanced around at me. He mouthed "Sorry" and winced at the realisation he may have disturbed me. I shook my head, dismissing his apology and not attempting to disguise my curiosity.

"Yeah, I thought that might be the case. I'll be in later and do what I can. I'll speak to Karen and see if I can talk her round. Thanks, Joe." He moved the phone away from his ear, tossing it onto the bed and rubbing his eyes with the heels of his hands.

"Dan? What's going on? What's happened?" I sat upright, no longer concerned with sleep.

He turned to me. "Sorry I woke you, babe. You look shattered." He gave me a sympathetic look. "That was Joe. The latest victim, the one that survived the attack, she's come round."

My belly flipped as though there was something trying to get out. Would she identify Phil as her attacker?

"Oh, right. That's great." I nodded with more enthusiasm than I felt.

"Hmm," Dan agreed, looking as conflicted as I felt. His skin was almost grey.

"So, she hasn't said anything yet? Will you go and see her?" I questioned, wanting him to do something, wanting to be able to tell Annie and Dalaja that he was working on finding out what was going on, but with no idea what I was expecting him to do.

"No. The big guns have pulled me off it. I can still be involved in the case, but not with the big stuff. Conflict of interest. They know I know Phil personally, and can't risk jeopardizing the case by having me too closely involved."

He gave a small shrug and pressed his lips together.

"Oh." I wasn't sure if that made me feel better or worse. "But surely they know you'd never…"

"See it from their side, Rach. They know my connection to him, that we spent time together outside of work. They have to cover themselves. When this goes to court, the case must be watertight, and me being too involved could cause questions to be raised."

I nodded, glad that he didn't, at least, seem too upset. "I guess."

"They haven't kicked me off. I'm still able to run things from the office. I'm going to go in and see what I can do to help, but it's fair that they don't want me involved with interviewing witnesses. I'd do the same if it was anyone else on the team."

He pulled himself to standing and stretched out his back, turning back to look at me. I felt myself squirm, aware of how I must look having spent the majority of the night crying.

"Look, Rach, I know this is the most awkward situation. It's totally crap for both of us that we are caught up in this, but neither of us have done anything wrong. I get that you need to support Dalaja. I want you to, but equally, I have to do my job. I wanted Phil to be innocent as much as you did, but *he* did this, not any of us. We shouldn't be suffering for his actions. Let's not let him cause any more damage, okay? I don't want this to come between us." He lowered himself, leaning on his elbows and stretching across the bed, planting his lips on mine. "I love you," he whispered, pulling back and searching my face.

"I love you too." I meant the words but couldn't bring myself to meet Dan's gaze.

THE REPORTERS HAD THINNED OUT, but there was still a small gaggle of them sipping cups of coffee and eating breakfast out of wrappers. I wondered if they had left at all or if they had been here all night. They dropped what they were doing and ran towards me, calling out questions and asking me if I believed the accusations that the police were making about Phil.

I made no reaction, continuing towards Dalaja's front door as though I hadn't heard them, until one of them shouted a question that caused me to stop in my tracks.

"You're married to the police officer heading up the investigation, aren't you? What does he make of you coming here?" The question blindsided me. Of course they were going to make the connection. Why hadn't I been expecting that? It was as though a bone had been thrown to a pack of starving animals. The barrage of questions bounced off me as I practically ran up the path, banging on Dalaja's front door with my fist.

The curtain twitched and I saw Annie's eye appear in the gap. Within seconds, I saw her shape behind the glass of the front door, which she opened just enough for me to squeeze inside.

"Jesus, they're relentless," she breathed as she stepped back and let me pass.

"It's a big story, I guess. They know who I am, my relationship to Dan." I winced.

Annie lifted one shoulder. "It was always going to happen at some point." She gestured towards the living room, and I reluctantly moved deeper into the house. The curtains were still drawn, and the room smelt faintly of body odour mixed with coffee. I placed the bag of supplies down on the coffee table, having almost forgotten I was holding it.

Dalaja was propped up on the sofa, staring at a point on the wall with a mug of coffee grasped between her hands. She looked better than she had when I had left, but only marginally. Her eyes were swollen and puffy, her hair a mass of greasy clumps, and her skin almost grey. He usual radiance seemed to have been extinguished and I wondered if it would ever return.

"Hey," I whispered. She flinched and turned to look at me as if I had just materialised from thin air. Annie appeared beside me, and Dalaja blinked at us both as though she couldn't work out if we were really there.

"We didn't get much sleep." Annie shrugged, retrieving her own coffee from the mantelpiece and taking a long gulp. "Do you want me to make you one?"

"No, that's okay, thanks. Actually, I can't stay this morning."

Annie looked crestfallen and I felt a twinge of guilt.

"I have to go into work for a while. We're so stretched as it is. It'll put so much pressure on if I don't show… I really can't leave them in the lurch." That part wasn't a lie, but I couldn't miss the irony that it was exactly what I was doing to my friends.

Annie nodded, offering a sad smile before glancing at Dalaja, who was staring into her coffee.

"I just wanted to call in and see if there was anything else you guys needed before I go. I can call back later too."

"I think we're good." Annie shrugged. "I've taken some personal leave from work and Dalaja's firm obviously know what's happening. I spoke with her boss, and they've granted her leave with full pay until she's back on her feet. They've also offered to cover her legal costs."

I felt another stab of guilt, but I needed to focus. It wouldn't help anyone keeping myself locked up there too. "That's good of them." I nodded.

"We can get anything else we need delivered for now, but we can't hide in here forever." Annie glanced at Dalaja, who didn't react.

"Did you speak to Dan?" Annie studied me, and Dalaja's head snapped up to stare at me.

"Has he spoken to Phil? What did he say? Why is he saying he killed those women?" Dalaja's questions tumbled from her, the first time she had spoken, and she appeared almost manic. I felt the heat rise to my face at the memory of Dan explaining that no one's family ever thought their loved ones capable of this kind of evil.

"I spoke to him. He's doing his best, but they've limited his involvement for the time being because of his relationship to Phil. He's going in this morning to see what he can do and how he can help."

"Help who?" Dalaja narrowed her eyes. "Is he on their side, Rach? Does he think Phil did this?"

"Of course he doesn't," I soothed, wondering what the right thing to say was. Hadn't she herself referred to Phil as a 'piece of shit', wishing harm on him only hours before? She had obviously had another change of heart. I was beginning to struggle with the emotional whiplash of it all.

"None of us do," I added. "We just need to figure out what the hell is going on. I promise, we are all behind you, Dala, and we won't stop until you have the answers you deserve." I chose my words carefully, keen not to make false promises of proving Phil's innocence, Dan's words still ringing in my ears.

"And how exactly is anyone going to do that?" she hissed. "Dan's kicked off the case so he can't do anything. Phil didn't even have the balls to speak to me unless it was through our solicitor. What exactly do you think we can do? I am going crazy here, with no idea if I have spent the last however many years of my fucking life shacked up with a serial killer, bouncing between being sure there is no way my Phil could have done that, but then remembering the fact he is refusing to talk to me and has admitted to it all. You have no idea what I'm feeling, Rach, so please don't swan in here with your patronising promises, telling me everything's going to be fine." Her face was thunderous.

"Dala..." Annie tilted her head, drawing out her name, appealing to our friend, a hint of warning lacing her tone.

"Don't Dala me," she snarled. "I don't need you here either, with your pity. It would be better for both of you if you just left. Who wants to be associated with the serial killer's girlfriend?" She paused. "To think I was so desperate for Phil to propose. The serial killer's wife would at least have had a better ring to it. But then at least I don't have to worry about a divorce. I wonder if your husband being found guilty of murder gives you grounds." She laughed before dropping her head into her hands, giving way to shuddering sobs that took over her body. We were silent, uncertain how to support her.

"I'm sorry. I'm so sorry. I didn't mean to be such a bitch," she whimpered. "I don't know why I said all of that."

Annie and I crossed the room and had her enveloped in our arms in an instant. I ached to tell her the truth about Dennis, to share with her the fact that I did understand, more than she knew, but I couldn't decide if it would just be a way for me to unburden myself at a time their defences were down. The last thing she needed was to carry someone else's problems along with her own. Annie and I wouldn't be pushed away by her self-destruction.

We could do nothing but hold her as her body seemed to deflate and she sobbed until she was spent. With nothing left to give, she gave in and succumbed to a restless sleep. We laid her gently out onto the sofa and Annie laid a blanket over her.

"What the hell is going on?" she whispered, shaking her head. "How is this happening?"

"I really don't know, Annie," I whispered back, exhaustion beginning to pull at me again. "But I meant what I said. We are going to support her and do all we can to make sure Phil at the very least tells her the things she deserves to know."

26

I had left Annie to get some rest whilst Dalaja slept, and drove over to work, wishing I could curl into a ball and sleep too. I wanted nothing more than to go to sleep and not awake until everything had been cleared up.

Work passed by in a blur and I fought to concentrate, thankful for the easy morning with nothing too serious to contend with.

There was none of the usual relief as I saw my last patient out. I had no desire to go home, nor to have to go back to Dalaja's to be submerged into the pit of misery again. But I had no choice, aware what a terrible friend avoiding them would make me. I made the drive as slowly as I could manage, stopping off for a Chinese takeaway and popping into a corner shop for some essentials.

Pulling up outside her house, I was relieved to see that the number of journalists had dwindled.

The ones remaining certainly wouldn't get anything from me. I was out of my car and up the front path before they'd had time to catch up, ignoring their pleading shouts and knocking on the door.

"Boy, am I glad to see you," Annie muttered, letting me quickly inside. She had dark circles under her eyes and her complexion had lost its usual glow. For the first time in all the years I had known her, she seemed defeated and withdrawn.

"Everything okay?" I whispered.

She raised her eyebrows and sucked in a breath.

"Well, she's certainly back with us now. But I'm not sure if it's better or worse than she was this morning."

She gestured with her head towards the kitchen. I walked through, taking in the sight before me. There was paperwork strewn over every visible surface, a laptop sat open on the kitchen table, and a calendar and diary lay abandoned on the floor beside the table. I threw a questioning glance over my shoulder at Annie, who offered a defeated shrug.

"Oh, hi, Rach. I didn't hear you come in." Dalaja barely glanced up from the papers in front of her. She had a wild look in her eyes and seemed wired, as though she might have taken something.

"Hey. I brought us some Chinese food." I held up the bag, but she didn't look up from her task.

"Thanks. I'm not really hungry but you guys carry on. You know where the plates and stuff are." She waved a hand over her shoulder.

Glancing over at the cupboard, I wondered if I would be able to find anything underneath the mountains of paperwork. My stomach growled, reminding me that I hadn't eaten in hours.

"Well, why don't you stop for a minute and have something to eat with us? Maybe afterwards I could help?" She paused in her task, and I saw my in. "You won't be able to carry on much longer anyway if you don't eat something."

Dalaja was clearly torn, throwing a glance towards the bag clutched in my hand and then shifting her gaze to take in the sight of Annie, who looked as though she might be about to pass out where she sat.

"Okay." She gave a sharp nod. "I'll have something quick. But let's eat in the living room and I'll catch you up. I don't want to mess up my system." She gestured around at the papers that appeared to me as though they had been scattered around haphazardly, but I said nothing. Annie visibly brightened at Dalaja's break in resolve and hurriedly pushed back her chair, almost tipping it over in her haste to grab the plates and cutlery.

It was only a few minutes before we were all sat, plates perched on laps, in the living room. The lights were on as the curtains remained drawn, and I fought the urge to throw them open, along with the windows to try to relieve the house of the thick atmosphere.

Annie was withdrawn and huddled in the armchair as Dalaja picked at her food, too desperate to catch me up on what she was doing to eat much. The women were in stark contrast to one another, almost as though the day spent together had caused them to reverse roles from when I'd last seen them, Dalaja seeming to have sucked all of the energy from Annie, using it to feed her mania.

"...Because clearly, we know Phil wouldn't have done this, so we just have to find a way to prove it. You said that yourself. So, I thought if I went back through all of our paperwork – appointments, that kind of thing – I would be able to find proof that he couldn't have killed any of those women because if I find out where he really was at the time any of them died, it'll show that he couldn't have been there." She stared at me, eyes wide and expectant, a bright look on her face.

"Right." I nodded, surprised. Maybe she could actually be on to something. "So, what have you found so far?"

"Well." Dalaja pushed the rice around her plate. "It's been a little bit more of a challenge than I anticipated because Phil doesn't organise in the standard way. He doesn't really keep a diary, or any kind of structured notes as to where he's going or what he's got planned." She swallowed hard. "He's more the 'keeps it all in his head' type."

I chewed on a spring roll, keen to seem supportive. "Right."

"Plus, you know... with his job... he can't write down *everything* he does. He meets sources and things. Some of it has to be kept under wraps."

I glanced at Annie, whose focus was fully fixed onto her plate. Clearly, she had been dealing with this for most of the day.

"Well, it's a great idea." My food sat heavily in my stomach as my hope dwindled. I dropped my fork onto my plate and ran my tongue over my teeth before I spoke again. "Do you think he might have been at work, or meeting sources some of the times the women were attacked, then?" I asked carefully, swallowing hard and trying to keep my face impassive.

Dalaja shrugged. "I'm not sure. He definitely could have been. It's just so hard to be certain when he hasn't got anything solid written down to pinpoint dates and times." She waved her fork around as she spoke.

"Could you ask his bosses or colleagues?" I pressed gently. Her face darkened as her eyes narrowed slightly.

"Those same people who are busy writing stories about him?" she scoffed. "Why would they want to help him? They're having a field day tearing apart one of their own." I wondered if she had missed the irony that it was only what Phil himself would have done had the roles been reversed.

"I just thought it would be in their interest if they had a way to prove the police had it wrong. Imagine *that* story." I cocked my head, but Dalaja remained quiet, crushing a prawn cracker.

"And you don't think he was with you any of the times of the murders? Or when that last girl was attacked?" I was aware I was beginning to sound desperate, but my head spun with the need for her to find something concrete, to end this.

"Not any of the times that I can recall. I don't keep a schedule of what I do in the evenings and stuff either, though. I don't have any need to."

"So, when the last girl was attacked, where they found the DNA, was he with you?" I didn't want to put into words that it had only been hours previously and that she must know.

Dalaja's eyes narrowed. She pursed her lips and cocked her head. "I've said I'm not sure. Why do you keep asking?"

I instantly regretted my inability to rein in my anxiety. Aware it was too late to backtrack, I attempted it anyway.

"Sorry. I didn't mean to. I just thought you were right; you're onto something. If we could prove where he was, especially during the last attack, we could be sure he was innocent. His DNA was only found at that one scene, so all the others—"

"What did you just say?" Dalaja glared at me, and I felt a heat claw its way up my body as I tried to figure out what I had said.

"I... Er... I..."

"I don't need proof to *be sure* he's innocent, Rach. I know he's innocent." Dalaja's tone was venomous.

"Of course you do. I didn't mean—"

"You think he did this, don't you?" she cut me off. "You think Phil, *my* Phil, is a murderer. Some kind of psycho. Don't you?"

I could feel the heat in my face, the damp prickle of sweat that had formed on the back of my neck and along my hair line. I wiped at the beads of it that were forming on my lip, the plate of food on my lap seeming to radiate heat.

Dalaja's eyes felt as though they had burrowed into my mind, leaving her able to read my thoughts.

"Of course she doesn't." I had almost forgotten that Annie was there. She sounded exhausted. "We're all tired and under a lot of strain. Let's not take things the wrong way or say anything we don't mean."

"Answer the question, Rachel," Dalaja continued as if Annie hadn't spoken. "Do you believe Phil could have murdered those women?"

27

BEFORE

I had assured the girls from the photographs that I would be able to protect them if they never spoke of my part in it. It hadn't been difficult.

I put on a great show, acting as though I was fighting to hold back tears as I explained that my father forced me to take their photographs for him. I told them stories about the kind of men my father associated with, what they would do to us all if we didn't do what they said. I held their hands as I begged them to tell the police my father had been the one behind the camera, that if they didn't, I would be arrested too, and we could never be together. I told them how much they had meant to me, and that it had broken my heart when my father had forced me to take those photos.

I assured them that in time, we could be together, in a real relationship, if they did this one thing to help me, to protect me from these people. I needed to be safe from my father before I could enter into a relationship. I couldn't put them at risk until I was safe from him, and I couldn't live with myself until I knew it was all done with and the photographs of them were gone, never seen again. After all, we didn't want them cropping up further down the line, their families potentially seeing them, or affecting their future career prospects.

They lapped it up, seeing it as a way to save the damaged boy they were falling for, at the same time as saving themselves. They truly believed they would be the ones to fix me.

They couldn't understand that I had never needed to be fixed.

I was so sick of seeing the looks my father reserved only for me, the way he was so desperate to drip poison into my mother and brother's ears about me, to regain power. But the look on his face as I entered the room and whispered in his ear, just minutes before the police arrived, was enough to erase all of that. From the way his skin turned grey, and his veins popped in his head, I was surprised he didn't drop down dead of a heart attack right then. But that would have ruined all my plans.

"You're about to see what happens when you make an enemy of me. Don't make this any worse for yourself. You won't be getting out of it. And if you try, someone else will have to suffer for your selfishness."

28

My heart was hammering, and I knew when I spoke again, my voice would be trembling.

I glanced at Annie, who looked as though she were either going to yell at us or burst into tears.

"Don't look at her," Dalaja spat. "I'm asking you to answer me. It's not difficult, Rach."

I opened my mouth, closed it again, at a total loss as to how I could respond. We had been friends for too many years for me to be able to convincingly lie directly to her face. She would see through me instantly. Yes, I had kept my secrets, but my friends had never had reason to suspect that my father was a convicted criminal, so it had been easy to mislead and change the subject when I'd needed to, never having been asked directly if my father was a killer.

"I knew it." Her voice was dangerously low. "Dan's got inside your head, hasn't he? Because he made the arrest, he can't lose face and admit he was wrong, and having you associated with me doesn't look good for him. Is that why he's been kicked off the case?" A strange look came down over her face, as though a blind had been removed. "Is *that* why you've been acting so weird recently? Did you *know* that Dan was going to arrest Phil?"

"What?" I choked out, barely able to speak.

"You've been acting so off, avoiding us and making up excuses. And when we have seen you, you're cagey and weird. I knew something was going on." A muscle twitched in her face as she glared at me.

"No. No, you've got it wrong. I didn't know anything. Dan didn't—"

"You're a liar. I can see it all written all over your face. You came to my birthday, drank the champagne that Phil paid for."

"Dala, I didn't know anything," I gasped. "I swear."

"Then what's going on? Look at me and tell me you aren't hiding something from us. That there isn't something making you act really weird."

I couldn't meet her eyes.

"Rach?" Annie's voice came as barely more than a whisper.

"You're a two-faced bitch, Rachel. How could you have pretended to be my friend? Pretended to be shocked when Phil was arrested, sat here with me, when all along, you'd known it was coming. What else do you know that you aren't telling me?"

I shook my head, silently begging for them to see they'd got it wrong.

"I let you speak to my fucking solicitor," Dalaja hissed. "I gave him permission. I trusted you. You left the room while you were on the phone to him. What did you ask? Did you pass information back to Dan? Whatever he said to you, that was confidential. *I trusted you.*" She was yelling now. She rose from her chair, allowing the plate of food to tumble from her lap and land with a clatter. I stared down at the scattered food, the upside-down plate, and fought the urge to start picking up the grains of rice.

"Of course I didn't. Dala, this is *me*." I pressed my finger tips to my chest. "I swear to you, I haven't... I didn't..."

She stood, fists clenched by her sides, her chest heaving, a look on her face like I had never seen before.

"Dala, please. You don't understand. I didn't..."

"I want you to get out of my house. Right now."

I felt the hot prickle of tears and attempted to blink them away, remaining motionless, willing them to see sense and allow me to stay.

"Get out before I force you out. That'll give the media something to write about." She spoke through her teeth. "I don't want you here, Rachel, and I don't want to see you again. Now get... Out." She drew out the last order and I slid the plate of food from my lap and onto the arm of the chair. I turned to look at Annie, praying that she would intervene and stop this horrific scene from playing out.

She was staring at me as though I was something alien to her.

Crossing the room I went back into the hallway. My feet ached from the afternoon spent on them, but it was nothing compared to the ache that was building in my chest.

I turned back, considering going back inside, insisting they listen to me and coming clean about everything. I could make them understand and repair the damage I'd caused. But I knew the timing wasn't right for that conversation.

Dalaja would never believe me while she was so angry. I

pulled open the front door, ensuring my car keys were at the ready in case of an ambush by the press.

Slipping out, I dashed towards my car, not even offering a glance in the direction of where they had set up their camps.

Could it really be coincidence that everything had begun to turn rotten at exactly the time that Dennis reappeared in my life? If his game was to destroy me, it was working. There had been no explosion, no sudden relief when he came for me. Instead, my life was being torn apart, inch by inch, until I had nothing left.

My body ached to just stop. To leave it all to the police, to wait for Dennis to totally destroy me. But I was a fighter. I had come through my entire life with the odds against me. I wasn't about to lie down and give up now.

I checked my phone, my mood lifting slightly at the text from Dan.

> Hey, where are you? I've just got home. Going to head to bed for a few hours. Wake me if you come back. It'd be really good to see you. D. xx

It was still early, only around six, but Dan's shift pattern had been so erratic he had to grab his sleep wherever he could. The thought crossed my mind that things might slow down now that they had someone in custody, before I remembered who that someone was, and my stomach plummeted once again.

My body sagged at the thought of Dan already being home, that I wasn't going back to an empty house – or worse. I placed my phone onto the magnetic holder on the dashboard of my car and started the ignition. Aware that the curtains would remain drawn and that I would see nothing, I still couldn't help myself from glancing over as I drove past Dalaja's house, picturing her and Annie inside tearing me apart for what they thought I'd done.

The radio played a cheery George Ezra song and I jabbed the button to silence it.

29

My mind was practically exploding with questions as I drove home.

I didn't even have a clear answer myself for what I had hoped would be the outcome of the day. If Phil was guilty, that meant that all of us had allowed a murderer to walk among us for the entirety of our adult lives. I had no idea if Dalaja would recover from it, all too aware of the damage to my own life through strikingly similar events.

But if Phil was guilty, that meant Dennis had to be innocent. And if that was true, did that mean that he was telling the truth of what I had done? The idea caused my legs to go weak.

My phone rang and I glanced up at it, hoping to see Annie or Dalaja calling.

My heart dropped at the sight of Dennis's name. I couldn't face him right now. I rejected the call. Almost instantly, my phone rang again. I pressed the button on the side to switch it to silent.

As I drove home, I thought of Dan, currently sleeping in

our bed, and decided once I got home, I would go and join him. I wanted to feel the warmth of Dan's body against mine, to have his arms wrapped around me and to be able to block everything else out, even for just a few hours. Once I'd given myself some time to rest, it was time to tell Dan everything. I wouldn't keep anything from him – about Dennis's reappearance or his allegations. He was my husband and had never wavered in his support for me. The least I owed him was honesty, even if it was hard for him to hear.

I turned my key in the lock of our front door, closing it as quietly behind me as I could manage and slipping out of my shoes. I went to the kitchen, opening the cupboard and reaching for a glass to fill with water, but as I stretched out my arm, a large hand clamped itself over my mouth and a strong arm went around my waist.

I tried to scream and watched as the glass that I'd been about to grasp wobbled on the edge of the shelf in the cupboard. I willed it to topple, to crash down onto the worktop and shatter into a thousand pieces so that my husband would come downstairs to check what had happened. The glass shimmied and shuddered to a stop. I let out a whimper, feeling the strength of the body behind me as I was dragged towards my back door.

"Shhhhh," Dennis hissed in my ear, and I felt suddenly disgusted with the close proximity of our faces. His breath was hot against my cheek as he spoke and I tried to turn my face away, but he had me pinned too tightly.

I bucked, thrashing my body around as much as I could and attempting to shout through the hand pressed over my mouth. I attempted to bite it, but the grip was too tight.

The voice in my ear caused me to freeze, the fight leaving my body for a second.

"JoJo, please stop fighting. If you promise you'll be quiet, I'll let you go. You *have* to be quiet."

I blinked, spots peppering my vision from the strain of the fight I'd put up. My breathing was loud as I fought to get as much air through my nose as I could, exhausted from the effort.

I nodded and the hand slowly loosened its grip. I waited a second before I sucked in a breath, ready to shout.

"DA—" It was as much as I was able to get out before something soft was pressed against my face and muffled my shout. The cloth squeaked against my teeth as he held it firmly in place.

The world seemed to tilt, everything around me going fuzzy at the edges and a blackness swarming in from my peripheral vision, leaving me only able to see what was directly in front of me. My kitchen cupboards turned hazy and the last thing I heard as I fought not to close my eyes was the whisper in my ear.

"I really didn't want to have to do this."

MY MOUTH WAS DRY, and my head pounded. The last time I had felt this bad was the morning after Dalaja's birthday, and mine and Dan's disastrous anniversary meal. Had I been drinking again?

I ran my tongue over my teeth, attempting to stop them from sticking to my lips and generate some saliva. Things seemed to come back to me in pieces. Work. Collecting the takeaway and driving over to Dalaja's. Our fight…

"Would you like some water, JoJo?" His voice was barely more than a whisper, but it startled me as though he had just bellowed at me. I sat up too quickly, blinking rapidly, trying to bring the room around me into focus. Everything was spinning.

"Hey, take it steady. You're okay. You'll feel a bit rough for a while, I'm afraid. I'm sorry about that. I really didn't want to do that to you."

I opened my mouth to curse at him, but instead, I retched.

My head was pounding and felt too heavy for me to hold up. My body trembled and I had no idea whether it was through the cold, or fear of what was about to happen to me. I swallowed down the nausea that rose again and placed my hands behind me, palms down on the floor, balancing myself and waiting for the need to vomit to pass.

My hands weren't tied, which was good – as long as I could keep it that way. My vision still swam, leaving me unable to focus on my feet to see if they were also free, but it felt as though I could move them.

Dennis moved into my periphery, offering me a plastic cup of water. I desperately wanted to grab it out of his hand and swallow it back in one, but self-preservation kicked in.

"No." The word sounded slurred as I reached out and attempted to push it away, misjudging where it was and almost falling forwards onto my face. Dennis caught me, sitting me upright again.

"It's just water, JoJo. Here, I'll prove it." He lifted the cup to his own lips and took a swallow of the liquid. I eyed him, aware he could have pretended to gulp the water, but my desperate thirst and pounding headache were eroding my resolve.

"Take it." He held it out again, and this time I reached

out a trembling hand, wondering if I would be able to get it to my mouth before I spilled it all.

I lifted it to my cracked lips and took a greedy gulp, regretting it instantly as nausea rolled my stomach.

"Drink it slowly. You'll start to feel better soon, I promise. It's just the effects of the drug."

Wiping my mouth with the back of my hand, I scowled at him again. How could I have fallen for his act? I had allowed him to tangle me up in his web of lies, let him infiltrate my barriers and take me down from the inside.

"I'm so sorry I had to do this. I had no choice. I had to bring you somewhere that no one would find you."

I couldn't read the expression on his face, but I was with it enough to understand what that meant. A ripple of fear set my body into another round of violent shaking, but I refused to allow him the satisfaction of seeing how afraid I was. If I was going to get out, I needed to be smart about it..

"Where..." The word came out as a raspy croak, so I cleared my throat, swallowing hard so as not to gag again. "Where are we?" My throat was dry despite the water, and my lips kept sticking to my teeth. My voice sounded odd, as though I had a lump of cotton wool stuffed inside my cheeks.

Dennis threw me a sideward glance and cleared his own throat, confirming that I sounded as awful as I thought.

"We're on the industrial site – where we met." He at least looked uncomfortable as he filled me in. "I noticed this unit was empty and that there was an easy way to get inside."

My heart rate sped up and I placed my hands on my knees to hide their trembling. A cold sensation of dread was rapidly consuming me as the reality sank in. I had no desire to ask him anything more. His intentions were pretty clear.

He had drugged me, kidnapped me and brought me to a place where, by his own admission, no one would find me. I didn't want to hear his reasons or his justification for what he had done. I never wanted to have to see or speak to him again, and although my lack of restraints showed how easily he believed he would be able to overpower me, I planned to fight him with everything I had.

I thought of Dan and what it would do to him, being informed by one of his colleagues that Dennis had got to me. I imagined the police officers crawling all over this space, whispering to one another about who I was and exchanging grim looks. If I was going to die here, I wanted Dan to know I didn't just give up.

Dennis glugged from a water bottle, leaning back against a desk.

"I *am* sorry, JoJo. This wasn't the way I wanted to... I know I need to explain it all to you. I just don't know how to start. I know you'll hate me."

I said nothing. I could indulge him, allow him his moment to share his monologue, but I despised the creature that had stolen my life from me once before and was about to attempt to do it again. I had one shot at getting away from the monster before me, and I planned to give it everything I had left. I shifted myself to sitting upright, leaning back on my hands, my knees drawn up in front of me.

"I... I..." I ensured I had Dennis's attention before I forced a strange noise from my throat. I allowed one of my elbows to give out and rolled my eyes as far back into my head as I could manage. I had no idea how convincing it was, but as a doctor I had witnessed my share of people passing out.

It seemed to work, as Dennis dropped the water bottle to the floor. He ran towards me, calling out my name.

I didn't hesitate. The second he was close enough I lifted my legs and kicked out as hard as I could physically manage. One of my feet made contact with his knee, forcing it backwards on itself with a sickening crunch. My other foot landed somewhere around his crotch, and I watched in relief as his body seemed to crumple, folding in on itself as he dropped to the floor with a stomach-turning howl.

I observed him for a second before coming to my senses, aware I might not have disabled him for too long and that I was not in the best condition myself to be having to run anywhere. I forced myself to my feet, having no choice but to pause for a few seconds as the world shifted under me. Nausea rose again but the adrenaline surged, and I was across the floor in seconds, yanking open the door and blinking, squinting in the weak sunlight. Dennis released another groan, followed by what I was pretty sure was him growling my name. I didn't look back as I took off as quickly as my trembling legs would allow.

30

BEFORE

The police had arrived quickly and, throwing glances at me and my brother, had asked our father to accompany them to answer some questions. My father had glared at me, a fire in his eyes like I had never seen before. It lit something within me too, causing mini explosions behind my eyes as justice was done.

He had pointed at me, telling them whatever they thought he'd done, it was all my doing. I watched the spittle fly from his mouth as he panicked, acting like a cornered animal. My mother had placed her body between the two of us, reaching behind her to take hold of my hand as the police cuffed him.

I kept my face impassive, self-aware enough to know it wasn't the time to allow my euphoria to show. I turned to see my brother staring at me. His eyes were wide, and his lips were slightly parted, pink against his rapidly paling skin.

We watched as my father was dragged from our dining room and I mirrored the reactions of my remaining family. The police spoke to my mother in hushed tones, advising her to take us boys away from the house while they conducted their searches. We were ushered out and taken to the local cafe for milkshakes.

My mother had quietly sobbed as we had sat around in silence. A middle-aged man whose hair was thinning, what he had left turning grey, had come in a short time later, offering me and my brother a sympathetic greeting before pulling my mother aside. I studied their faces as they spoke, my mother covering her mouth with her hand, fighting to hold back the emotions that threatened to engulf her.

They had arranged for us to go to a hotel for the night, informing my mother that they wouldn't be done with our house for some time. He told us he would return to our house and pack us a bag each with the essentials we would need.

I had ensured to meet my brother's gaze when our mother informed us later that the police planned to speak to us both the following morning. It hadn't been difficult to convince him to go along with the next part of my plan. He was malleable. As soon as he had made that call to the police, I'd had him. It would be a case of building slowly on those foundations, never allowing him to see how badly he was entangling himself. I would use what he had done to force his hand into my next requirement of him and continue that way until he was too deep to refuse anything. It was almost too easy.

My brother spoke with them first and I didn't hold up my part of the bargain, shaking my head with wide eyes when the officers asked if our father had ever behaved inappropriately around me. It was in that moment I knew without doubt the level of control I could gain over him.

31

I ran towards the sound of the traffic, disoriented and unable to think clearly enough to decipher which direction would be best to head. All I could think was that if I could make it to an area where there were enough witnesses, I would be safe. I wasn't sure how true that was, but I wouldn't allow any other thoughts to swamp my mind.

I kept running until my lungs burned with the desperate need for oxygen. The sensation hit me as if I had run into it, and I stumbled to a stop before turning toward the hedge, resting my hands on my knees, bending, and vomiting relentlessly.

Certain Dennis would be right behind me, I risked a glance back towards the unit I had run from, wiping my mouth on the back of my hand and forcing myself to set off again, unable to run on legs that threatened to give out altogether. I reached the main road and weaved my way along the pavement, still no idea where I was going. Clambering up a hill, I released a cry of relief as I made it over the crest.

Right ahead of me was a supermarket. There would be people there. It would be too risky for Dennis to follow me.

I made it as far as the entrance, leaning on a row of trolleys for support. A middle-aged woman in a brown, shin-length coat threw me an odd look, struggling to disguise her look of disgust at the sight of me.

I staggered into the supermarket toilet. Seeing the state of myself in the smeared mirror, I made an attempt to clean up my face. The paper towels felt too rough against my sensitive skin and I winced against my pounding head. Whatever Dennis had given me, I was still feeling the after-effects of it, so I grabbed a bottle of water and some paracetamol. A sudden realisation that I didn't have my purse dawned, and automatically, my hand went to my pocket in search of my phone, thinking I could use it to pay. I froze, perplexed when I found it still there. Dennis hadn't even taken my phone? I'd had it in my pocket the whole time.

Needing to get home but feeling too wobbly and shaken to consider walking anywhere, I decided to arrange a Uber.

Dennis had tried to call me five times. I scoffed at the audacity of him. How could he think he could drug me, abduct me, and then give my mobile a call as though nothing had happened?

The Uber driver eyed me as though I may be infectious. He turned to give me another look as I lowered myself into the back seat, clutching my head as I did.

"Everything okay, love?" he asked, frowning.

"Fine." I didn't take my hands away from my head. It felt as though if I let go, it might explode.

"No shopping?"

I stared at him blankly and he nodded towards the supermarket.

"Oh. No. I just need to get home." I swallowed hard, desperate for him to just get the journey over with.

"Right. Just so you know, if you vomit in the vehicle, it is an extra charge."

I blinked at him, watching his eyes drop to my grime-covered jumper. Slowly, I lowered my gaze and took in the state of it. The filth from the warehouse floor. The vomit stain over my left breast.

"It's okay," I stuttered, unable to care enough to conjure up any shame. "I won't."

There had been no time for me to process what had happened with Dennis and it was only as I sank into the back seat of my Uber that it hit me square in the chest.

There was also a text message from Dennis, along with one from Dan that had come through a couple of hours before. I opened Dan's first.

> Hey, babe, where are you? I was hoping you'd be back by now. Can we grab some food together or something in a bit? I just want to spend some time with you and have a normal evening. I hate all this drama and the way it's coming between us. I know how hard this all is for you and I want us to support each other like we always have. I miss you, Rach. xx

Dan clearly hadn't realised anything was amiss. It was far from unusual for me to go out without my car, often favouring a walk or the use of the train to save the hassle of parking. He wouldn't have noticed my bag either, aware I didn't always take one.

I wondered if Dennis had replaced the glass, closed the

cupboard, or whether Dan hadn't yet been back into our kitchen.

His message would usually have lifted my spirits, but it did nothing to make me feel better. The unread message from Dennis caused my heart to plummet further, a harsh, hard-hitting reminder of the day's events. I would have given anything to go home and have the evening with Dan that he was suggesting, but I was all too aware that was impossible given everything I was about to go home and drop on him.

I opened Dennis's message, too curious to just press delete, swallowing hard, fingers beginning to tremble as the memories of our last encounter flooded my already thumping head.

> I am so sorry about earlier. Please, please let me explain it to you. I know what you must think but you've got it wrong. You're not safe and I did what I did to try to protect you. I know it was a stupid thing to do. I just panicked, reacted to the situation, and I realise that now, but please let me explain. I thought it was for the best. I still think you'll understand if you let me tell you the truth. Please call me. I'll meet you anywhere, any time. I just need you to be safe.

I screwed up my face, feeling my lip curling. Did he honestly think I was that stupid? Granted, I had fallen for his bullshit before, but that was before he had done what he had. How could there be any doubt in my mind after that?

Furiously, I started tapping out a reply, informing him what I thought of him and where he could shove his meeting and his concern for my safety. I wanted to scream at the phone, my fury bubbling, torrid. My thumb hovered over the button, prepared to send it, but something stopped me. Contacting him in any way couldn't bring anything good. Although I didn't believe I would ever let him get inside my head again, hadn't I been certain of the same thing just a few short weeks earlier? Look at where that had landed me.

I was a mess. There was too much happening all at once for me to trust myself or my judgement. It was time I was honest with Dan about everything. If I even so much as communicated with Dennis, he would worm his way in, twist things around and lay out excuses for everything he'd done. My resolve was too weak to take on that battle right now, and he knew it. It would be opening the door for him once more, and I would never be that foolish again. I knew without doubt what he was now.

The Uber pulled up outside my house and I dragged myself out of the back seat and up to the front door. I sucked in deep breaths, realising my keys would still be inside where I had left them earlier.

Hesitating, I checked again to make sure Dan's Toyota was on the drive before I knocked on my own front door.

I saw the shape of Dan behind the glass, distorted by the frosted glass but unmistakably him. My legs shook as though they might have been about to give out now that I was so close to the safety of my husband. I had never felt so weak, so shamelessly willing to hide behind my husband and let him protect me. How had I gotten to this point? Wasn't I the same woman who had fled everything I knew to build a new life for myself, fearless and unafraid to risk everything to turn it all around?

Dan opened the door, his face appearing in the gap, a look of confusion instantly chased away by concern.

"Rach? Christ. Are you okay?" He clutched a tea towel

he'd been wiping his hands on, reaching out to me before hesitating. He stared at me as though I might shatter if he touched me.

The sobs escaped my body before I was even aware I was going to break, rushing from me in loud gasps as I released the torrent of emotions that had been building all day.

Dan caught hold of me, whispering reassuring things as he practically carried me through to the living room, lowering me onto the sofa with such compassion, his touch so tender that it only led to another round of uncontrollable sobbing.

"Rach? What the hell happened?" he asked, pulling back from me gently.

He took my hands in his.

"I'm not going to ask if you're okay, because clearly..." He nodded towards me, shaking his head. "Do we need to get you seen?"

I sniffed loudly and shook my head, unsure of how to even begin to fill him in on everything.

His face creased as he cocked his head.

"You need to tell me what's happened." He squeezed my hands, his eyes dark with urgency and fear at what I was about to tell him. I felt a surge of love for him, desperate to unburden myself and get things back on track with the man I loved more than anyone. Things might get worse before they got better, but I was done with secrets.

"I'm going to tell you everything, Dan, but it's going to be a lot to hear." My voice cracked with emotion. Dan pulled his head back and widened his eyes, visibly unsettled further by my admission.

"Okay. I'm sure I can take it. Tell me everything."

I HAD no idea how long we had been sat there but my legs were starting to go numb, and my hands were sweaty in Dan's. The urge to remove them from his and wipe them on my jeans was almost overpowering, and I was also conscious of how regularly I was having to sniff to stop the snot dribbling from my nose. But I was too afraid to release the grip on Dan's hands, petrified that if I did, he may start to drift away from me and I'd never pull him back.

My voice had become croaky as I spoke, and I felt as though I had been talking for so long that once I stopped, I would be incapable of generating any more words. I was desperate for water and wished I had brought the bottle from the supermarket. I must have dropped it when I ran to Dan and hadn't even realised it. Dan had listened intently, gracious enough not to interrupt my story at any point. He hadn't been able to hide his shock, his reflexes. His face gave him away a few times throughout my admissions. At the mention of Dennis's name, his lips had parted, and his nostrils had flared, but he had managed to rein himself in, clenching his jaw closed, the muscles in it flexing with his effort not to interrupt me.

Once I was done, we sat, neither of us looking at the other while we both processed everything I had just said.

Dan was the one to release his grip on my hands. Launching himself from the sofa, he slammed the palms of his hands against the wall as he let out a stream of expletives. I flinched, both hands flying up to cover my mouth. At least he hadn't punched a hole through the wall.

I eyed him cautiously as he bent over double, panting

and holding his fists at the side of his head as though to regain control of himself and his thoughts.

Neither of us said anything, the only sound the ticking of the clock and Dan's heavy breathing.

"Say something," I squeaked, already missing the physical contact, unable to imagine how he must have been feeling hearing everything I had just told him. The least he deserved was a minute to let it all soak in, but I craved his touch, his reassurance that it was okay, that he wasn't furious with me.

"I really don't know what to say," he growled, his voice gravelly. "I can't believe you didn't come to me with any of this before now. I mean, what the fuck, Rach?" I flinched as the tone of his voice rose. "You're sitting here, telling me that psychopath has been in our house? With you? He broke into our home. And you didn't think to tell me, or call the police? Not only that, but you then went on to meet him, by yourself, and show him the perfect, secluded spot to hold you when he then, later, abducted you? I mean, honestly, do you even understand how reckless you have been? The danger you've put yourself in?"

His nostrils flared and his eyes flashed.

"For all we know, Dennis and Phil could've been working together. I'm old enough to remember your father's crimes being reported. Phil isn't that much younger than me. He would have been young and impressionable – maybe he hero-worshiped him. I'll bet he was some kind of copycat." He was almost manic in his ranting, seeming to be talking to himself more than me.

"That's a big assumption," I whispered, shocked by the sudden change of direction. I was knocked sick at the idea of my father and my friend, plotting and comparing the way they enjoyed killing women.

Dan turned to stare at me, as though he had just realised I was still in the room.

"You don't know what these kinds of men are like. You let Dennis so close to you. I really thought you knew better. You let your guard down and allowed him to get inside your head. Do you see him for what he is now? Do you accept that he isn't the good guy he'd like you to believe he is, now he drugged you, kidnapped you and held you in an abandoned warehouse? Tried to convince you that you'd killed your sister?"

A muscle twitched beside his eye as he glared at me, and I clenched my jaw. I had no right to feel sorry for myself. Dan was right in everything he had said. I needed to accept the consequences of what I had done and start working to put it right.

"I'm so sorry, Dan. I know I've been unbelievably stupid. I was so ashamed when Dennis told me what I'd done. Of course, I can see now that it was just his mind games, his way of making me believe he was a decent person and that I owed him. You just had so much on already I didn't want to add to it all. And then Annie and Dalaja were mad at me. I managed to mess that up too." The desperation was bleeding into my voice. I snapped my jaw closed to stop my pity party before I went into a full-blown whine. I needed to face up to my actions. Dan didn't deserve to be guilt-tripped into feeling sorry for his overemotional wife.

Dan flopped into the armchair, dropping his head into his hands, his elbows resting on his thighs. The urge to reach out for him was so strong I balled my hands into fists and wedged them under my legs, aware he deserved to absorb this in his own time.

Dan lifted his head, puffing out his flushed cheeks and blowing out his breath.

"I'm sorry. I was harsh just then. You've been through a lot – we all have. I didn't mean to react like I did. I just love you so much, Rach. What you did... You've been so reckless. I'm a bloody police officer and just discovered that my wife was abducted from my own home this afternoon while I slept..." He trailed off, looking away from me. His jaw was clenched and a vein in his neck pulsed. He swallowed hard. "Christ knows what he would have done to you if you hadn't managed to get away from him." He pressed his lips together and I noticed his fists were clenched on his thighs. He was struggling to keep his anger in check.

"I know. I was stupid. I don't know why I fell for anything he said. He got into my head, and I am furious with myself for allowing him to get to me so easily." I couldn't stay away any longer. I stood, crossing to him, and reaching down, I wrapped my fingers around his clenched fist.

He looked up at me, his eyes instantly softening, and turned his hand over, releasing his grip and linking his fingers with mine. He pulled me onto his lap, and I curled in against his chest, listening to his heart hammering.

Neither of us said anything for a while, but there was still one more thing I wanted to broach, and I knew if I let the time pass, I would never be able to do it. I took a deep breath.

"I think I should request a visit with Phil." I blurted it out before I could second-guess myself.

Dan gripped me by the shoulders, sitting me upright to look into my face, his brows dipped so low his lids hung over his eyes. "What? Phil? Why would you even…? What?" His reaction was exactly what I had expected.

"I know it sounds crazy." I held both of my hands up. "But hear me out. Dalaja is furious with me because she thinks I believe Phil is guilty. The truth is, I don't even know if that's what I think. He won't see Dala, but what you said earlier got me thinking. If he really is working with Dennis, he probably knows who I am. He might just agree to see me. Especially if we can make him think Dennis sent me."

Dan stared at me as though I had just started speaking in a foreign language. No part of me actually believed Phil and Dennis were working together. It was a wild theory and I had no idea where Dan had plucked it from, but if he thought it was possible, it was my best chance of convincing him that me visiting Phil would be a good idea.

"I really think it could work, Dan. We all need answers here. One way or another, this whole shitshow is tearing our lives apart. All of us. For us to start picking up the pieces, we all need some clarification on just what the hell really happened." My emotions were rising again, my breathing matching time with my pounding heart.

"I understand why you want to do it, Rach. Really, I do. But I don't think you're prepared for what you might have to face. What if he does admit everything to you? How are you going to feel having to sit and listen to Phil talking to you about things like that? And if he and Dennis are working together, it's likely Dennis will have let him know you aren't on side with them. All of this is assuming that he would even consider seeing you in the first place. He won't even see his own girlfriend." He paused, seeming to consider whether to say more. He let out a sigh.

"I really don't want to sound like an arsehole here, but at

the risk of it, after what's just happened, I'm not sure you would get anything out of speaking to him anyway."

I stared at him blankly, missing his point. He ran his hands through his hair before dragging one of them over his face.

"Please don't take this the wrong way, Rach, but look how easily Dennis suckered you in. Do you not think Phil would do exactly the same, manipulating you into thinking what he wanted you to?" He had to good grace to look uncomfortable, shifting on the sofa as he spoke.

I wanted to bite back, to fight my corner on it, but although his words stung, in all honesty, he wasn't wrong.

"You're not the one who needs to solve this case. You're not a detective and it's not your job to try to put everything right. If anything, pushing your way in is going to hinder the case. You're too close. You need to take a step back." He spoke softly but there was an edge to his voice telling me in no uncertain terms I needed to let go.

All of the fight had left my body.

"If Phil speaks to you at all, it's going to be for his own gain. It'll be because he wants to use you in some way. It won't help repair things between you and your friends if Dalaja thinks he'll see you and not her. Imagine how that would feel to her. Then it's only going to be made worse if you somehow get caught up and become a pawn in his game. No good could come of seeing him, babe."

I nodded slowly, feeling completely defeated and as though the last breath of wind had been whipped out of my sails. Seeming to sense my deflation, Dan took hold of my hand, cupping it in both of his.

32

As I had expected, Dan was still livid with Dennis for what he'd done to me. So much so, I was truly afraid of the idea of him tracking him down.

Despite the fact that Dennis had broken the law, Dan hadn't even mentioned calling it in, instead snarling out a barrage of expletives in between graphic explanations of what he would do once he got hold of him.

Not that I felt anything for Dennis, but I was terrified that Dan would let his temper and fury towards my father get the better of him. The professional Dan was currently lost, his emotions clouding his judgement and rational mind.

Not only would that have the potential to destroy his career, but he could go to prison himself if he didn't keep a hold on his rage.

Dennis had called me so many times I was seriously considering blocking his number. The only thing that stopped me was Dan saying we may need to use it at some point to trace him. He'd sent countless texts too, all pretty vague but with the same basic outline – that he needed to speak to me urgently. I had stopped reading them soon after the quantity of them reached double figures.

I had asked Dan why we couldn't just have him rearrested there and then, but Dan suddenly seemed convinced that Dennis was working with Phil. He wanted to have him watched, see what his next move was. If they could make any connection between the two of them, they'd be able to charge him with much bigger offences than breaking the conditions of his release. There was no proof that he had abducted me, and Dan gently asked how I would feel about having to go to court and admit that I had met with him previously. Not only that, but when he had broken into my home, I hadn't informed the police. The lines were too blurry. Admittedly, it didn't sit particularly comfortably with me that he was still roaming free, nor that the police seemed to think that they could suddenly outwit someone so highly skilled at lying and manipulating. But I understood Dan's reasoning. He swore to me that they were keeping tabs on him, ensuring he didn't get an opportunity to hurt me or anyone else. If I let Dan's plan play out and he took the bait, walking into their trap, my father might never see the light of day again. I still wasn't convinced of any kind of connection between Dennis and Phil, but that was why Dan was the detective. Perhaps he and his team knew more than he was telling me. I honestly couldn't say if I would feel better if Dennis had been involved and would be arrested again, or if he was proven innocent. Unable to think of the repercussions of either of those outcomes, I pushed it from my mind.

Dalaja was still refusing to take my calls, and after numerous texts, I had decided to allow her some space until we knew more. Annie had begun to reply to my messages, but her responses were curt and much more abrupt than normal. I'd come to the decision that I was going to go over there as soon as I felt strong enough. It was time I put my trust into my friends. I was going to tell them who I really was.

Regardless of the outcome, I had spent enough of my life running and lying to those I loved. The last few weeks had been the worst of my life and I had nothing left to lose. I prayed selfishly that our shared betrayal, by men we had loved, would bring us back together, repairing the cracks that had formed and spread so quickly.

Maybe Dalaja would understand why the whole situation had been so hard for me to deal with, and why I had let her down so badly.

"I've made you a cuppa."

I flinched, having been totally unaware of Dan's presence in the room.

"Sorry, babe. I didn't mean to scare you. Penny for them." Dan tapped the side of his head before tilting it to one side, waiting for me to speak.

My thoughts were a jumbled mess. The effects of the drug Dennis had used on me were lingering. My head felt as though it was going to split in two every time I moved too quickly, and I had an almost unquenchable thirst. Everything tasted slightly odd too, with a tinge of something I couldn't put my finger on.

Dan had told me my symptoms sounded classic of chloroform. He said they would wear off over a few days, but it was a sickening reminder of what Dennis had done, and what he may have been planning to do to me.

I released a heavy sigh. "I was just thinking, as soon as I can clear my head enough to think straight, I'm going to go over to Dalaja's." Leaning forward, I took the mug of tea from Dan.

"What for?" Dan frowned at me. "I thought the girls weren't speaking to you." The reminder that my two closest friends currently despised me and had shut me out of their lives stung like a physical slap.

"I know. But I've made a decision, Dan. I've decided it's time I told them the truth about Dennis. About who I am. Everything. I'm sick of all the lies, and look at where they've got me. I won't let him control any part of me anymore. I'm taking back my life." My words held much more conviction than I felt.

Dan's eyes widened before his face creased with shock and concern.

"Do you really think now is the time? What with everything she's going through?" Dan spoke slowly, keeping his voice even and choosing his words carefully. It didn't prevent them from irritating me. He should be on my side, telling me I was being incredibly brave and that I was doing the right thing.

"Yes, actually. I do," I snapped. "I hope it will help them to understand. Help Dala realise that *I* understand. More than she could know. The best way to prove to them that they can trust me is by putting my trust in them. Confiding in them the thing I have always been most afraid to tell anyone." My face felt flushed, but I continued, "And besides, Dan, when exactly would you suggest is a good time to approach your best friends of over a decade to say, 'Oh, hey, guys. It's me, your bestie. Guess what? I'm also the daughter of a murderer. Surprise.'" I made jazz hands sarcastically.

Dan rolled his eyes.

"Alright, Rach. There's no need to be like that. I was only

thinking of you. Of all of you. But I can't do anything right at the moment, it seems."

Before I had time to say anything else, he had turned and left the room, leaving behind a heavy atmosphere. I dropped my head into my hands. What was wrong with me? Why was I so determined to push everyone away?

I counted my breaths, trying to recentre myself. The flashbacks of Dennis appearing behind me flooded my mind, but I wouldn't let him make me afraid in my own home. Pushing myself from the sofa, I checked the kitchen, ensuring the back door was locked. When I was sure I was alone, I tipped away the tea and filled the mug with cold water. I gulped the entire contents before refilling it and drinking most of that down in one. Even the water tasted odd. I leaned back against the worktop as Dan appeared in the kitchen doorway.

"Are you going back to work?"

I glanced at the clock, the anxiety of being left in the house alone already causing my body to tense. "No. I need to be here with you tonight."

Guilt prickled at the idea of my actions resulting in him feeling the need to stay and babysit me, but I couldn't deny the relief that flooded me at the knowledge I wouldn't be spending the night alone.

"Are you sure? I'll be fine if you need to..."

"No. He cut me off. "The gaffers will want me in first thing but I'm staying here tonight. I'll arrange some kind of protection for you before I go tomorrow."

Before I had chance to argue he held up his hand.

"It's non-negotiable."

Despite the fact that I hated the thought of him having to speak to his colleagues about my father, what had happened, plus my reflex reaction to refuse it, I knew he was right.

"This will all be over soon. We've got a survivor now – a witness. We have to make sure we get this all right. Make sure we nail Phil for this." His eyes had that manic look to them again as they drifted, and his fists clenched as he spoke. I felt a prickle of concern that he was headed for a breakdown, that this had all gotten too much for him too.

"You really think he did it?" My question was barely more than a whisper.

Dan blinked, refocusing on me. "I think with the evidence, plus his confession..." He shrugged, twisting his mouth to one side, his eyes having softened as he took in my pain.

"Can you tell whoever you send that I need to go and visit Annie and Dalaja in the morning? Do you think they'd take me?"

He paused, studying me for a few seconds, obviously weighing up whether to say what he was thinking. "Let's think about that tomorrow, okay? You went through one hell of an ordeal earlier today. Just... let yourself rest for a little while, please."

I felt my entire body sag, and I tried not to cry. I was afraid to rest, afraid that the reality of everything that had happened in such a short space of time might just catch up with me. If it did, I knew there was a very real chance that I would crumble under the weight of it all, the veil of the charade I had worked so hard to hide behind having worn too thin to conceal any of the darkness that consumed me. I had believed that I had left Joanna in the past, that she had been buried along with my mother and sister, but I had been stupid to believe that the ripples of my past would never catch up with me.

"Yep," I whispered, afraid to say anything more, aware that it would only take the tiniest knock to shatter me. My body suddenly felt too heavy, weak with exhaustion.

He crossed the kitchen, taking the mug from my grip and topping it up. "You look wiped out, babe. Let me help you upstairs." He paused, lines etched deep into his face.

I HAD ALLOWED Dan to help me up the stairs as if I were a child who was too tired to climb them myself. It was as though my body had run on adrenaline for as long as it could manage, but it had burnt out, leaving nothing more than embers.

I had dropped onto our bed, feeling the safety of Dan's weight on the mattress beside me. The pull of sleep was now so strong I couldn't believe I had been considering going anywhere. All I could think about was resting my head on the pillow and pulling the duvet up around myself, enveloping myself in the softness of our bed.

The last thing I remember was focusing on my phone screen with one eye, the other seemingly having fused itself shut. Every blink felt as though I had grit under my eyelids. I wondered if I should send a message to Dalaja, see if she would agree to see me, hear me out. Remind her I was still here for her.

I must have fallen asleep almost instantly as I awoke with a jolt, my ringing phone still clutched in my hand.

I blinked, disorientated, trying to figure out why my phone was ringing and what time it was. I stared at the time on my phone screen, trying to decipher if it was morning. No, it was dark. I'd gone to bed early, only been asleep for a couple of hours. It was only nine thirty.

My phone stopped ringing before I could gather myself enough to answer it. I shifted myself backwards, propping myself up against my pillows and widening my eyes, stretching them out and attempting to chase away the drag of sleep.

Glancing over, I was surprised to find Dan's side of the bed empty and cold. I checked the missed call.

Dalaja.

I frowned, double-checking the time and date of the call. Had I sent that message before I fell asleep? I couldn't remember sending anything. The pull of sleep had been too strong. Perhaps she had called me by mistake, or maybe she'd decided to put everything behind us. I hoped the call was just her reaching out, but would she be calling me at this time just for a reconciliation? A pang left me brimming with anxiety as I considered whether to call her back. What if it was more news about Phil?

Before I had time to make my decision, my phone rang again. Her name flashed on the screen, and I took a deep breath before accepting the call.

"Dala? Sorry, I was asleep." I pulled the duvet up around my midriff as if she could see me. Somehow, even being on the phone made me feel exposed, unusually on edge at speaking to my friend.

"Rachel, I need you to do something for me." Her tone caused my stomach to plummet. I had been fiddling with the corner of the duvet, twiddling it between my fingers, but I froze, instantly feeling my insides turn to ice.

"Dalaja?" I repeated dumbly.

"I'm so sorry, Rachel. I'm so sorry I'm doing this to you."

Fear laced her voice. Nausea rose and I swallowed hard, a hollow feeling in my stomach.

"What?" I squeaked, desperate for her to tell me what was going on and yet wishing I could cover my ears and refuse to hear any more.

"You need to come here. I need you to come here. He says you'll know where to come."

"Wait, what? Who? Who told you? Where are you?" I stuttered, refusing to believe what I already knew.

"I'm with Dennis. Rachel, please. You have to come." The line cut out.

A second later, my phone buzzed with a new message. A photograph.

33

I launched myself from the bed so quickly the duvet got entangled with my legs and I only just managed to right myself before I fell.

I had stared at the photo for a solid thirty seconds before it had actually processed what I was seeing. It was a photo of Dalaja, standing outside of the abandoned warehouse, her eyes wide, like that of a child being asked to pose but who didn't understand the instruction. She looked lost, but worse than that, she looked as though she had given up.

I had no idea what Dennis had done to her to get her there, but there was no way she was going to pay for my mistakes. She had already suffered that fate once thanks to Phil.

"Dan?" My voice sounded too loud in the otherwise silent house, and I waited for his reply. It didn't come and I paused, straining to listen, confused as to why he wouldn't answer.

Maybe he had gone downstairs and fallen asleep. I called out again as I yanked the first jumper I could lay my hands on over my head, and scraped my hair back into a ponytail as I thundered down the stairs. I frantically ran around the downstairs of the house, fumbling with my phone, unable to get my trembling fingers to do what I needed them to. Eventually, I found Dan's number and jabbed at the screen, desperate to know where he was, for him to tell me what to do.

"Please, please. Come on, Dan. Please answer," I pleaded, my voice no more than a whisper.

Had Dan been right? Had Dennis been working with Phil and had abducted Dalaja in an attempt to help him somehow? I shook the thought from my head, barely pausing to grab my keys as I yanked open the front door, slamming it closed behind me as I raced towards my car.

Dan's Toyota wasn't on the drive. Something major had to have happened for him to have left me alone. Had Dennis got Dalaja in some sort of hostage situation? Maybe Dan had tried to wake me, but I had been in too deep a sleep? Perhaps he hadn't been concerned about my safety if he knew Dennis was surrounded by police somewhere. My head was spinning out of control with images of Dalaja, Dennis, Dan, the news breaking, the world discovering that the evil predator responsible for ruining so many lives was my father.

The ringing cut to Dan's voicemail and I cursed, tossing my phone onto the passenger seat as I slid behind the wheel.

The engine fired into life, and I pulled at my seatbelt, cursing as it jammed in retaliation to my attempts to wrench it out. I put the car into gear with my free hand and released the handbrake, allowing the car to pull away as I continued to wrestle with the belt.

It finally released its hold, and I jerked it across my body, jamming it into place. My phone had connected to the car by then, and I jabbed the button, waiting to be connected to Dalaja's phone.

The automated voice of the answerphone cut in instantly and I cursed again as I cut the call, pressing the button to redial without hesitation. When the same thing happened, I scrolled down through my history to the torrent of missed calls I'd received from Dennis, doing what I swore I never would and returning the call.

"Please, please," I whispered as I involuntarily tapped my hand on the steering wheel. It came as no surprise when his phone cut straight to answerphone too.

"Fuck," I yelled, slamming my palm into the steering wheel and accidently blaring the horn. I caught the shocked expression of the driver who was edging around a parked car on the opposite side of the road, and as I lifted my hand by way of apology for my unintended blast of the horn, he screwed up his face and gave me the finger as he slammed his foot onto the accelerator.

My hands were trembling as I went back to my call list. Picturing Dan as I hovered over his name, I wondered what this would do to us all. I just hoped Dan hadn't gotten to Dennis before any of his colleagues. I did not want my husband to end up going to prison because of the creature that had helped to give me life and now seemed to resent it.

I looked up from my call log just in time to see the brake lights of the car ahead of me and slammed my own foot down onto the brake with my full force. I glanced at my rear-view mirror, watching the car behind echo my exact action, the horn blaring at my sudden standstill as they stood on their own brake to prevent rearending me. My cheeks burned. I was likely to find myself reported for dangerous driving at the rate I was going. My mind was anywhere but behind the wheel of my car.

At the thought of being reported, something clicked in my mind. Perhaps I couldn't contact Dan, but I absolutely should be contacting the police. I had made this mistake before. It would be stupid of me not to let anyone know where I was going, and the police would surely inform me if they were already there, if they had it in hand.

Tapping in the three digits, I hesitated for a second before dialling, and waited for the call to connect. After hurriedly telling the operator which service I required, I was put through.

Everything came out of me too fast, like air trying to escape a deflating balloon, as I filled in the call handler on the situation I had entangled myself in. I knew I was making no sense as I went backwards and forwards, trying to fill in as many of the details as I could whilst desperate to convey the urgency of the situation.

"I'm sorry, I'm not sure I'm following. Could I just ask you to slow down a little and tell me exactly what's happened? Your best friend... you said she's in danger, but she's with your father?"

I tried again to explain to her who Dennis was, why we needed to get to Dalaja.

"Are there already officers there? Were you aware of something happening?"

The line went quiet apart from the sound of other call handlers in the background and the clicks as I pictured her navigating her computer.

"Not that I'm aware of." I could almost hear her frown through the phone. "I'm going to send a unit over to the industrial site as soon as I can. I do have to warn you, though, due to a number of other incidents, we are stretched extremely thinly at the moment, and it may be a while until we are able to get an officer to the scene."

"What?" I screeched at her. "Have you heard what I've been saying to you?"

"I've passed on everything you've told me and, as I explained, we will be out to you as soon as we can. We have been experiencing an unusually high volume of calls and, unfortunately, it leaves us no choice but to prioritise. I do understand your concerns, but the only thing we know Mr Raiker has done wrong is breaking his curfew, which we already have highlighted. That will be dealt with. He isn't breaking his conditions by being with your friend. We don't know if she's there of her own free will, and as there doesn't seem to be an immediate threat to life—"

"How can you make that call? You really don't seem to be listening to what I am saying to you. He's a convicted murderer. He has her against her will. How can you not—"

"I have highlighted this as an urgent response. If anything changes you can call us right back, but due to the volume of calls and demand on our units, we don't have any officers able to be diverted immediately. They're all dealing with equally pressing reports. We will have someone out to you as soon as we possibly can. In the meantime, I suggest you wait until an officer is present to approach the area. I understand your concerns, but putting yourself in danger is only going to add to the—"

I cut the call, releasing a scream and slamming my palms against the top of the steering wheel. How could they let Dalaja down so badly? I scrolled up and selected Dan's number, jabbing the button to connect the call again.

His phone went straight to voicemail this time, and I let

out another scream, fighting the urge to completely lose control. Instead, I pulled myself together and left a message, letting him know exactly what had happened and where I was going. I asked him where he was and insisted he call me as soon as he got my message. In an attempt to soften the blow of what I was about to do, I hurriedly added that I had already called the police but emphasised how fruitless that had been, before trying to explain why I couldn't wait, why I couldn't leave Dalaja. I knew he would be livid that I had given in to Dennis's demands, but I hoped he would understand my reasons. My best friend was just a pawn in his game. He was using her to get to me and I couldn't allow her to be put through any more suffering. Especially suffering that was because of me, that I could prevent.

I rounded the last corner. The industrial site came into view, and I tried to bring my breathing under control. The pounding of my heart matched the pounding in my head, and I sucked in deep breaths, gripping the steering wheel to keep control of my trembling. My tyres popped as they drove over the gravel before bumping over the uneven and potholed tarmac covering the ground. I was thrown around in my seat as I made no attempt to avoid them, taking the fastest route towards the unit. My phone rang out in the silence of the car, a withheld number calling. I knew it would be the emergency call handler returning my call, and so rejected it, holding down the button to turn my phone to silent. They were either coming or they weren't, but I was going in.

Yanking on the handbrake before the car had even come to a complete stop, I pushed open the door at the same time as yanking my keys from the ignition.

I swung my feet around onto the ground and launched

myself from the car, in the exact same way that I had launched myself from my bed. It seemed impossible that I had been asleep, in the safety of my own home, less than an hour before.

I slipped my phone into my back pocket, feeling some reassurance from having it on me regardless of the knowledge that I had already exhausted all my options of people to call.

Weaving my way through the junk, I avoided standing on anything that may cause me to lose my footing. As I went to make my way around the side of the building, I stopped in my tracks, freezing and unable to make sense of what I was seeing ahead of me.

A whimper escaped from me as Dalaja's eyes met mine and reality hit me with the force of a speeding train.

34

Dalaja held her finger against her lips and waved her hand up and down, signalling for me to be quiet.

"What the..." My mouth hung open as I took in the sight of her. She moved away from the grime-smeared window she had been peering through, seemingly of her own free will, not bound or being forced in any way. My best friend looked as far from someone being held against their will as she ever had.

"You... you..." It was all I could force out as she jogged towards me. My eyes blurred with hot tears, and I felt the ground shifting beneath me. How could I have misjudged everything so badly? My best friend was setting me up. I had come here thinking I was going to save her, willing to sacrifice my own life if it meant that hers could be spared, and the whole time she was luring me here, working with Dennis to reel me in.

Stumbling backwards, I willed my legs to break out of the shock, to force my body to turn and run. I had already escaped from here once; I could do it if I could just make myself turn and run. My exhausted body betrayed me, and I took no more than a few stumbling steps before Dalaja stood in front of me.

"Rachel." There was a look in her eyes like I had never seen before, but the grieving woman whom I'd held as she cried, that had thrown me out of her home, was nowhere to be seen. I couldn't believe it could have all been an act. I hadn't doubted her for a second. She had seemed so broken.

I stared at her. My vision swam as I tried to piece it all together – Dalaja, Phil, Dennis. Were they all in this together? Had she always known who Dennis was? Who I was? Did they plan to use me, or were they hoping to bring me on board with whatever they planned next?

I waited for it all to fall into place, but somehow, none of the puzzle pieces seemed to fit. There was no sudden moment where it all made sense. My thoughts bounced around, moving to Dan. What would he think if they found my body here? Would he believe that I didn't know anything about any part of this, or would he doubt my innocence once he knew how deep this all went? I hoped he knew me well enough never to think of me that way.

My knees trembled, and I struggled to hold myself upright, afraid that they may give way any second.

Dalaja's face clouded with concern, and she tentatively reached a hand towards my arm, seemingly planning to hold onto my elbow for support, but I yanked my arm backwards away from her outstretched hand and angled my body away from her as though she was a venomous creature striking out at me.

Her hand hovered awkwardly for a second before she withdrew it, her shock softening to a wounded look as she held both hands against her chest as though she herself had been bitten.

"Rach, I know this is going to all be a huge shock... I understand..."

I scoffed, cutting her off and screwing up my face, taking another step back from her.

"Don't even try to tell me you understand *anything*," I hissed at her, jabbing my finger towards her. Rage bubbled up from deep inside me. It had been suppressed too long, allowed to fester until it had become putrid, swelling until it had nowhere left to go and was finally bursting its way out.

"How could you?" I spat the words at her, feeling my lip curl.

She recoiled as if I had slapped her.

"Rach. I don't know what you think—"

"Don't. Don't insult my intelligence any more than you already have. You lured me here. You made me think..." A thought popped into my mind, causing the air to leave my body. "You know... About Dennis." It wasn't a question.

Dalaja studied me for a second before nodding.

"Is this – all of this – to get back at me for what Dan did?" My voice broke as it rose in pitch.

"Of course it's not." Dalaja's face fell. She looked at me as though I had accused her of something unforgivable. That was something, at least.

Her gaze shifted as she gathered herself, holding up both of her hands in front of her body, as though surrendering. I wanted her to explain it all away, to make it all okay again, but how could she possibly explain this?

"Please, Rach... We really don't have time. If you just let me—"

"Did he come to you? Did Dennis come to you?"

She stared at me for a few seconds, considering how she should answer, before she closed her eyes and nodded.

I drew in air, unable to fill my lungs, stars peppering the edges of my vision.

I wanted to shout at her, to pound my fists into every part of her body they could make contact with, but I did nothing, rooted to the spot as a nausea rose, clawing its way up my windpipe. I couldn't speak.

"He did," she finally broke the atmosphere. "I know who he is. But that's not why we're here, Rach. There's something you need to know. Something you need to see. We really didn't want to do this to you, but you need to—"

"I don't care," I snarled. "I don't care what you want me to know, or see, or think. I don't want any part in any of this. I won't comply with any part of it. I don't know what he planned to do to me, but you're wasting your time. He will not get into my head again. That's what he's done to you, and if… if it's worse than that, if you… and Phil… Well, you'll have to kill me because I won't be involved, and the second I get any opportunity, I will make sure everyone knows everything."

Dalaja's face seemed to crease. It was her turn to take a step back, and she opened her mouth to say something but I cut in again.

"I've already called the police. They're on their way." I stuck out my chin in defiance.

Dalaja didn't seem fazed by my admission, and it took the wind from my sails. I had expected that to knock her off balance, even if only slightly.

"That's good." She nodded, seeming to pull herself together a bit. "We have too." The use of the word we, along with her statement, blindsided me. "Although they don't seem to be in any sort of rush, considering the magnitude of it all. Hopefully your call will make this more of a priority."

She glanced up at me, taking in my confusion. "Rach, I don't know what you think is going on here, but Dennis doesn't want to hurt you."

I scoffed. "You believe that, do you? Did he tell you he drugged, abducted, and brought me here once already?" I narrowed my eyes at her, waiting for my words to sink in, hoping to shock her, but although she flinched slightly, this clearly wasn't new information to her. Her eyes slid off to one side and she bit her bottom lip.

"Oh." I barked out a humourless laugh.

"I know how it must look." Her hands were up again.

"Do you?" I didn't recognise my own, shrill voice.

"You've got it wrong, Rach. We've *all* had it wrong." She held up her hands as if I were pointing a gun at her, moving them in time with her words. "We thought maybe, if you saw it for yourself..." She trailed off, throwing a glance towards the warehouse over her shoulder. "Please, Rach. This is me." She moved both of her hands and placed them against her chest, echoing my own words and actions from the last time I saw her. Her eyes were brimming with a silent pleading and I ached to strip everything away and go back to when she really was her. My shoulders sagged and I felt the overwhelming urge to drop to the floor, curl into a ball and bury my head until the police arrived to deal with it all.

"We needed you to come here. We need you to hear what we have to say. It's Dan." My head shot up, my heart rate reaching an impossible rate within a second. I felt my legs wobble beneath me and held my hand to my chest, afraid that my heart might actually give out if it had to endure much more.

"Where is he?" I breathed. Dalaja eyed me, weighing up her options. "Where is he?" I repeated, speaking through my teeth.

Fear flashed in Dalaja's eyes as she glanced towards the warehouse again. She swallowed hard as she darted glances around her before finally speaking in a measured tone.

"He's inside. Rach, Dennis did tell you what—"

I didn't wait to hear the rest of her sentence, suddenly finding the ability to move, lurching forwards and sprinting towards the entrance to the warehouse. Dalaja called after me as I took off, but I wasn't stopping for anyone. I had to see what they had done to Dan. I had to know that he was, at the very least, still alive.

35

I burst through the doors, the sound reverberating off the walls in the near silence, Dalaja's footsteps close behind me.

The dusty air filled my lungs, which burned in protest. Blinking in the gloomy half-light, I willed my eyes to adjust.

I heard Dennis before the shape of him came into focus, struggling, grappling with the taller figure.

"I told you not to come in here," he growled.

"I know." Dalaja sounded breathless. "But what was I supposed to do?"

Glancing around at Dalaja, I returned my glare to Dennis, who had his arms wrapped tightly around Dan, wearing a thunderous expression.

"Rach?" Dan's familiar voice called out across the empty space. As my eyes adjusted, I could make out a lump on the floor a few metres in front of me. There was a tarpaulin spread out over a large area, and I squinted into the dim light, trying to piece the scene together.

"Dan?" I called out. My body sagged with relief that he

was at least alive. If the police got here soon enough, we could both still get out of this.

I considered turning to Dalaja, begging her to get help, but then I remembered the look she and Dennis had shared when she had run in behind me. She was his ally now, no longer mine.

"JoJo, Dan isn't... He's not who you think he is." Dennis spoke evenly, his words calm.

"You didn't tell me you hadn't told her. If I'd have known, I would never have let her find out like this," Dalaja hissed at him, her face twitching with fury. "Rach, I'm so sorry."

I scoffed, rolling my eyes, fighting the tiny part of my exhausted brain that was beginning to fire and make connections I already wanted to rebuff.

"I'm serious, JoJo," Dennis growled. My lungs felt more compressed than when he'd held his thick fingers over my mouth, and I tried to steady my breathing.

Dennis inched the two of them further into the light, an unreadable expression on Dan's face as his eyes moved from me to Dennis, and finally to Dalaja. The tiniest hint of unreadable emotion crossed his features as he studied her, but it was gone before I could be sure. His stare flicked between us as he weighed up the situation.

I fought my rising panic, my conflicting thoughts colliding with one another, battling for dominance. Dennis had Dan restrained because he was guilty. Dan had known he was working with Phil, and Dennis hadn't had a choice but to stop him.

But as I took in the sight of Dan, something twisted in my gut. He was dressed in a full paper suit, his hood drawn up over his head, gloves on, and blue plastic covered his shoes. I couldn't tear my eyes away from him.

"What's going on?" I fought to keep the tremble from my voice, needing to sound more in control than I felt.

"Did he hurt you?" Dan barked.

"No." I shook my head, still unable to take my eyes off my husband. "What's going on, Dan? Why are you here? Why are you wearing that?" I gestured towards his suit.

Dan glanced down at himself as though he had forgotten what he was wearing and then looked back up at me.

"They got to Hayley," he replied seriously. "There was a mass search on for her. I heard the calls over the radio and had a feeling they'd have brought her here. I didn't want to contaminate the scene." He nodded towards the lump on the floor, and I allowed my eyes to fall to it. Now that they had fully adjusted to the half-light, I could make out the dark hair, the pale skin, the jeans of the woman whose face had been kept out of the public eye for her own protection. If this was Hayley...

My hands flew to my mouth, and I let out a whimper as I took in what I was seeing. I crossed the room without taking the time to think about it. I dropped to my knees and placed my hands on the woman, desperate to know if she was still breathing.

"It's over, Dan." Dennis's gruff voice startled me, but I didn't stop, Dalaja joining me, falling into a crouched position beside us and brushing Hayley's hair back from her face.

I held my own breath as I listened for hers, grabbing her wrist and checking for a pulse. It was weak, but it was there. I rolled her into the recovery position, steadying myself, meeting Dalaja's questioning stare and giving a tiny nod. I witnessed the relief flood her features, telling me all I needed to know about my best friend.

"The ambulance is on its way. I called it as soon as we knew she was definitely in here," Dalaja whispered.

I stared at her, at a loss for how to help the woman before us much more without medical equipment, my mind processing everything that was happening around me, refusing to even accept the possibility.

"He took her, JoJo." Dennis's tone was flat, his arms still gripping Dan.

My head spun as I slowly rose to my feet, my focus back on Dan.

I didn't miss the flicker in his eyes. Fury? Panic? Was this aimed at Dennis due to his lies, or...

The woman on the floor let out a groan, and all eyes dropped to her for a second. I returned my focus to Dan in time to see him swallow hard, a hard look on his face before it softened again at the realisation I was watching him. The first wail of sirens came from somewhere in the distance and Dan's head snapped around like that of a dog who had just heard a whistle. None of it was making any sense, but at the same time, I knew now that it did.

The atmosphere was electric whilst we all waited for someone to make a move. Dan turned his head slowly back towards me, and I gasped at the twisted features of a man I didn't know. Dennis must have loosened his grip because in an instant, he was doubled over, gasping, and Dan was sprinting towards the back of the warehouse. There was a rush of air as Dennis's heavy footsteps thundered past us, and I watched helplessly as he tore after my husband.

The sirens grew louder as I stood, unable to move, my entire body shaking, my teeth chattering as I stared at the spot where Dan had stood seconds before. My legs gave way beneath me.

36

DENNIS

The young woman still threw frightened glances at me as though I was something to be afraid of. The nurse had been in, cleaning and bandaging my wound as the female officer had asked me her questions. The officer stood back from me as though I may be about to spring from the bed any second and grab her. I had been over what had happened at least three times now, but she still asked me to repeat the answers as though I may have something new to add to my version of events.

"So, you ran after him, managed to catch up to him, and that's when he hit you?" She fixed her stare on me, her pen poised above her pad.

"From what I remember." I shrugged vaguely.

"And then everything is a blur from then until we found you back at your flat?" She raised an eyebrow.

"Uh huh. I'm afraid so." I tentatively touched my fingertips to the lump on the side of my head.

"Right. And you have no idea whatsoever where DCI Thatcher was heading when you took off after him?"

"I'm afraid not." I shook my head, wincing as it pounded in protest. "Why would I hide anything? I have no reason to want to protect that scumbag." I couldn't disguise my hatred towards Dan. "Can I see Jo... Rachel now?" I asked again.

"Mrs Thatcher is being treated. We will take you to see her once she's been given the all-clear, if she wishes to see you." The officer pursed her lips and raised one perfect eyebrow.

No one could blame JoJo if she refused to see me. I could only imagine what she thought of me. I hadn't planned to drug her, or to take her, and had replayed the moment countless times in my mind, wondering how I could have done it differently. That had all been meant for Dan. I had been expecting JoJo to be out. I had planned to wait for Dan, to drug him using his own chloroform and take him away from the house, so that I knew she was safe from him. But then JoJo had come into the kitchen. She'd caught me completely off-guard and I panicked. She would have shouted for Dan and he would have come, and she'd have been convinced he'd saved her. She would have refused to speak to me, and she would have been left with him, believing he was the good guy. There had been no time to think it though and so I acted on impulse, out of desperation to keep her safe. He would have had me put away again for the rest of my life. I would never have hurt her – that was exactly what I was trying to avoid. She was supposed to wake up and I could have explained everything, but then she kicked me and ran before I had chance to tell her anything.

"Well. I'd like to rest now. Unless there's anything else I can help with? Or do you plan to arrest me?" I raised my eyebrows at the officer who still lingered in my hospital room.

She sniffed, making a point of scanning her pad before placing the lid carefully back onto her pen and slipping them both into her bag.

"That'll be all for now. You'll need to come in and give a full statement as soon as you're feeling up to it." She pursed her lips again, struggling to keep the irritation from her voice, standing and slipping her arms into her coat.

"Of course." I gave a salute and winced again as another wave of pain throbbed through my head.

The officer left the room without saying anything more. It was no surprise that I wasn't being treated as a victim. Once a criminal, always a criminal.

I reached for the water on the table beside my bed, thinking back over the events of the past few days. I couldn't believe it could have only been days.

It hadn't been my intention to reappear in JoJo's life. I really hadn't wanted to cause her any pain. Quite the opposite; I had just needed to see that she was doing okay. I *had* broken into her house, but not for anything more than to check in on her, to feel close to her, just for a few stolen moments. It had been my plan to leave again, just as quietly as I had come in, to make sure she was happy, looked after, and when I knew that was the case, I planned to leave her alone, only ever watching her from a distance. She was all I had left, and although I felt no resentment, I had as good as given my life for hers. I had just needed to be within touching distance. And then I saw that card.

Everything I told JoJo was the truth. I only left out a few details. I never killed her mother, and the part about how her sister died, that was all true.

Of course, I'd been painfully aware of how deep her mother's addictions had burrowed, that there was no way she should have been left to care for two infants – a tough enough job for those in the best state of health and mind. Overwhelming concern for the girls' welfare caused me to make an excuse at work that day, inventing an appointment and leaving early. When I got home, both girls were in the sitting room. The TV was blaring, and JoJo was playing on the floor, whilst Julia was sleeping in her bassinet.

I had poked my head into the room, noting Ruth's absence straight away. JoJo hadn't noticed me, too engaged in what she was doing, and so I had slipped along the corridor to find their mother, dreading what state I might find her in. Our bedroom door had been closed, and I had approached quietly, stopping in my tracks when I heard noises coming from inside.

The sound of her moaning, the sound of a man grunting had left me unable to move. I didn't wait to hear any more. Sick to my stomach and ablaze with fury towards her, I hadn't barged into the room to confront them. Instead, like a coward, I turned and fled. It's my biggest regret that I didn't scoop up my girls when I left, but I was too livid to think, needing to be alone.

By the time I had cooled off enough to return, I was prepared to tell Ruth that she had to leave. I didn't believe that she was having an affair, but instead that she was allowing those animals to use her body in exchange for the poison she was injecting into it. It had gone too far; I wouldn't allow her to continue that kind of behaviour – especially whilst our girls were under the same roof. I had no idea how I was going to cope, but I was going to throw her out, tell her she couldn't come back until she had cleaned herself up. I knew there was a chance she would take it too far before she got to that point, I knew how deep her addiction was rooted by that point, but the girls had to be my priority. So, I made my decision. My wife was going to leave.

Only, when I got home, Ruth still hadn't appeared from the bedroom. JoJo had run right out to me, telling me that she was hungry, and that Mummy was still sleeping. JoJo's underwear had been wet. She was barely out of nappies, having just turned three. I had promised her I would make her a snack as soon as I had woken her mummy, and stormed off down the hallway, my rage sizzling white-hot that Ruth had neglected our children, more concerned with getting her fix.

The bedroom door had been left ajar and I'd shoved it open. It nearly came back to smack me in the face as it ricocheted off the wall behind and creaked back. The smell had been what had hit me first. It had taken me what seemed like forever to take in what I was seeing, unable to drag my eyes away. She was face down on the bed, her scarf still wrapped around her neck. Ruth had soiled the bedsheets beneath her. Her staring eyes were bloodshot, broken blood vessels making them appear as though she had been possessed.

I fled the room, my thoughts instantly turning to the girls, to getting them out of there before they saw their mother that way. I shook out my hands as though to try to remove the stench and clutch of death that felt as though it clung to my skin, contaminating me, my entire body shuddering.

The image of my wife was burned into my brain as I stumbled back into our living room, but I felt no emotion. I reached for the landline phone as JoJo asked again for a snack, telling me that Mummy had been sleeping all afternoon. I had turned to check on Julia at that point, and that's when the bottom had fallen out of my world.

JoJo had shushed me, proudly informing me that she had managed to stop her sister crying when she had woken up. She had told me Mummy had insisted she was not to go into our bedroom, no matter what, and that she was to look after Julia until she came out.

I couldn't even remember making the call, or the police arriving. They told me I never cried.

I never told anyone that I had been home earlier that day, or that I heard what I can only assume was my wife being murdered. There were no signs of sexual intercourse discovered in the post-mortem.

When the police found out I had left work early, it only added to the weight of their certainty that I was guilty. I didn't even have work as an alibi for the time of her death, and could give no decent explanation for why I'd left or where I'd been after lying about a fictional appointment.

I have had to live with my decision every single day since. I wasn't lying to JoJo when I told her I was the one to blame for the death of her mother and sister, regardless of who had physically taken their lives.

I hadn't planned to tell JoJo anything about the past, aware that I owed it to her to shoulder the blame, let her live in blissful ignorance. I deserved to carry the guilt; she absolutely did not.

But then I had seen the card.

I had recognised the handwriting immediately. It was an anniversary card from husband to wife, signed off by Dan, written in the exact same hand that those letters I had received in prison had been. Those same letters that had told me exactly where to find my daughter.

It made no sense that Dan would write to me, that he would tell me about JoJo when she'd made it so clear that she hadn't wanted to see me again. So I started following him. It didn't take long for him to lead me to everything he was keeping hidden.

He was visiting a lock-up. Later, I discovered it to be where he stashed his trophies, a variation of drugs, a whole drawer of burner phones, and sealed packs of the coverall suits that the police wear when they are working a crime scene. There was a barrel out the front with ash in it, and I shuddered to think what he may have been burning. There is a reason I failed to tell the police about it. Dan remains the only other person who knows of its existence.

It didn't take long before he led me to the house of his next intended victim.

He would have killed Hayley had I not banged on the back door. It was enough to cause him to panic and scarper from the scene as soon as she lost consciousness, afraid he was about to be discovered.

I heard on the news that Phil was to be released pending further investigation, so I can only assume that his arrest and confession were also something to do with Dan.

I didn't graffiti their wedding photo. Despite what I thought of Dan, I wouldn't have done anything that might have scared JoJo or left her vulnerable. I still don't know who left that message, or whether it was aimed at Dan, or my daughter.

There's only one other thing I haven't been totally honest with her about – what really happened when I went after Dan.

37

TWO WEEKS LATER

There was nothing but blank space from the moment my legs gave out in that warehouse. I wasn't even sure where my memories started again, the whole time after I arrived in hospital nothing more than a hazy nightmare that I seemed to float in and out of.

There were parts I thought I could remember, but even with those, I wasn't certain whether they were real memories, or ones I had created based on what people had told me, to fill in the gaping void.

It hadn't been a surprise to hear I had been verging on hysteria each time I had come close to consciousness. There had been nothing too much wrong with me medically. I was suffering shock, exhaustion, and dehydration thanks to the effects of the drug Dennis had given me. The hospital staff had been left with no option but to sedate me several times, until I finally came round without screaming.

When I awoke that last time, I couldn't bring myself to

say a word, staring ahead of me as I allowed the horror of the situation to sink in. The nurses had offered me water, and I had taken it gratefully, my throat feeling as though someone had been continuously scraping their nails down the inside of it.

The whole situation was impossible to wrap my head around. I couldn't comprehend that the man who had been murdering women as a pastime was the same man I had been sharing my home with, my bed with. I had suspected my father, one of my closest friends, but never would I ever have questioned Dan. I still struggled to accept it could be true.

The monster they had described in the press simply didn't fit with the man I had married, the police officer, my Dan.

I went through every scenario in my head, considering every possibility. That someone had forced him to do it. That he had been set up. That he had taken some drug and he hadn't been responsible for his actions.

Hayley had identified him as the officer who had arrived to collect her, showing his badge to the sergeant who was guarding her, informing him that he was taking over. The sergeant had no reason to doubt his superior officer. There had never been a conversation between Dan and any other senior officer about getting Hayley somewhere safe.

The hospital staff believed she was being discharged into the care of a high-ranking police officer who had been part of an arrangement to keep her release under the radar, stopping too many people from finding out where she was going and shielding her from the press. They never questioned it.

He had drugged her as soon as he'd got her to the car,

and driven her over to the warehouse, from what we had pieced together, planning to kill her and make it look as though Dennis had ambushed him and killed Hayley.

Phil and Dalaja had visited me regularly. I was sure Dalaja felt guilty. It was as though we had swapped places and she had handed me her suffering on a silver platter. Still, I was grateful for their support despite everything. The police had drawn the conclusion that Dan had planted Phil's DNA at the scene. None of the work Dan had done on the case could be used since his involvement had come to light, so the case against Phil was likely to be completely dropped. Phil avoided going into too much detail but had made a statement to say that Dan had gotten to him while he was being held in custody. He'd told Phil that if he didn't accept responsibility for the murders, he could be certain that neither I, nor Dalaja, would ever be safe.

Phil knew it would be his word against Dan's, and that Dan would run rings around him as a high-ranking, well-thought-of police officer. Plus, with the DNA evidence against him, he hadn't felt like he had a choice and had done what Dan had demanded of him, willing to sacrifice himself to protect Dalaja. I burned with shame at the admission.

Dennis had also been in to see me. He had discharged himself after having his head dressed and being monitored for a concussion for a few hours. I considered refusing to allow him to visit, but I needed answers.

He explained the reason he had drugged me and why he'd come back into my life in the first place. Of course, it was all plausible, but I wasn't sure I would ever fully trust him. Or anyone.

We didn't discuss my mother or sister. I wasn't ready to

know the truth of that for certain on top of everything else, and he didn't offer anything up. I wondered, if what Dennis had said was true and I had been the one to kill my sister, perhaps I deserved all of this. Maybe it was karma. Was there something deep-rooted and evil within me that Dan had recognised, and had that drawn him to me? I decided that once I'd had a chance to speak to Dennis properly, to be sure of the truth, I would go to the police myself and tell them everything he had told me. I was too tired to rebuild my life again and would never allow it to be built on another lie. Plus, Dennis deserved to have his name cleared.

Dennis went over the same story the police had reiterated to me about chasing Dan before Dan had bashed him over the head with something and left him out cold. Possibly assuming he was dead. Dennis had eventually come around and stumbled to the nearest road, flagging down a taxi and going back to his flat in a state of confusion. The taxi driver had confirmed his story.

Something didn't sit right about it all, but I didn't push it. I didn't have the energy and wasn't sure I even wanted to know.

Dennis had apologised profusely for not telling me about Dan as soon as he'd worked it out, explaining that he knew I would never believe him and that he was afraid of pushing me closer to Dan and freezing him out entirely. I didn't respond. The knowledge that he was right stung. Dennis wanted us to try to build a relationship, but I told him I needed some time and space to process everything. I can't look at him without being taken back to that warehouse.

It's been two weeks since I came home from the hospital.

Annie picked me up. She begged me to stay with her and Tim, but I can't run from reality forever. I have spent my entire life hiding, pretending. I won't ever do that again. The girls now know every part of the truth of who I am. They must have hundreds of questions, but they've been good enough not to ask. It's ironic that my biggest fear was them discovering the truth, and that I would lose them, but instead I have found out I was the one being deceived and have lost the one constant in my life.

The press were waiting for me outside the hospital and there was also a small cluster of them on my street. Dalaja and Phil were waiting for me inside, having tidied up after the police had ransacked the house, searching it for evidence. It had offered me only the slightest relief to hear they had found nothing in our home.

It had never crossed my mind until that moment that Phil might take any part of the story to print. As though reading my mind, he had opened his arms, wrapping them tightly around me and pulling me into his body.

"Really sucks to be on the other side of it." He released me, moving his hands to the tops of my arms and giving me a gentle squeeze.

Dalaja and Annie had barely left my side since I'd returned home, but I was starting to feel suffocated. I had gently explained that I needed a bit of time and watched them leave with a false smile and reassurances. The second I closed the door, I ran up the stairs and into our bedroom. I hated that I still thought of it as 'our' bedroom. It was as though a force outside of my body had taken control of me as I tore around the room, destroying anything within reach and the clean-up operation my friends had carried out. I yanked clothes from drawers, swiped his bottles of perfectly lined-up aftershave from the unit. I ran to his bedside table, pulling out the drawers there too, and turning them upside down. I tossed the room like I myself was the FBI, searching for something, but my only aim was to destroy.

Dan had always liked things to have a certain order to them. He was borderline obsessive about neatness. I had always convinced myself it was a good thing, reminded myself how many women complained about dealing with men who couldn't pick up after themselves. A hysterical laugh bubbled up at that thought. What I wouldn't give for the biggest issue in my relationship to have been my husband leaving his dirty washing lying around. The laugh instantly turned into a sob, and I threw myself onto our bed, burying my face in his pillow and screaming into it.

The scent of Dan made me feel crazy. I longed to have him here, to have his arms wrapped around my body and for him to tell me everything was going to be okay. I physically ached for him, the longing causing a pain like I had never felt. How could I love someone so much, and yet despise him? The thought of him made me want to melt into him, but also to scratch, rip, fight and claw at him.

My emotions were too much. The mental tug of war was pushing me close to the edge of sanity and I felt the sudden urge to be out of the four walls of our house. Every tiny sound had me listening, convinced it was Dan. When it wasn't, the agonising struggle between relief and excruciating disappointment would jolt me again, making me uncertain if I was more afraid of seeing him, or not seeing him. I couldn't take it for another minute, afraid I was about to completely lose the thin shred of control I was clinging to.

Thoughts of Dennis entered my mind uninvited, and I suddenly wondered if this was close to the anguish and torment that he had felt when his family had slipped through his grasp and the world had turned its back on him. I needed to speak to him. I didn't know why or what I wanted to say, but it suddenly made sense that there was so much more for us to say to one another. Jumping into my car, I started up a playlist from my phone, turning the volume up loud enough to drown out my thoughts.

I couldn't even say how long it had taken me to drive over to his street. My body seemed to physically draw in, and I wished I could close my eyes and not have to see the area he was living in. The fences of the front gardens had fallen, apparently long enough ago to have begun to rot. One of the gardens looked like a graveyard for bikes. There must have been close to thirty of them, not one of them usable. Black bags of rubbish piled up against the wall in the alleyways between the houses, the bags splitting and gaping open, rubbish spewing out like it had become too bloated to be contained. Old electronics and a filthy mattress were propped up against the wall.

He had sent me his address, but this was the first time I had visited his maisonette. I turned the stereo off and crawled along, trying to see the house numbers in the fading light, wanting to be anywhere but that street, considering just leaving again. Just as I had decided to drive off, my headlights caught on a figure appearing from the front gate of one of the houses.

Squinting into the darkness, I was in two minds about launching myself from the car and calling out after him, but I didn't move.

I watched as Dennis got into a car parked a few spaces

ahead of mine. I had no idea why I felt the need to follow him, but some little voice in my head told me it was important. Keeping my distance, I was thankful for the late hour and the quiet roads making it possible for me to tail him from a safe distance without the issue of heavy traffic. There was just one time that I thought I might have lost him, when he went through a set of traffic lights just ahead of me that turned amber just as I reached them. I cursed, slamming my palm against the steering wheel and pulling off in a screech of tyres the second they began to change. Thankfully, he had been stopped himself by the next set and I caught up with him in time to see him turn left just ahead of me.

We arrived in an area I didn't recognise, and Dennis pulled his car into a side street. I wondered whom he could be visiting here. I didn't think he had anyone to visit.

He stepped out of his ancient car and walked briskly off down the street. I allowed him only a few more seconds before I was off, scurrying after him.

He crossed allotments and walked through a small group of garages that seemed to be abandoned. Old car parts, a few rusty tools and piles of tyres made it look like an automobile graveyard. We were in the middle of nowhere. A lump formed in my throat as I thought about what I was doing – what I might be about to unwittingly witness or expose myself to if Dennis was on the way to meet someone questionable. I pushed the thoughts aside, reminding myself of how little I had left to lose, and trudged on after him.

He crossed a large area of overgrown wasteland, and I kept back as he looked around him, checking to ensure no one was close by. He reached into his pocket and withdrew something as he approached a concrete building. After another glance around him, he closed the distance between himself and the door, sliding a key into a padlock and removing it from the door. He slipped inside, pulling the door closed behind him.

I chewed the inside of my lip, an internal battle raging inside me on how I should handle this. I could turn, go back the way I came, return to my car, and no one would ever be any the wiser that I had been here. But I would also never know what Dennis was hiding. He could be involved in drugs. This could be some kind of huge operation. Regardless of feeling as though my life may as well be over, I really didn't want to get myself caught up in something like that. I tapped my fingertips against my thigh, willing something to happen so the decision would be taken out of my hands. After another uneventful few minutes passed, something clicked in my head.

Hadn't I found myself in the situation I was with Dan because of my blind trust, my lack of desire to ever rock the boat and question anything, always finding it easier to bury my head in the sand with any tiny thing that didn't sit right or caused red flags to rise? I would quietly shut it down inside my head, convincing myself I was overreacting. Look where that had gotten me.

"Fuck it." I spoke the words aloud as I crossed the wasteland after Dennis before I could change my mind, no longer trying to keep myself hidden.

Peering in through the grime-covered window, I squinted through, trying to make out anything inside. There was something stacked up against the other side of the glass, and I couldn't see anything. A moment of doubt caused my stomach to plummet. I could still turn and walk away. But how would I live with the idea of being so naive around the people closest to me again?

I walked around to the door. The padlock was missing from the bolt, which remained open. I took hold of it and pulled open the door, holding my breath as I took in the scene in front of me.

Nothing could have prepared me for that moment.

38

Dennis's head turned so fast I was surprised he didn't tear ligaments. His eyes were wide and filled with panic, his skin instantly turning grey as he took in the sight of me. He had been bent over and stood so quickly he wobbled on his feet, gripping the table beside him for support as he stared at me, unblinking.

"JoJo?" he breathed as though he was clinging to the hope that I may be an illusion, that I may just vanish before his eyes. I felt my lips part, heard the gasp escape them, followed quickly by a wail. The floor seemed to shift beneath my feet, and I lost the ability to breathe properly, unable to get enough air to stop my head from spinning, a tingling sensation turning my skin to pins and needles. My vision swam and I was certain I was going to pass out, certain I wasn't seeing what I thought I was. This couldn't be. It wasn't possible.

"Rach?" His voice was raspy, as though he hadn't had a drink in days.

"Dan?" I breathed his name, unable to believe that he

was real. Tears formed in my eyes, which I couldn't tear away from him. The overwhelming combination of emotions that slammed into me felt as though I was being beaten, like fire and ice was being applied simultaneously to my skin. I wanted to laugh, scream, hold him, inflict every bit of pain imaginable on him. The carousel of emotions seemed to gain speed, with all of them fighting for dominance, none of them victorious.

"Dan?" I repeated, unable to get anything else to pass my lips.

He had lost weight, the skin hanging lose from his cheekbones. His stubble had gone from designer to unkept, and his hair looked long, lank, and greasy. He wore the same clothes I had last seen him in, and they were grimy, unidentifiable stains in patches all over them. There was a sour odour to the room, mixed with the stench of human excrement. His arms were drawn up to his left, bound with what looked like cable ties and attached to something I guessed was a bike chain to give him a little extra range of movement. It was looped around a metal pole that seemed to be part of the structure of the building, and within a few feet of where he sat, there was a large, blue bucket which explained the foul odour.

"Rach, oh, thank God. You have to untie me, please. He has been keeping me locked up here like some kind of animal. I thought I was going to die in here. I'm so happy to see you, babe."

I stared down at him blankly, aware of Dennis, who eyed me cautiously.

"And isn't that what you are?" My voice trembled as I spoke, barely more than a whisper.

"What?" His features folded in on themselves, his eyes darkening.

"Some kind of animal? Isn't that exactly what you are?" I cocked my head, glaring at him.

Dan drew his head back. His brows dipped as his face twitched.

"Rachel, there's still so much you don't know." Dan paused, allowing his words to sink in.

For just a second, I considered telling him I didn't need to know. I could cross the room, release my husband, and we could go home. We could shut out the world and everything could just go back to how it was before. I could have my Dan back; we could be us. I wouldn't have to spend another night alone, reaching out into the cold space where his body should have been, sleeping beside mine. I wouldn't have to wake up in the morning and face that second or two before I opened my eyes where I had forgotten that my husband was a monster, before it all came down on me again, crushing me with the same force as if the walls around me had collapsed in, the agony of it physical.

As though he could sense my resolve wavering, there was a tiny twitch in Dan's eye, the slightest tug to the corners of his lips that someone who didn't know him like I did would never have been able to spot.

I clenched my teeth, aware of how rapidly my chest was rising and falling. Dennis remained motionless beside Dan.

"I'm not stupid, Dan. Please don't treat me like an idiot. There is no way that you can explain any of those things." Dan opened his mouth to argue but I held up a hand.

"Don't. Please don't insult my intelligence. I know what you are, and I know what you did." I paused, watching him processing what was happening, trying to figure out his next move.

"But that doesn't mean I don't still love you."

Both men stared at me, horror tugging at Dennis's features whilst a desperate hope took over Dan's.

"I want to hate you," I spat, screwing up my face. "Despise you for what you've done. Part of me does. But you're my husband and I have loved you for more years than not. I can't just switch that off." Dragging my hands down my face, I puffed out my cheeks and blew out a breath. "I can't help what I feel." I shrugged, feeling exposed for being so raw and honest, dropping my eyes to the ground.

"JoJo." Dennis spoke my old name as though afraid a sound too loud might cause me to shatter. I had almost forgotten he was still in the room. I turned my gaze on him, meeting his eye, his searching mine, desperation carved into every line of his face.

"I know this must be hard. Beyond what I can imagine, but—"

I held up my hand, cutting him off. "Don't. Please, just don't. I am sick of being told what to do. Running away, pretending not to feel. In my whole life, I have never been able to just be who I am and not hide behind a façade. So just stop trying to tell me what to feel."

Dennis snapped his jaw closed, his eyes falling away from mine and his shoulders sagging. He moved away from Dan and crossed the room, slumping onto an old desk chair that released a cloud of dust.

Dan's eyes were ablaze, fixed onto me. My skin broke out into goosepimples.

"I love you too, Rach. Please. If you'll just let me explain."

He tilted his head, lowering it to move himself into my line of sight.

Dennis mumbled under his breath. I couldn't be certain, but I was pretty sure I heard something about how he should have killed Dan while he had the chance. I threw him a look, but he refused to meet my glare.

"So, all those evenings. I thought you were working..." My voice caught in my throat.

"No. Most of the time, I really was working." He licked his lips. "I left the house at other times. Times you weren't aware of. I needed an alibi. Someone who'd say they'd been with me and not doubt it, even themselves." He glanced at me before his eyes dropped to the floor again.

My chest felt as though it was being crushed, all the air forced from my body.

"Me? But... How?"

"Your intolerance to wine. I'm so sorry, Rach. I didn't want to but I needed..."

"You were drugging me?" I squeaked out, stepping back to lean my weight against the wall.

Dan nodded, and I watched him put on a perfect show of a person filled with shame and remorse.

"Yes. It was the only way to be certain you never knew I was missing. Plus, you would genuinely have no idea you weren't telling the truth when you said I was beside you all night. I never wanted to implicate you in any—"

"When did this all start?" I breathed, cutting him off. I couldn't stop, or I would never start again. "Was it after you joined the force?" He couldn't look at me.

"No." He looked wretched but I knew he felt nothing. How could he? "That's what I need to tell you. It started years ago. I was barely out of my teens. Dennis never killed those women back then." Dan lifted his hand as high as the restraints would allow, pointing to his chest. "That's how I came to meet you." He paused. "When I found out the man who'd taken the fall for everything I did had a child, I couldn't..." He trailed off. "I wanted to tell you. I wanted to so badly, but I fell in love with you. He swore if I told you anything he'd kill you, and..."

I'd stopped listening.

"And my mother?" I breathed.

"No." He shook his head vigorously. "It was just a coincidence. I never—"

"Liar," I half-screamed, half-whimpered. "You're a fucking monster," I growled, unable to hold back, realising I didn't need to hear anything more. I had never felt an anger so fierce, so white hot. It caused a pressure to build behind my eyes, my vision to blur as I pictured myself running at him, picking up anything within my reach and smashing it into his skull.

"That's not true, Rachel." He shook his head rapidly, yanking on his restraints as I glowered at him. "I'm just trying to be honest, tell you everything. You don't know the full—"

We both turned at the sound of Dennis's growling tone cutting off Dan's protests.

"We don't need to hear any more. You really don't see it, do you? A quick death is too good for you. You're chained up in your own lock-up. A lock-up that, if you are as intelligent as you think, is likely completely untraceable?" The question hung between them. "As I thought." Dennis nodded. "You're not going anywhere, Daniel. I do hope you like it here, because this will be where you'll be spending the rest of your days, until we believe you've suffered enough for everything you've done."

Dan's face fell slack for a second before he turned slowly to look at me.

"Rach? You can't... Please let me tell you... There's more to this. I need to know you'll be safe..."

He was still shouting after me as I turned and left the lock-up, but I was no longer listening.

39

DAN

I heard the clunk of the padlock being released before the bolt slipped across.

"Hello, Daniel." He had always called me Daniel when it was just the two of us.

There was no need to look up. I was already aware I would see that same smug smile he had given me the first time I had gone into his room.

I had known he would come; I just hadn't expected it to take so long.

My father had tried to get me to keep away from him. He told me there was something wrong with him – he was someone to be feared and avoided. I think the actual term he had used was 'wired wrong', as if a visit from an electrician could fix him. But his warnings had only served to make me more curious about him, like a child who couldn't resist poking the ant's nest.

"My, my, what a situation you find yourself in." He let out a low chuckle. "Did you really think I would let you put this all on me and allow you to walk away?" He clicked his tongue three times, tutting at me.

My mind was torn. Part of me was flooded with relief at seeing him finally arrive. The anticipation had been almost too much to bear. But now that he stood there in front of me, I wasn't honestly sure if my new, physical prison wasn't preferable to the trap I had been tangled up in before. As long as I was alive, regardless of whether I escaped this room, I would never have any sort of freedom, forever his puppet, his plaything.

There had been plenty of time to think during the time I had been chained up here.

I would have given anything to go back to that fateful night, to never enter my brother's room and poke the beast, hinting at what our father was thinking and how he was just waiting for Phil to slip up so that he could see him taken away. I still replay the conversation with my father in my head some days, in the moments I feel most like I deserve to be punished.

"It's not that I don't love your brother, Daniel. I do. But to be quite honest, he scares the hell out of me. I want to see him get the help he needs, but your mother would never hear of it. I can't do anything but wait. I'll be there, when he slips up, and I'll prove what he is. Then we'll all be safe, and your brother will be where he belongs."

I knew my brother. There was no way he was going to slip up. He was meticulous in every single thing he did. He was younger than me, by almost ten years. I had watched him grow up, witnessed the type of person he was. Even being so much younger, he had managed to manipulate me into doing exactly what he wanted me to.

It had started so small. Our parents had been religious,

often talking of God and how important it was for us never to sin. He had mentioned the porn magazine so casually. It wasn't even mine. One of the boys at school had hidden it in the back of my folder during science when the teacher had come to check his work. I didn't want to be a snitch so had left it there, forgetting about it until it was already in my bag. I have no idea how he knew it was there, but as I listened to him talk about how hard our mother would take it, finding out I was a pervert, indulging myself in filth, it had seemed like the world would end.

My mother adored my brother, never doing well at hiding her resentment for me. She had fallen pregnant with me at barely seventeen, and after my biological father's promises to love and support her, he had left when I was only a few weeks old. She had met my stepfather not long afterwards and he had led her to religion, going on to marry her and take me on as his own. My mother often commented on how much I resembled my dad, and I knew her feelings towards him. She took her anger for him and directed it at me, meaning I had to work hard to be noticed beside my perfect brother.

Once he had agreed to keep the porn a secret, refusing to believe that it wasn't mine, he told me I owed him. It escalated slowly, with him forcing me to nick a few quid from the church collection plate, keying cars of anyone he didn't like the look of. It spiralled until he made me set fire to the woodshed in the garden of one of the kids at his school for calling him a freak. The fire had spread to their house, and although the family had made it out, it had been a close call.

By then he had me completely under his control. There was barely a day where I didn't wish I'd allowed him to tell my mother about that fucking porn magazine.

I was still living with my parents into my twenties after finishing uni and taking a gap year – that turned into a couple while I applied to join the force. It must have been my self-preservation instincts that made me go running to him about our father's intentions, believing that if he saw me as an ally, I'd be much safer than if I was his enemy. I think part of me knew what that meant I was doing to my father, but I refused to allow those thoughts in.

My brother had instructed me to call the police, telling them that I had found something on Dad's camera. Despite the fact he wasn't actually my biological father, Dad had taken me on as his own and we had loved one another like father and son. I actually believe he preferred me. Perhaps that was part of the problem, part of the reason my brother wanted to see our relationship destroyed. He made it quite clear that I had been the one to inform him of Dad's intentions, that I couldn't now refuse to follow through on it. He hadn't had to make his threats verbally; I had been perfectly aware just from his insinuations and from the looks he gave what my life would be like if I didn't do what he wanted me to. So, I made the call, naïve enough to believe I would finally be proving myself to him and it would be the last thing he would ask of me.

Then came the next demand. I say that, but my brother never had to demand anything. He could word these things so perfectly, as no more than a simple, reasonable request, as though he were asking for you to pick up milk on your next trip to the shop. It was the way he delivered his instructions that left you with no choice. I couldn't even describe it, but I would never have dared say no to him.

I heard myself telling the police officer about the times my father would sneak into my room, after my mother had gone to sleep, the things he would force me to do while he watched, sometimes took photographs. The lies had slipped from my lips easily. I refused to think of my mother or father, instead picturing my brother's face – the church plate, the charred house – reminding myself why I was doing it. I was so detached from it; it was as though I was watching someone else saying those things.

If only I could have known back then that I was only digging myself in so much deeper, so deep into a black hole that I would never be able to clamber back out of it for the rest of my life. Doing what my brother forced me into never liberated me, or offered me any freedom from him. Instead it wrapped me tighter in his restraints, gave him more and more to hold over me, to blackmail me with. Each time I would succumb to him, the next time it would be worse.

I had betrayed the only other person who would have helped me escape him, landing my father with a lengthy sentence in prison thanks to my lies. Our mother was never the same after Dad's arrest, taking to the drink to mask the agony of what her life had become. We became a target for the parents of the girls who believed our father had abused us. Life for me and my mother was hell, but my brother continued his day-to-day life as though nothing had happened, completely unfazed by any part of what was happening around him.

Eventually, we were forced to move. We had always had different names thanks to our paternal roots, but when I changed my surname, he chose to keep his.

My brother's power over me never relented. I was in my late twenties when we received the news that my father had been killed in prison. Mum had never recovered; I believe it was a mixture of the alcohol and a broken heart that caused it to finally give out on her.

Somehow, even though our parents had offered no protection, life with just me and my brother felt even worse. He assured me that if he was forced to tell anyone what I had done to our father, the arson, the stealing, I would be prosecuted as a murderer, arsonist and thief. The other prisoners would despise me for what I'd done to my own family. Even convicts had a moral compass, and what I had done to my own father had crossed a line.

So, when he told me what I had to do, how he was going to support me and ensure there was no way I was going to be caught, I barely had any fight left in me. I still found myself clinging to the hope that, one day, it would all be enough. I prayed for the day he would tire of me, or agree that I had given him sufficient enough sacrifices, that I was free to live the rest of my life. I even found myself daydreaming about him stepping out in front of a car, or falling down the stairs and breaking his neck, anything to offer me release from his hold over me. But it never came. I considered suicide, even got as far as getting the antidepressants from my GP, saving them up in the hope they'd get the job done quicker than anything I could buy over the counter. But I was a coward, choosing to preserve my own life at the detriment of others.

I tried to get him to change his mind, begged him not to make me hurt anyone else, pleaded, trying to get him to see reason, to understand the magnitude of what he was asking me to do. But I had known it was all a waste of time. There was no reasoning with someone who felt nothing, who cared for no one. There were no bargaining chips with someone with no fear of anything and who held all of the cards. He had simply smiled at me the entire time while I had cried and begged, and when I was done, panting from the effort of my desperation, he had reiterated his instructions without faltering, his facial expression as unreadable as it always was.

I hadn't wanted to kill those girls, truly. I still have no idea why he made me do it. It was probably no more than a game to him. I don't even believe he would have killed them himself if he didn't have me to force into doing it for him. It just seemed to fascinate him. Was it an urge that he had to have fulfilled or would he have never gotten his own hands dirty? I wasn't even sure if it was about the killing or if he just wanted to ensure he held that power over my head. He would watch while I carried out his instructions, his eyes turning almost black with the excitement. The longer it went on, the more I believe it was my suffering he enjoyed over that of our victims. When I told him I wouldn't hurt them, refusing to inflict any injury, and would only do it by strangulation, he had shrugged, unfazed, as though bored with the conversation.

I had almost been able to fool myself into believing what I was doing wasn't as bad if I didn't have to inflict wounds or witness them bleeding out. That's where my aversion to blood began.

It was true that I was more desensitised to it than most – I had grown up with a psychopath in the next room, after all – but it was never something I had wanted to do.

I managed to block it from my mind, took my career as a police officer and threw myself into climbing my career ladder as a way to make amends for the alternative life I was trapped into leading. Of course, my brother was only too happy with my career choice, which made it even easier for us to ensure our horrific games could continue on whilst I gathered inside information. I had played right into his hands, even in my desperate efforts to rebel against him.

He had insisted on me meeting Rachel, on trying to figure out if Dennis had been the one to kill her mother and sister, sizing her up and deciding if she needed to be eliminated if she was likely to be protesting her father's innocence once he was freed. I didn't mean to fall for her. I liked to think it was the one part of my life that really was mine, but realistically, I knew our relationship only developed because he allowed it to. And how much she would despise me if she ever found out the truth. I never told Rachel – or anyone – about my brother.

It had also been his idea for me to write to Dennis in prison. He thought if we drew him back, had him close by once he was released from prison, we'd have a scapegoat if we needed someone easy to pin things on. The selfish part of me had needed Rachel to blame him but I didn't want to see either of them suffer. I had tried to refuse, even considered suicide once again at that point, but it was as if he could see inside my head as he casually mentioned how sad it would be if I was to make things difficult. I still remember the words he had spoken, feeling as though ice had been dripping down my back whilst he studied his nails.

I'm considering getting myself a new cat. I think I'll name it Rachel.

Somehow that betrayal of Rachel's trust had hit me harder than anything else, but it was better than handing her over to him. I really did love her.

Phil had never settled down, of course, favouring one-night stands with countless women he felt nothing for. But when I had met Rachel, he had realised that it was normal behaviour to meet a partner, start a relationship, and so he had too. With Dalaja.

He would never have gotten married. And I knew of his inability to remain faithful. But he could certainly act the part and was always one step ahead, smart enough to cover his tracks in every aspect of his life. I wished I could save her from him, but I had never even been able to save myself. He infiltrated all our lives and hid in plain sight, with only me ever aware of who he truly was. No one was even aware I had a half-brother.

I was sick of being his puppet, so done with him looking over my shoulder, feeling his presence and hearing his voice inside my head every single day. This had been my last-ditch attempt at ridding myself of him for good. I hadn't wanted to leave Rachel. I had been making plans in my mind of ways that I could convince her to leave with me before she discovered the truth. But then Dennis had gotten involved before I'd had a chance to tell her anything. He had led her right to me in that warehouse and left me with no option but to run. If only he knew the damage he had done. I couldn't blame him, though. I hadn't wanted to hurt Hayley, but I knew there was a chance she would identify me, and I couldn't take that chance if Phil was ever going to be prosecuted and I wanted to be truly free.

I could never explain that part to Rachel, though. How could I expect her – or anyone – to understand that? So I fled. Part of me had still hoped I would get the chance to tell her everything one day. Dennis had chased me. He was surprisingly athletic for someone his age, and I knew we couldn't run forever. I'd hidden and waited for him to catch up, striking him over the head with a small rock. He had wobbled on his feet before he had crashed to the ground. I should have run but I made the mistake of leaning in to check if he was still breathing. He kicked out at my kneecaps, swiping me clean off my feet. He already had the rag in his hands, soaked with my own chloroform. He had since told me he had swiped it from the warehouse while he was trying to stop me hurting Hayley. He'd only held off using it on me in the hope I'd admit everything to Rachel before my arrest. It was the last thing I remembered before I had woken up in one of my own lock-ups.

The irony wasn't lost on me that I had been so careful to ensure the lock-up was untraceable back to me, no one would ever find me here. No one else had known it existed, apart from my brother. And of course, Dennis, from all the times he's followed me.

I desperately tried to tell Rachel the truth, but perhaps it's for the best she doesn't know. Maybe she's safer that way. If she doubted my brother, began to wonder about what he really is, he would sense it, worm his way out of it even if she ever got as far as going to the police. She would become a threat. I'd already tried to take him down, to have him arrested, and even after he had confessed, he'd still managed to walk free. There was no way any of us would ever win against him.

My best hope was that Dennis would kill me, and that my brother would leave, with no reason to stay once I was out of the picture. But instead, they decided to let me suffer for what I'd done. If only they knew the true extent of that.

"What do you want?" I muttered under my breath, my voice gruff from lack of water.

"Oh, come on. Don't be like that, big brother." Phil sniggered. "We've always made such a great team."

I scowled at him. I was weak from being kept prisoner for

so long, but knew, given the chance, the adrenalin would have coursed through me and allowed me to tear him apart with my bare hands.

"It's a shame it has to end this way. You really thought you could outsmart me? Planting the DNA was a bold move, I'll give you that. Did I get you when I confessed? Did you think I'd decided to give it all up and live out my days in a prison cell? You'd have liked that, wouldn't you?" A sickening smile spread, twisting his features into the look I knew so well, the one that was reserved only for me. "It was fun making the confession, telling the police everything, admitting to it all right there in an interview room. It was so easy to tell them everything I'd done and then just... take it all back." He waved his hands around with a snigger. "They had me, had my admissions, and still, here I am, a free man. It was delightful to think what it must have done to Rachel too – her buddy, confessing to murder, arrested just like her old man. Must've pushed her to the brink." His smile was so wide I imagined it splitting his face. "It didn't take much for me to ensure Dennis was on to you. Luckily for me, he was like a dog with a bone once he had put it together. It reminded me of that line in *Scooby-Doo*, '*You'd have gotten away with it too if it hadn't been for that meddling old man.*'" He mimicked the voice of one of the characters whose name escaped me and barked out a laugh. I clenched my jaw.

"Oh, that reminds me. Did you like the note I left for you on your wedding album? I couldn't resist. It was so much fun knowing how much panic it would inflict on poor little Rachel, thinking it had been written to her. The best part was, I knew whichever one of you found it, you'd believe it was meant for you. The irony is, I didn't actually know

Dennis had been there at that point. I needn't have bothered trying to freak her out." He sniggered.

"Don't worry, we've been taking great care of Rachel." He winked at me. "I can't see what you see in her. She's not exactly a stunner – looks too much like her old man – and she doesn't half know how to whine and feel sorry for herself, eh? Still, it'll be interesting to see how easily I can find my way into your bed. Imagine what that would do to Dalaja too." He laughed again, a throaty sound that made me want to wrap my hands around his neck and squeeze until no more sound could ever escape.

"I just wanted to come and say my goodbyes. We've had some really great times together, haven't we, Daniel? My cat in the shed." He crossed the room, crouching down in front of me and cocking his head, that smirk still fixed in place, his eyes holding no sign of the emotion he now feigned every day.

He reached into his pocket and withdrew something, holding it up between us. The sight of the flame as he flicked the lighter caused my insides to turn to ice. This was my comeuppance for everything I had done – and I deserved it. A grin spread across his face as he watched my reaction.

"I'm sorry it has to end like this. Truly. I thought we had years in us yet." He tutted, flicking the lighter again, this time feeding the flame and letting it burn. He stood, crossing the room, pulling open a drawer and retrieving some of the paper suits. They were still in the plastic, but they caught quickly when held over the flame. He dropped them into the drawer, and I watched in fascinated horror as the fire gathered momentum, consuming the old wooden desk.

I didn't even attempt to pull on my restraints, aware they wouldn't give. This was it; he had won.

The sound of the door creaking caused me to snap my head up, aware my brother still stood by the desk. Dennis's face appeared around it, his shock evident at the sight of the fire, and then he took in the pair of us.

"What... what are you doing here?" His face was slack, his eyes wide with panic that his secret had been discovered.

My brother's mask was back in place in an instant.

"I just found Dan. Someone tipped me off that he was here, and I came and..." He trailed off.

Dennis glanced behind him at the fire, his eyes flicking to the lighter still clutched in his hand. He had no time to react before my brother was on him, punching him square in the face before shoving him into the centre of the room, turning and fleeing, slipping the bolt into place as he left.

The smoke was causing my eyes to stream, my throat closing up as I choked on it. There wasn't enough air. Dennis sat up, turning to look at me as blood trickled from his nose. I hated the sight of blood but in that moment, I barely registered it.

"You have to go after him," I choked out, the effort causing me to cough so hard my chest ached.

I had to tell him more. "He's... my brother. He's been forcing me to do what I did... blackmailing me... If he gets away, he'll... he'll... Rachel." It was as much as I could splutter out. I just prayed it was enough.

Dennis's eyes locked on mine for a second and he shoved himself to his feet.

"Please, go," I croaked.

EPILOGUE
ONE WEEK LATER

Staring down at the newspaper clutched in my hand, I kept the scarf wrapped tightly around my face and my hat pulled down to just above my eyes.

I glanced at my watch. There was less than an hour before I could collect my new passport from my contact. It hadn't been difficult to find someone to arrange it for me with the connections I had from my work in the police force. Everyone had seen the news, so they knew I was no longer working as an officer.

I had been prepared to die in that lock-up, embracing the idea that I would finally be free of him and allowing the last of my fight to seep out of me.

Dennis had faltered for no more than a second before he had made his decision. I had expected him to leave me, as he believed I deserved to perish, but he had run to me, releasing a growl of frustration before cutting through my restraints with a pen knife he pulled from his pocket. I resisted, screaming at him to go after my brother. He had snarled something about having to let me go, that he wouldn't go down for whatever he was about to do to Phil, and that I wouldn't be held responsible if they then discovered my body. His words told that story, but his eyes told another.

He had broken the window, dragging himself out of it and running around to undo the bolt. He pulled me from the lock-up, lying on the grass beside me, panting, while I sucked back air. We both knew Phil was long gone, but Dennis pushed himself back to his feet, throwing one last look over his shoulder as he took off, pulling up his hood and sprinting across the wasteland and out of sight. I had laid there, gasping, spluttering as I waited for my head to stop spinning.

Eventually, I knew I had to risk it and move, regardless of my fear that my legs wouldn't take my weight. I'd been staying in drug dens and homeless shelters since, cleaning myself up and changing my appearance as much as I could to avoid being recognised. Thankfully for me, it's been my brother's face that has dominated the news.

I skimmed my eyes over the article once more.

The Times
Reporter attacked in the line of duty.

The Met are still investigating following the vicious attack of one of our own last week.

Phil Metcalf, a reporter for the Times, was due to meet an unknown source as part of the story he was writing on Daniel Thatcher, the DCI who was responsible for the murder of multiple women across the country.

Metcalf himself was originally arrested for the crime, but was released after it came to light that he was being blackmailed into his confession. He was seen by multiple witnesses, waiting to cross a busy road when an unknown assailant shoved him in front of oncoming traffic, fleeing after Metcalf fell into the path of a bus.

Police have said they are unable to confirm or deny that the identity of the assailant was missing Thatcher, who has been on the run since his abduction and attempted murder of Hayley Larkin, witnessed by his wife and the partner of Mr Metcalf.

There have since been reports that DCI Thatcher and Phil Metcalf are closely related. The police are yet to release a statement on this.

Mr Metcalf survived the attack, but remains in hospital on life support, with life-threatening injuries.
All parties involved refused to comment.

If you think you may have seen Daniel Thatcher, please call 999. Please do not approach him.

Dennis hadn't caught up with Phil, but I could only assume it wouldn't have taken a lot for him to convince Phil to meet with him once he knew Dennis hadn't perished in our lock-up. I folded the newspaper and dropped it onto the tabletop, standing and stretching out my back.

There was just one more stop I had to make.

I knew from a previous recce of the area it wasn't the type of place where neighbours watched out for each other, or concerned themselves with who came and went. Still, I kept my hood covering as much of my face as I could.

I turned into the alley, not risking a glance around, and hopped over the back fence before crossing the garden and opening the back door without hesitation.

As I stepped into the kitchen, I jumped as I turned to see him, facing away from me, busy pouring boiling water into mugs. I held my breath, wondering how he would react when he turned and spotted me. Especially with kettle in hand.

"Hello, Daniel. Are you going to tell me why you're in my kitchen?" His tone was flat. He turned, fixing me with a stare that gave away nothing.

"I need to know she's safe. Before I leave her for good, I need to know he can't get to her again."

Dennis's eyes flicked to the left, towards the doorway of the kitchen for a second. I hadn't missed the shadow that appeared, or the two mugs he tried to hide behind his back.

"She is. His injuries are serious. Enough that the doctors say survival with at least partial paralysis is the best-case scenario."

My body sagged, and I nodded, at a loss for how to reply.

"Why didn't you leave me in there? I deserved it. After everything I've done..." The question came in a rush. Part of me wished he had.

"Because I'm not a killer, Daniel. I never have been, and I wasn't about to change that for anyone."

An image of Phil flashed through my mind, but I supposed he was still right; he hadn't actually killed him. "If I'd let you die like that, I knew what it would do to JoJo. Taking a life doesn't bring back another."

The silence hung thick between us for a few seconds.

"I hope you manage to build a relationship with her. You both deserve that. Can you make sure she knows that I really did love her? I'm sorry for everything. So sorry. I know she won't ever understand any of it, but I truly hope she finds happiness." I paused. "It's going to be hard on Rachel and Dalaja. I know they'll never understand what I did, but hopefully they'll know it was never what I wanted."

Dennis's eyes widened for a second before shooting towards the doorway again, a look of understanding crossing them before his features softened.

Our actions were incredibly different, but we had both been prisoners in our own way due to the actions of others.

"You freed yourself of him in the end." Dennis crossed his arms over his chest. "I think Rachel already understands why you pushed him, and I'm grateful he will never be around my daughter again."

I stared at him blankly for a few seconds, trying to make sense of what he was saying.

"Pushed him? I didn't... I thought you..." Our eyes met as we sized one another up, trying to figure out if this was some sort of trap. There was a shuffling sound and the shadow disappeared from the kitchen doorway. Dennis turned to stare at the gap, his eyes wide when they came back to meet mine, lips slightly parted.

The echoes of the conversation from Dalaja's birthday slammed into my mind. *Anyone is capable if they find themselves in the right circumstances.*

"You told her the truth about him?" I breathed. He nodded slowly and we stood in silence for a few seconds, the realisation of what had happened dawning on us both.

I turned, placing my hand on the door handle.

"Daniel." I paused, turning my head to face him. He gave

a small nod before he spoke, a beat of silence passing between us.

"You should know, there was an anonymous tip-off to the police about the lock-up. I've ensured the police will find a set of keys for it belonging to Phil. When I realised I wasn't going to catch up with him, I went back to get you. You'd already gone so I called the fire brigade. A lot of it had burned but I managed to put out the fire before everything was lost. I believe they'll find evidence in there. There have also been details accidently leaked to the press – rumours that you'd been kept there, imprisoned, that he may have been moving you at the time of his accident. They'll find what he was trying to destroy." He glanced towards the door again and gave a small shrug.

I closed my eyes, truly breathing for the first time in my life.

It was time for me to leave. The cat, finally free of my shed.

THANK YOU FOR READING

Did you enjoy reading *You Can Run*? Please consider leaving a review on Amazon. Your review will help other readers to discover the novel.

ABOUT THE AUTHOR

After spending her working life searching unsuccessfully for a fulfilling career, Laura George found her passion for writing psychological thrillers whilst on maternity leave with her first child. She took a leap of faith and didn't return to work, instead running with her dream of continuing to write.

Now a mum of two, she lives with her children, husband and springer spaniel, Dougie, on the beautiful Devonshire coastline. In the little spare time she gets, she loves nothing more than writing twisty thriller novels for the reader to untangle.

She spends most of her days with her children, in soft plays, on the beach or jumping in puddles, grateful that no one can see inside the corners of her mind as she conjures up the next dark character and plots their fate.

ALSO BY L C GEORGE

The Sleepwalker

You Can Run

Printed in Great Britain
by Amazon